MONT-ORIOL

Stories by Guy de Maupassant
Translated by Marjorie Laurie

BOULE DE SUIF
THE HOUSE OF MADAME TELLIER
A LIFE
YVETTE
BEL-AMI
TALES OF DAY AND NIGHT
MONT-ORIOL
PIERRE AND JEAN
THE MASTER PASSION
NOTRE CŒUR

MONT-ORIOL

By
GUY DE MAUPASSANT

Translated by
MARJORIE LAURIE

TURTLE POINT PRESS

103 Hog Hill Road, Chappaqua, New York 10514

CONTENTS

Part I

Part II

PART I

II

UNDER the lofty trees fringing the stream, which flows down from the glens above Enval, the earliest risers, singly or in pairs, were taking their leisurely constitutional after the morning bath. Late comers from the village hurried into the establishment, a pretentious building with the hydropathic section on the ground floor, while the floor above served the purposes of casino, restaurant and billiard room.

Dr Bonnefille had discovered in the heart of Enval a copious spring, to which he had given his name. Certain of the neighbouring landowners, speculative but cautious, had ventured to erect in this magnificent valley of Auvergne, so wild and yet so smiling, with its great chestnut and walnut trees, a spacious building to serve all purposes, whether of cure or entertainment. Medical waters, douches and baths were available on one storey; beer, liqueurs and music on the other. Part of the valley on either side of the stream had been enclosed and turned into a park, the first essential of a watering-place. It had two winding paths, while a third led almost straight to an artificial fountain, fed from the main spring and bubbling up into a large concrete basin under a thatched roof.

The fountain was in charge of a country woman of imperturbable demeanour whom everyone called familiarly Marie. The placid Auvergnat in her little bonnet of spotless white, with a vast apron, equally clean, over her working dress, rose slowly from her seat at the approach of a client. As soon as she recognized him she would select his glass from a small, movable, glazed cupboard, and slowly fill it by means of a zinc cup at the end of a wooden handle. With a melancholy smile the patient would empty the glass, hand it back, and murmuring " Thank you, Marie," turn away. Marie would resume her straw-bottomed chair to await the next visitor.

Patients, however, were few. Six years had elapsed since the opening of the spa, and at the end of that experimental period it could hardly boast more visitors than in its first season. They numbered some fifty, most of them attracted by the beauty of the scenery, and the charm of the little village, embowered in mighty trees, whose twisted trunks seemed as massive as the cottages they overshadowed. They were lured thither by the fame of its glens and ravines and its curious blind end of valley, leading from the vast plain of Auvergne, and ending abruptly at the very foot of a lofty mountain, riddled with extinct craters, where it formed a gorge of wild magnificence, threatened by overhanging rocks and strewn with huge boulders, over which a torrent dashed in a series of cascades and pools. Like all other watering-places, the spa of Enval had been brought to the notice of the public by a pamphlet extolling the virtues of its spring. It had been written by Dr Bonnefille in a florid, grandiloquent style, adorned with choice and extravagant epithets, full of sound but signifying nothing. All the surroundings were declared to be " picturesque, abounding in grandiose prospects and in scenes of gracious homeliness," while to every walk in the vicinity was ascribed " a quaintness all its own, guaranteed to appeal to artists and ordinary visitors alike." Then abruptly, without any transition, the author plunged into an enumeration of the medicinal properties of the Bonnefille Spring : its bicarbonate, its soda, its lithia, its combined chemicals, its acids, its iron and so forth, warranted to cure all imaginable ailments which he included under the heading : " Chronic or acute diseases, especially amenable to the Enval waters." It was a long list, astonishingly varied and calculated to encourage invalids of every category. The pamphlet wound up with practical information as to cost of living, price of lodgings and terms at the hotels. Simultaneously with the Hydro-Casino, three hotels had sprung into existence : the brand-new Hôtel Splendid on the brow of the hill overlooking the Baths, the Hôtel des Thermes, an old inn with a fresh coat of plaster, and the Hôtel Vidaillet, which consisted simply of three contiguous houses knocked into one.

One morning, obedient to the same impulse, two doctors were found to have established themselves at Enval, no one quite knew how : in watering-places doctors seem to rise out of the springs as naturally as gas bubbles. One of them, Dr Honorat, was a native of Auvergne, while the other, Dr Latonne, came from Paris. A deadly feud sprang up at once between Dr Latonne and Dr Bonnefille, while Dr Honorat, who was sleek, well-groomed, and forever bowing and smiling, held out a hand to either and remained on good terms with both. Still, by virtue of his title of Inspector of the Springs and of the Hydropathic Institute of Enval-les-Bains, Dr Bonnefille remained master of the situation. From this designation he derived his authority, as well as his autocracy over the Baths. All his days were spent on the premises, and some said his nights too. A hundred times in the course of the morning he went from his house, which was close by in the village, to his consulting-room on the right of the corridor near the entrance. Lurking there, like a spider in its web, he watched the invalids coming and going, with a disciplinary glance for his own patients and a furious scowl for those of the other doctors. He was as despotic as the captain of a battle-ship and inspired newcomers with awe, or, possibly, with amusement.

On this particular day, as he was hurrying to the Baths, with the voluminous skirts of his old frock coat flapping about him like wings, he heard someone call him. He stopped short and turned round. His gaunt face, seamed by deep, sinister furrows ingrained with black, was disfigured by a grizzled, unkempt beard. He endeavoured to muster a smile, as he raised his tall hat, shabby, stained and greasy, from his long locks, which were pepper and salt in colour, a phrase altered by his rival Dr Latonne to " pepper and scale." Stepping forward with a bow, he said politely :

" Good morning, Marquis. I hope you are quite well."

The Marquis de Ravenel, a trim, dapper little man, shook hands with him.

" Yes, thank you, Doctor; at least, not too bad. Kidneys still giving trouble, but on the whole I'm better, much better, and I have only had ten baths so far. Last year, as you may remember, I had sixteen before there was any improvement."

" I remember perfectly."

" But that's not what I came to talk about. My daughter arrived this morning and I want to consult you about her at once, because my son-in-law, Monsieur Andermatt—William Andermatt the banker . . ."

" Yes, I know."

" My son-in-law has a letter of introduction to Dr Latonne. Personally I pin my faith to you, and I should be glad if you would come to the hotel before. . . . You understand . . . I prefer to put the case frankly. . . . Are you disengaged just now? "

Full of perturbation, Dr Bonnefille resumed his hat.

" I am at your disposal this very minute. Shall I go with you? "

" I wish you would."

Turning their backs on the Baths, they went quickly up a winding path leading to the Hôtel Splendid, which was built on the side of the mountain for the sake of the view. They entered a sitting-room on the first floor, which communicated with the suites occupied by the Ravenels and the Andermatts. Here the Marquis left the doctor and went to find his daughter. He returned with her almost immediately. She was a very pretty young woman, small, pale, fair-haired, with the features of a child, but the unwavering and resolute gaze of her frank blue eyes invested her dainty and exquisite person with a singular and charming expression of firmness and force of character. There was nothing seriously wrong with her, merely a general feeling of lassitude and depression, which showed itself in causeless bursts of tears and fits of temper; in short, a tendency to anaemia. Her one desire was to have a child, but her hopes had been disappointed during the two years of her married life.

Dr Bonnefille declared that the waters of Enval were a specific in such cases, and proceeded to write out one of his prescriptions, which always presented the grim aspect of a charge sheet. Written on foolscap, his formulae displayed themselves in a series of paragraphs, each two or three lines long, dashed off in a frenzied hand and bristling with spiky letters. Draughts, pills and powders, to be taken before breakfast, and morning, noon and night, succeeded one another in battle array, as if to say:

" As Monsieur X is attacked by a chronic, incurable and mortal disease, he will take:

" 1. Sulphate of quinine, which will make him deaf and cause loss of memory.

" 2. Bromide of potassium, which will ruin the coats of his stomach, cover him with boils and taint his breath.

" 3. Iodide of potassium, which will dry up the secretory glands in his system, including those of the brain, and will shortly render him impotent and imbecile.

" 4. Salicylate of soda, of which the remedial qualities have not yet been proved, but which seems to promise a sudden and violent death to the invalids who take it.

" And in addition to these:

" Chloral, which induces insanity; belladonna, which affects the sight; and all the vegetable and mineral preparations which corrupt the blood, prey upon the organs, eat into the bones and destroy with medicaments those who are spared by disease."

He spent a long time over this document, wrote on both sides of the paper and finally signed it like a judge signing a death warrant.

The girl sat watching him, the corners of her mouth quivering with suppressed laughter. As soon as he had bowed himself out of the room, she seized the inky sheet, crumpled it into a ball and tossed it into the fireplace.

"Oh, father," she exclaimed, laughing uncontrollably, "where did you dig up that old fossil? He looks like a rag and bone man. It's just like you to unearth a doctor of pre-revolutionary days. What a funny old thing! and how grubby he is! I really believe he has left a dirty mark on my penholder."

The door opened and Monsieur Andermatt's voice said :

"Come in, Doctor."

Upright, slim, correct, of indeterminate age, Dr Latonne entered the room. With his clean-shaven face, his well-cut clothes and the inevitable tall hat, the hall-mark of every medical practitioner in all the spas in Auvergne, this doctor from Paris looked like an actor on a holiday.

Utterly disconcerted, the Marquis did not know what to say or do, while his daughter pretended to smother a cough in her handkerchief to keep herself from laughing in the newcomer's face.

Dr Latonne bowed with easy confidence, and at a sign from Madame Andermatt, took a chair. Monsieur Andermatt, who followed him into the room, gave a minute account of his wife's state of health and symptoms, and the opinion of the doctors she had consulted in Paris. He wound up with his own views, which he supported with special arguments expressed in technical terms.

Andermatt was a Jew, still young in years, and engaged in business enterprises of every description, to which he brought a penetration, adaptability, swiftness of perception and sureness of judgment, which were nothing short of miraculous. He was already rather stout for his very moderate height, bald-headed, with fat hands, short thighs, and chubby cheeks, which gave him an infantile air; he looked too pink to be healthy, and he talked with bewildering fluency.

He had ingeniously contrived to marry the Marquis de Ravenel's daughter, in order to extend his financial operations to a sphere outside his own. The Marquis, indeed, had an income of thirty thousand francs and only two children, but Andermatt, who was barely thirty at the time of his marriage, was even then worth five or six millions, and had made investments likely to yield another ten or twelve. A man of vacillating, irresolute, fickle and feeble character, the Marquis had at first indignantly rejected the overtures towards this match, outraged at the idea of marrying his daughter to a Jew. But after six months of opposition, he had yielded to the pressure put upon him by so much accumulated wealth, merely stipulating that the children should be brought up as Catholics.

There was, however, no sign of the hoped for son and heir. The Marquis, who for the last two years had been a devotee of the Enval waters, finally remembered that the promises in Dr Bonnefille's pamphlet included the cure of sterility. So he sent for his daughter, and Andermatt came with her to see her comfortably settled and to entrust her to the care of Dr Latonne, who had been recommended to him by his doctor in Paris.

Andermatt, who had called on Dr Latonne at once, continued to enumerate his wife's symptoms and finally expressed his deep concern at having his hopes of paternity disappointed.

The doctor heard him out, and then turned to the young wife.

" Have you anything to add, Madame Andermatt? "

" No, nothing at all," she replied solemnly.

" Then will you be so kind as to remove your dress and corset and put on a plain white dressing-gown? "

Noting her surprise, he hastened to explain his system.

" Really, Madame Andermatt, it's very simple. Formerly it was believed that all diseases were caused by corruption of the blood, or some organic defect. Nowadays we hold that in many cases, and especially in a case like yours, the vague indisposition from which you suffer, and other more serious, nay mortal, diseases, may be due, through causes easily traced, entirely to the abnormal development of one particular organ of the body, which has a detrimental effect on the rest, and destroys the harmony, the equilibrium of the human frame, modifies or arrests its functions and impedes the working of all the other organs. Thus an enlarged stomach is sufficient to produce symptoms of disease of the heart, which, restricted in its movements, beats violently, irregularly, and even at times intermittently. An enlarged liver, or enlarged glands, can work havoc, which doctors, unskilled in diagnosis, ascribe to a thousand irrelevant causes. Our first step, then, is to discover if a patient's organs are normal as to size and position, for a very small thing is sufficient to undermine one's health. With your permission, therefore, Madame Andermatt, I will examine you carefully and mark upon your dressing-gown the extent, dimensions and position of each organ."

He had deposited his hat on a chair and was talking at his ease. As he spoke, two deep parentheses on either side of his large mouth gave him almost an ecclesiastical appearance.

" Just fancy," exclaimed Andermatt, much impressed. " That's capital; very ingenious and novel and up-to-date."

" Up-to-date," on his lips, was a supreme expression of admiration.

Much amused, Christian went to her room and returned in a few minutes wearing a white dressing-gown. The doctor made her lie down on a sofa, and, producing a pencil with three points, red, blue and black, he sounded and tapped his new patient and covered the white dressing-gown with little coloured marks, to denote the result of each observation. After a quarter of an hour of this labour, she looked like a map showing continents, seas, capes, rivers, kingdoms, and cities with their geographical names, for on every line of demarcation the doctor scribbled two or three Latin words, intelligible only to himself. After he had tapped all the resonant and non-resonant parts of her body, and had auscultated her thoroughly, he drew from his pocket a note-book alphabetically divided and bound in red leather with gold tooling. After consulting the index, he wrote as follows :

" Examination 6347, Madame A. . . . aged twenty-one."

Then, like an Egyptologist deciphering hieroglyphics, he read off the coloured scrawls on the dressing-gown and noted them in his book.

" Nothing to worry about," he declared when he had finished. " Nothing abnormal; only a slight, a very slight irregularity, which a course of thirty carbonic acid baths will put right. And you must drink three half-tumblers of our waters every morning before luncheon. That is all that is necessary. I will pay you another visit in three or four days."

He jumped up, bowed, and was out of the room with a celerity which left them gasping. This trick of abrupt departure was a whim of his, a pose, which he considered the height of good form and calculated to impress his patients.

Christian ran to look at herself in the mirror and burst out laughing like a happy child.

" Oh, aren't they funny? Aren't they absurd? If there's another one, I must see him immediately. Will, do go and hunt. There must be a third, and I insist on seeing him."

A third? " asked her husband in surprise. " A third what? "

The Marquis had to explain matters. Apologetically, for he was a little in awe of his son-in-law, he said that as Dr Bonnefille happened to be visiting him, he had asked him to see Christian. He was anxious to have his opinion, as he had great confidence in the old physician, as a man of experience, a native of Auvergne and the discoverer of the spring.

Andermatt shrugged his shoulders and said that no one but Dr Latonne should attend his wife, and the Marquis, much disconcerted, wondered how he could smooth over matters and avoid offending his irascible medical adviser.

Christian asked if her brother Gontran had arrived at Enval.

"Yes," said her father, "he has been here three or four days with a friend, whom you have often heard him mention, Monsieur Paul Brétigny. They are doing a tour in Auvergne together. They have just come from Mont-Dore and Bourboule, and are leaving for Cantal at the end of next week."

He suggested that she must be tired after her night in the train and had better rest till luncheon. But she said she had slept splendidly in the sleeping-car, and merely stipulated for an hour to dress. Afterwards she wanted to see the village and the Baths. The two men went off to their rooms to wait for her. Presently she reappeared and they left the house together. She went into raptures over the village, which lay embowered in woods in the depths of the valley, shut in on all sides by chestnut trees, that seemed to rival the mountains in height. They had seeded themselves in all directions and had sprung up haphazard through the centuries, by cottage doors, in yards and streets. Everywhere there were fountains consisting of an upright slab of black rock with a hole in it, through which a jet of clear water shot out, and fell in a graceful curve into a basin below. Beneath the leafy canopy was diffused an aromatic smell of stables. Country women were wending their way gravely along the streets, or standing by their cottage doors, their nimble fingers spinning black wool from distaffs tucked into their girdles. Their short skirts revealed lean ankles in blue stockings; their bodices were secured with narrow shoulder straps, and from their linen blouse-sleeves emerged hard, stringy arms and bony hands.

Suddenly the three visitors heard strange, spasmodic snatches of music, like the strains of a barrel organ, a wornout, wheezy, broken-winded barrel organ.

" Whatever is it? " cried Christian.

" The Casino orchestra," laughed her father. " It takes four performers to make a noise like that."

He pointed to a poster on the wall of a farmhouse, with the following announcement in black letters on a red ground :

ENVAL CASINO

Under the management of Monsieur Petrus Martel, of the Odéon.

Saturday, July 6th : A grand concert, under the direction of Maëstro Saint-Landri, second Grand Prix at the Conservatoire. At the piano, Monsieur Javel, Gold Medallist at the Conservatoire. Flute : Monsieur Noirot, Medallist at the Conservatoire. Double-bass : Monsieur Nicordi, Medallist at the Royal Academy of Brussels.

The concert will be followed by a special performance of—

" LOST IN THE FOREST."

Comedy in One Act.

by

MONSIEUR POINTILLET.

Dramatis Personae:

Pierre de Lapointe .. Monsieur Petrus Martel of the Odéon.
Oscar Léveillé ... Monsieur Petitnivelle of the Vaudeville.
Jean .... Lapalme of the Grand-Théâtre, Bordeaux.
Philippine .... Mademoiselle Odelin of the Odéon.

The orchestra, which will play during the performance, is also under the direction of Maëstro Saint-Landri.

In laughing astonishment, Christian read the bill aloud.

" The orchestra will amuse you; let's go and hear it," said the Marquis.

Turning to the right, they entered the Casino grounds. Some of the visitors were slowly and solemnly pacing up and down the three paths, and after drinking their glasses of water, a few of them went away again. Others were resting on the seats and idly tracing figures in the sand with the tips of their sticks or sunshades. None of them spoke. Their minds seemed a blank, and they themselves paralysed, bored to extinction, by the deadly monotony that characterizes all health resorts.

The only sounds that troubled the mild, still air were the weird vagaries of the orchestra, wafted from some strange, mysterious source, which, ere they died away among the trees, seemed to set the mournful pedestrians in motion.

" Christian ! " cried a voice. She turned and saw her brother, who ran up to kiss her. After shaking hands with Andermatt, he took his sister by the arm and carried her off, leaving his father and brother-in-law together.

Gontran was a tall, immaculately dressed young man, merry like his sister and alert like his father. He took things as they came, but had always an eye to the main chance.

" I thought you would be asleep," he said, " or I would have paid my respects to you at once. And besides, Paul took me this morning to the Château of Tournoël."

" Who is Paul? Oh, I remember, your friend."

" Paul Brétigny. I forgot you hadn't met him. Just at present he is having a bath."

" Is he ill? "

" No, but he's doing a cure all the same. He is just getting over a love affair."

" And he's taking carbonic acid baths—isn't that what they call them?—to set him up again? "

" Exactly. He does whatever I tell him. Oh, he was badly hit. He's a terribly violent fellow. He nearly died of it, and he wanted to kill the girl too. She's an actress, a well-known actress. He was madly in love with her. And of course she deceived him. It was a fearful tragedy. So I made him come away. He is getting over it, but he can't keep his mind off it."

Her face, a moment ago all smiles, had suddenly become serious.

" I shall enjoy meeting him," she murmured.

As yet the word love had for her little meaning. Sometimes she thought about it, as a penniless girl might dream of a string of pearls or a diamond tiara, with a dawning desire for a thing remote yet not unattainable. Her idea of love was derived from novels she had read in idle hours and she did not consider it of great importance. Endowed with a happy, placid, contented disposition, she was not given to daydreams. Though she had been married over two years, she was like an innocent girl. Her heart, her mind, her senses, were still unawakened, a condition in which many women remain till their dying day. Life seemed to her simple and pleasant, without any problems, and she had never sought to probe its meaning and significance. She lived her life, dressed well, slept well and was happy and contented. What more could she desire?

At first, when Andermatt's proposal was put before her, she had refused him, childishly disgusted at the idea of marrying a Jew. Her father and brother, who shared her prejudice, endorsed her answer with a formal refusal. Andermatt lay low for a time; but within three months

he lent Gontran more than twenty thousand francs, and
the Marquis had reasons of his own for changing his
mind. It was characteristic of him invariably to yield
to pressure, from a selfish love of a quiet life.

"All papa's ideas are in a muddle," Christian used to
say of him, and it was the truth. He possessed no fixed
principles or beliefs, but was swayed merely by gusts
of enthusiasm which never remained the same for two
minutes on end. Now, in a romantic but passing
transport, he clung to the time-honoured traditions of
his caste, and was all for a monarchy, but an intelligent,
liberal-minded, enlightened monarchy, moving with the
times; again, after reading Michelet or some other
democratic thinker, he was seized with a passion for the
equality of men, for modern ideas, for the rights of the
poor, downtrodden, afflicted masses. He was ready to
accept any doctrine that happened to suit his mood, and
when his old friend Madame Icardon, whose many links
with the Jewish community induced her to favour
Christian's marriage to Andermatt, began to urge the
proposal, she knew exactly what line of argument to
pursue. She explained to him that the Jewish race, which
had hitherto been oppressed, much as the French lower
classes before the Revolution, had now reached a stage
when they would avenge themselves and use their wealth
as a weapon to hold the rest of the world in subjection.
With no religious beliefs whatever, convinced that the
idea of God was merely an invention of the governing
classes, a more effective device than the idea of abstract
justice for sustaining the foolish, the faint-hearted and
the ignorant, he regarded all dogma with the same
respectful indifference and extended a sincere, but indis-
criminate, esteem to Confucius, Mohammed and Jesus
Christ alike. The incident of the Crucifixion seemed to
him less a fundamental crime than a grave political error.
Within a very few weeks he had been brought to the
point of admiring the secret machinations, incessant.
irresistible, of that race, which had been universally

persecuted. Regarding the situation from a different angle, he now came to consider their triumphant success as a fitting compensation for ages of humiliation. He beheld them masters of kings, who themselves are masters of nations, upholding thrones or suffering them to collapse, bringing about the bankruptcy of a state as easily as that of a wine merchant, treating humiliated princes with arrogance and flinging their tainted wealth into the half-opened treasury of the most Catholic monarchs, who rewarded them with titles of nobility and concessions for railways.

In the end he gave his consent to the marriage of his daughter Christian to William Andermatt.

Christian herself was swayed unconsciously by Madame Icardon, her mother's old friend. Since the Marquise's death this lady had become the girl's confidante and counsellor; her persuasions were combined with pressure on the part of her father, and assisted by her brother's disingenuous indifference. This stout but exceedingly wealthy suitor, who, although he was not positively unprepossessing, did not appeal to her in the least, she accepted much as she would have consented to spend a summer in some unattractive neighbourhood. She now thought him a good-natured soul, kind and quite intelligent, and easy to get on with in private life. But she often made fun of him with Gontran, whose gratitude was merely skin deep.

"Your husband," he remarked, "is balder and pinker than ever. He looks like an overblown cabbage rose or a clean-shaven sucking pig. Where does he get that colouring?"

"It's nothing to do with me, I assure you. Sometimes I feel that I must stick him on the lid of a chocolate box."

At the door of the Baths they caught sight of two men, one on either side of the entrance. They were seated on straw-bottomed chairs, and were leaning their backs against the wall, smoking their pipes.

"Just look at them! Aren't they typical? The one

on the right, the hunchback in the smoking-cap, is old Printemps, who used to be jailor at Riom. Now he's hall porter here and practically runs the show. It's no change to him. He bullies the patients just as he used to bully his prisoners. To him the male patients are convicts, the dressing-rooms cells, the main bathroom a dungeon, and Dr Bonnefille's private room with its stomach pumps a mysterious torture-chamber. He never troubles to touch his hat to a man, on the principle that all convicts are beneath contempt. Women, however, he treats with more respect, respect mingled with surprise, because he had none in his charge at Riom. That retreat was reserved for men only, so he isn't used to addressing the fair sex. The other fellow is the cashier. I bet you won't get him to spell your name properly. You'll see."

Addressing the man on the left of the entrance, Gontran said slowly and deliberately :

" Monsieur Séminois, this is my sister, Madame Andermatt, who wants to put down her name for twelve baths."

The cashier, a very tall, gaunt, cadaverous-looking man, rose and went into the office, which was opposite the Inspector's room. Opening his book, he said :

" What name did you say? "

" Andermatt."

" I beg your pardon? "

" Andermatt."

" How do you spell it? "

" A-n-d-e-r-m-a-t-t."

" Very good."

He wrote with much deliberation, and when he had finished Gontran said :

" Would you mind reading out my sister's name? "

" Certainly, sir. Madame Anterpat."

Laughing till she cried, Christian paid for her tickets.

" What's that noise upstairs? "

" Come and see," said Gontran taking her arm.

Two furious voices greeted them as they climbed the

steps. They opened a door and found themselves in a large coffee-room with a billiard table in the middle. Two men in shirt sleeves, with cues in their hands, were abusing each other across the green cloth.

" Eighteen."

" Seventeen."

" I tell you I've made eighteen."

" You haven't. It's only seventeen."

The manager of the Casino, Monsieur Petrus Martel, was playing his customary game of billiards with the low comedian of the Casino Company, Monsieur Lapalme of the Grand-Théâtre, Bordeaux. Petrus Martel, whose vast and flabby paunch bulged out above his trousers, which were held up in some mysterious way, had had a chequered career as a strolling player, until he had undertaken the management of the Enval Casino. He spent his days imbibing the liquid refreshments which were intended for the visitors, and his huge military moustache was steeped from morning till night in foaming bocks and sticky liqueurs. He had discovered in the old comedian, whom he had engaged, a devouring passion for billiards. As soon as they were out of bed they made for the billiard table, bandying insults and threats, hardly allowing themselves time for luncheon, and refusing to be ousted by other players. Having put everyone else to flight, they passed the time pleasantly enough, although Petrus Martel had bankruptcy staring him in the face at the end of the season. Bored to death, the cashier watched their interminable game from morning till night, listening to their endless dissensions, and from morning till night she supplied the two indefatigable players with beer and liqueurs.

" Come into the grounds," said Gontran. " It's cooler there."

Round the corner of the building they came upon the orchestra in a Chinese kiosk. A fair-haired young man was frenziedly playing the violin and at the same time conducting a queer trio of musicians seated opposite him, with gestures of his head, his floating locks, and his whole body, which he managed like a baton, bending it, straightening it and swaying it alternately to the left and to the right. This was Maëstro Saint-Landri, with his assistants, a pianist, whose instrument was wheeled on castors every morning from the hall of the Casino to the kiosk, a flautist of enormous size, who seemed to be sucking a match and tickling it with his fat puffy fingers, and a double-bass of consumptive aspect. Together they laboured to produce that perfect imitation of a worn out barrel organ, which had surprised Christian as she wandered through the village. As they stood watching them, a man bowed to Gontran.

" Good morning, my dear Count."

" Good morning, Doctor. Let me introduce you to my sister. Christian, this is Dr Honorat."

She could hardly repress her laughter, when she was confronted with yet a third medical adviser.

" I hope you are not in bad health," he said with a bow.

" Only a little out of sorts."

He did not pursue the subject.

" I daresay you know, my dear Count," he said, " that you will have an opportunity of witnessing a most interesting spectacle, just outside Enval."

" What is that, Doctor? "

" Old Oriol is going to blow up that boulder of his. Oh, that conveys nothing to you, but to us it's a tremendous event."

He went on to explain that old Oriol, the richest peasant in the whole neighbourhood, known to possess an income of more than fifty thousand francs, owned all the vineyards, where Enval slopes down to the plain of Auvergne. Just beyond the village at the end of the valley, he continued, there was a little hill, or rather a large knoll, covered with Oriol's best vineyards. In the middle of one of them, close to the road, and two steps away from the stream, stood a gigantic rock, which interfered with cultivation and overshadowed a large portion of ground. Every week for the last ten years, Oriol had announced his intention of blowing up the boulder. But he could never make up his mind.

Whenever one of the village lads went off to do his military service the old man would say to him:

"When you come home on leave, bring me some gunpowder for that there rock."

And all the little soldier boys used to bring back in their knapsacks some gunpowder they had stolen for that there rock of old Oriol's.

He had a whole chestful of gunpowder, but the rock still stood.

At last, however, Oriol had spent a whole week drilling a hole in the rock, with the help of his tall son Jacques, who was nicknamed "Colossus," or, in Auvergnat, "Coloche." That very morning they had filled the cavity with gunpowder and had tamped it, leaving only a space for the fuse, which consisted of a length of pipe-lighter bought at the tobacconist's. The fuse was to be lighted at two o'clock and the explosion would follow five minutes or even ten minutes later, the fuse being very long.

Christian was much interested. The prospect of the blasting appealed to her ingenuous nature like an amusing game. They came to the end of the park.

"What is on the other side?" she asked.

"The '*Bout du Monde*,' Madame Andermatt, the 'End of the World,' a gorge with no outlet, famous throughout Auvergne. It is one of the most curious natural phenomena in this part of the country."

Just then they heard a bell ringing in the distance.

"Luncheon already!" said Gontran, and they turned back.

A tall young man came to meet them.

"Christian, my dear, let me introduce Monsieur Paul Brétigny. Paul, this is my sister."

At first she thought him unprepossessing. His eyes

had a somewhat hard expression and were too round for beauty, and his head, a powerful, bullet head, with close-cropped straight black hair, was likewise round; he had the shoulders of a Hercules, and there was something fierce, heavy and brutal about his whole appearance. His clothes and his whole person exhaled a delicate, subtle perfume, which Christian tried in vain to define.

" You arrived this morning, Madame Andermatt? " he said in a rather toneless voice.

She assented. Gontran caught sight of the Marquis and Andermatt beckoning to them to come in to luncheon at once. As Dr Honorat took leave of them, he asked if they really intended to watch the blasting. Christian promised to be present.

As she went towards the hotel, arm-in-arm with her brother, she whispered :

" I'm as hungry as a wolf. I shall be ashamed to let your friend see what a lot I eat."

II

Luncheon dragged on after the way of table d'hôte meals. Christian knew none of the other guests, and confined her conversation to her father and brother. After luncheon she went to her room to rest until it was time to go and see the blasting. But she was ready far too early and insisted on everyone starting, so as not to miss the explosion.

At the lower end of the valley, just outside the village, rose a large knoll, almost a hill, which they climbed under a burning sun, by means of a little path winding in and out among the vines. On reaching the top, Christian uttered a cry of astonishment at the magnificent panorama unfolded before her eyes. Beneath her lay a plain, stretching away into infinity and suggesting to the mind a boundless ocean. Veiled in soft, blue, airy haze, it rolled away to the foot of distant mountains, dimly discerned some forty or fifty miles away. Visible through the delicate, transparent mist floating above this vast expanse, lay towns, villages, forests, broad yellow acres of ripening crops, alternating with broad green acres of pasturage; factories with tall red brick chimneys, pointed church spires built of dark lava from extinct volcanoes.

"Look behind you," said her brother.

She turned and gazed upon the mountain, the great mountain, pitted with craters. In the foreground lay the valley of Enval, an undulating sea of verdure, which almost cloaked the deep, mysterious ravines. Trees mantled the steep slope, leading to the ridge of the first hill, which shut out from view the higher hills beyond. This was the boundary line between plain and mountain. The latter stretched away to the left towards Clermont Ferrand, and, in the far distance, reared against the sky its strange, truncated summits, extinct volcanoes, like monstrous pustules. Yet more remote, on the dim horizon, between two summits, rose another mountain, loftier still; upon its rounded, majestic brow were strange outlines, suggesting architectural remains. This was the Puy de Dôme, the massive and mighty monarch of the Auvergnat mountains, bearing upon its crest the ruins of a Roman temple wherewith earth's mightiest race had crowned it.

" I know I shall be happy here," cried Christian, conscious already of a thrill of joy; permeated by that sense of wellbeing, which pervades body and soul and makes each breath a delight and every movement a sudden rapture, as when a traveller suddenly enters a land, which bewitches his sight and ravishes his soul, a land which seems to have been waiting for him, the land of his heart's desire.

" Madame Andermatt ! " cried a voice.

A little distance away she saw Dr Honorat, whom she recognised by his large hat. He hurried up and escorted Christian and her party to a grassy slope on the other side of the knoll, where some twenty or thirty spectators, visitors and peasants mingled, were waiting by a clump of little trees. The hillside sloped sharply down to the Riom road, which was lined with willows, that fringed a tiny rivulet. In the middle of a vineyard on the banks of the stream rose a pointed rock. Two men were kneeling at its base in the attitude of prayer. This was the famous boulder, and old Oriol and his son were inserting the fuse. An interested crowd looked on from the road, the front line consisting of an excited swarm of village boys.

Dr Honorat found Christian a comfortable place and she sat down, her heart beating as if she expected the whole assembly to be blown up together with the rock. The Marquis, Andermatt and Brétigny threw themselves down on the grass beside her, while Gontran remained standing.

" My dear fellow," said Gontran banteringly to the doctor. " You can't be nearly as busy as your colleagues. They evidently haven't an hour to spare for this little performance."

" I'm not really less busy," replied Dr Honorat good-temperedly, " only I don't fuss so much about my patients. Personally I would rather amuse them than drug them."

He had a sly humour, which Gontran found attractive. Other spectators joined them, their neighbours at the table d'hôte, Madame Paille and her daughter, both of them widows, Monsieur and Mademoiselle Monécu, and a very short, stout man, who puffed like a leaky boiler. This was Monsieur Aubry-Pasteur, a retired mining engineer, who had acquired a fortune in Russia. The Marquis had already made friends with him. He sat down slowly and laboriously, after sundry preparatory movements, carefully and circumspectly performed, which roused Christian's mirth. Gontran went off to take stock of the other sightseers on the knoll, while Paul Brétigny pointed out to Christian the various features of the landscape. In the foreground lay Riom, its tiled roofs forming a patch of red upon the plain; then Ennezat, Maringues, Lezoux, a sprinkling of villages, barely distinguishable, tiny dark specks on the mantle of verdure. In the far distance, at the foot of the mountains of Forez, he tried to show her Thiers.

" It's over there," he cried eagerly, " where I'm pointing with my finger. I can see it quite plainly."

She herself could make out nothing, but she could well believe that it was clear to those round, steady eyes of his, which gazed into the distance like the eyes of a bird of prey. She felt that they must be as strong as the lenses of binoculars.

"The Allier runs through the middle of the plain," he continued, "but one can't make it out. It's too far away, about twenty-five miles."

She made no further effort to distinguish the points he indicated; her sight and mind were completely engrossed by the boulder. She reflected that in a few moments that great rock would cease to be, blown into a thousand fragments, and she felt for it the vague regret of a child for a broken toy. It had stood there so long, and besides, it was so fine, so picturesque. The two Oriols had risen from their knees and were heaping pebbles round the base of the rock, plying their spades with clumsy energy. The crowd on the road was steadily growing and pressed forward to look. The children frisked round the two men at work, leaping and gambolling like young animals at play. To Christian on the height above, all these people looked microscopically small, a swarm of insects, a busy anthill. The hum of voices reached her, now hardly perceptible, now more distinct: a medley of shouts and noises of human activity, diffused upon the air and reduced to minute atoms of sound. The crowd on the knoll was increasing, as more and more people streamed up from the village and spread all over the slope overlooking the fated rock. They hailed one another, and split up into little groups, according to social standing, caste and their respective hotels. The noisiest set was that of the actors and musicians, presided over by their director Petrus Martel of the Odéon, who for once had abandoned his absorbing game of billiards.

In a panama hat and open alpaca coat, his vast corporation bulging like a huge white protuberance, for in the country he dispensed with a waistcoat, the moustachioed actor behaved as if in charge of the situation and described, explained and criticised every action performed by the two Oriols. His subordinates, Lapalme, the low comedian, Petitnivelle, the leading man, and the musicians, Maëstro Saint-Landri, Javel the pianist,

Noirot, the bulky flautist, Nicordi, the double-bass, all clustered around him attentively.

In front of the group sat three ladies in the shade of three parasols, red, white and blue, which in the afternoon sun composed a quaint and dazzling tricolor. They were Mademoiselle Odelin, the young actress, her mother, described by Gontran as a mother of convenience, and their constant companion, the cashier from the café. This symphony of national colours was an idea of Petrus Martel, who early in the season had remarked the blue and white parasols carried by the Odelins, and had presented a red one to his bookkeeper.

Near the group, and scarcely less conspicuous, were a set of eight cooks and their underlings from the different hotels. Vying with one another in their efforts to impress the spectators, these miserable turnspits had clothed in white all their subordinates down to the dishwashers. Standing there with the pitiless sun beating down on their flat caps, they combined the appearance of a grotesque general staff of white-clad lancers with that of a deputation from the kitchen.

"Where do all these people come from?" asked the Marquis, turning to Dr Honorat. "I should not have thought Enval had so large a population."

"Oh, they come from far and near, from Châtel-Guyon, Tournoël, La Roche-Pradière, Saint-Hippolyte. This affair has been the talk of the countryside for a long time, and besides, old Oriol is a well-known character, something of a personage with his fortune and his influence. He is a true son of Auvergne, content to remain a peasant, working with his own hands, living frugally, amassing wealth, intelligent and full of ideas and schemes for his children's future."

Gontran came back, his eyes sparkling with excitement.

"I say, Paul," he said in an undertone. "Come here. I'll show you two such pretty girls, both perfectly charming."

Paul looked up.

c   *33*

" My dear Gontran, I'm very happy here, and am not going to stir."

" You are making a mistake. They are perfectly delightful. I must get the doctor to tell me who they are," he added, raising his voice. " Two girls of eighteen or nineteen, ladies, but evidently country-bred, and quaintly dressed in black silk gowns with tight sleeves, like the uniforms they wear in convent schools. Two brunettes."

" I know," broke in Dr Honorat. " They are old Oriol's daughters, two pretty little maids, educated by the Black Nuns of Clermont. They are sure to marry well. They are typical, absolutely typical of the race. They come of sound Auvergne stock. I'm an Auvergnat myself, Marquis. Let me show you these two children. . . ."

Gontran interrupted :

" Are you their family doctor? " he asked slily.

" Certainly," he replied gaily to Gontran's innuendo.

" How did you manage to get hold of a wealthy client like that? "

" By advising him to take plenty of good wine."

He told them stories about the Oriols. He was distantly related to them and had known them for years. The father was a character, and very proud of his wine. The produce of one special vineyard was reserved for the family and their guests. Some years, the emptying of these barrels of choice vintage presented no difficulty; in other years it was no mean task. Towards May or June, the old man would realise that he would be hard put to it to finish the remainder, and he would urge his tall son Colosse :

" Come, lad, we must get through it."

And they would keep tossing off pint after pint of red wine from morning till evening. A score of times at each meal, the old man would tip the jug over his son's glass and say :

" We've got to get through it."

At night, feverish and wakeful with all the alcohol he had absorbed, he would rise, slip on his trousers, light the lamp and rouse " Coloche." Together they would go down to the cellar, each with a crust of bread to dip in their glasses, which they kept replenishing straight from the hogshead. When they could actually feel the wine splashing about inside them, the old man would tap the resonant wood to see how much the level of the wine had fallen.

" And those are the two working at the rock? " asked the Marquis.

" Quite so."

At this moment the two men moved rapidly away from the rock, which was now ready for blasting, and the crowd that had gathered around them fled like a routed army, some in the direction of Riom, others towards Enval. The great boulder remained solitary on the little mound covered with turf and gravel, which divided the vineyard into two parts, the ground immediately surrounding it having never been cultivated.

On the height above, the crowd, which now equalled that on the road, was quivering with delighted expectation. Petrus Martel exclaimed in his loud voice :

"Look out. The fuse has been lit."

Christian gave a shiver of anticipation. But the doctor muttered in her ear :

" If they have used all the fuse I saw them buying, it will take at least ten minutes."

All eyes were fixed on the rock. Suddenly a small black pug dog ran up to it, and prowled all round, sniffing ; then, evidently detecting a suspicious smell, he began to yap with all his might, his legs rigid, his coat bristling, his tail straight up, and his ears cocked. A shout of brutal laughter went up from the crowd, some of whom hoped that he would not get away in time. Others whistled to call him off, and threw stones, which, however, fell short of their mark. The pug did not move, but continued to bark furiously at the rock.

Christian shuddered with horror at the idea of seeing the poor little creature blown to fragments. Her pleasure was completely spoilt. She started to her feet to turn away, frantically exclaiming in an agony of pity :

" Good heavens! Good heavens! He will be killed. I can't bear to see it. I can't bear it. I can't bear it. Let's go away. Let's go away."

Without a word Paul Brétigny sprang up, and ran down the side of the knoll as fast as his long legs could carry him. Cries of dismay were uttered, and a wave of horror swept over the crowd. As soon as he saw this big tall man coming towards him, the pug took refuge behind the rock. Paul gave chase ; and the dog scampered to the other side. For a couple of minutes they dodged each other round the rock, as if they were playing hide-and-seek. At last Paul despaired of catching the little creature, and climbed back up the slope, while the dog went on barking in a new access of fury.

Angry remonstrances greeted the panting adventurer ; few can forgive those whose rashness has made them tremble. Christian was choking with emotion and clasping both hands to her throbbing heart. She was so completely distraught that she exclaimed wildly :

" But at least you are uninjured ! "

" The fellow is quite mad," cried Gontran petulantly. " He is always playing the fool like that. I never knew such an idiot."

The ground quivered and heaved. A tremendous explosion shook all the surrounding country and for a full minute it thundered and reverberated among the mountains like a cannonade. All that Christian saw was a great mass of stones which shot up into the air, and fell back sheer upon itself in a cloud of dust. With shrill shouts the crowd swept down from the knoll like a torrent. The cohort of cooks scrambled down the slope, outdistancing the company of actors, who followed in the wake of Petrus Martel. The tricolor parasols were almost carried away in the rush. Men and women, peasants and visitors, they all raced along, tumbling, picking themselves up and running on again, while the two sections of the public who had been swept in opposite directions by their panic, now converged again, intermingling and elbowing one another as they drew near the scene of the explosion.

"Let us wait till the rush is over," said the Marquis, "then we'll have a look."

"Personally," remarked Monsieur Aubry-Pasteur, struggling to his feet with a mighty effort, "I shall take the path back to the village. I have seen all I want to see."

He shook hands and went off.

Dr Honorat had disappeared and they began to discuss him.

"You have only known him a day or two," the Marquis said to his son, "but you are always chaffing him. You will offend him if you are not careful."

Gontran shrugged his shoulders.

"Oh, he's a philosopher, a regular cynic. I assure you, he does not mind. When we are alone, he makes fun of everything and everyone, including his own patients and the waters. I bet you a presentation bath-tub you won't see him put out by my nonsense."

In the meantime there seemed to be great excitement on the site of the vanished boulder. The vast, seething crowd were shouting, jostling one another and swaying backwards and forwards as if thrilled by some startling new development.

Always interested and alert, Andermatt kept exclaiming:

"What is it, I wonder? What is it?"

Gontran volunteered to find out and left them. Christian, who had recovered her composure, reflected that, if the fuse had been but a little shorter, that great idiot of a man would have been killed, blown to atoms, simply because she had been concerned for the safety of a dog. She thought how headstrong and impetuous this man must be to risk his life so recklessly for the whim of a woman whom he hardly knew.

People were seen running along the road towards the village.

"Whatever is it?" asked the Marquis in his turn.

Unable to restrain his curiosity, Andermatt began to descend the slope to join Gontran, who was beckoning to them from below. Brétigny offered Christian his arm, which she accepted. It felt to her as rigid as iron. When her feet slipped on the sunbaked grass, she leaned on it as confidently as if it were a railing.

"It's a spring," cried Gontran, coming to meet them. "The explosion has released a spring."

They plunged into the crowd of excited spectators, through whom, heedless of protests, the two young men elbowed a way for Christian and her father. They stepped over ground littered with sharp, splintered stones, blackened with powder, till they reached a hole full of muddy water, bubbling up and flowing over the feet of the onlookers down to the stream. Andermatt, who had slipped through the throng by what Gontran called his own peculiar methods of insinuation, was already on the spot, absorbed in watching the water as it gushed out of the ground and trickled away. On the other side of the hole stood Dr Honorat, looking on with a mingled expression of surprise and boredom.

"We ought to taste it," said Andermatt. "It may be mineral."

"It's undoubtedly mineral," replied the Doctor. "All the water here is. There will soon be more springs than patients."

"Still, we really should taste it," repeated Andermatt.

"In any case we must wait till it runs clearer," said Dr Honorat indifferently.

In their eagerness to see, the people behind pushed those in front into the mud. A child fell down and everyone laughed. The two Oriols were solemnly viewing this unexpected phenomenon, and wondering what to make of it. Tall, sinewy, gaunt, clean-shaven, the father had the bony head and serious face of a peasant; the son, equally thin, a giant of a man, taller even than his father, wore a moustache and looked a cross between a vine-grower and a trooper. The water was bubbling up more freely and beginning to run clear. There was a stir in the crowd and Dr Latonne came hurrying up, panting and perspiring, with a glass in his hand. At the sight of his colleague, Dr Honorat, standing with one foot on the edge of the new spring, like a general, first to enter a captured town, he halted in dismay.

" Have you tasted it? " he gasped.

" No, I'm waiting for it to clear."

At this Dr Latonne dipped his glass into the water, and tasted it with the solemn air of a connoisseur tasting wine. He pronounced it excellent, an opinion which in no way committed him. He offered the glass to his colleague. But Dr Honorat had evidently no predilection for mineral waters.

" No, thank you," he said with a smile. " Your approval is sufficient. I know the taste."

He knew the taste of all existing brands of mineral water, and had his own opinion of their merits.

" It's not equal to your choice vintage," he said to old Oriol, who was gratified by his remark.

Christian had seen enough and wanted to go home. Again her brother and Paul cleared a way for her through the crowd, and taking her father's arm she followed them. Suddenly she slipped and almost fell. Glancing down, she saw that she had stepped on a morsel of bloodstained flesh, covered with black hair and sticky with mud. It was a fragment of the pug, which had been blown to pieces by the explosion and trampled upon by the crowd. Shocked and horrified, she gasped for breath and could not restrain her tears. She dried her eyes with her handkerchief, murmuring:

" Poor little thing! Poor little thing! "

She felt she could not bear another word of conversa-

tion.   All she wanted was to hurry home and shut herself
up in her room.   Her day, which had begun so happily,
had ended in gloom.   Was it an omen?   Her heart felt
a pang and began to beat violently.

They had the road to themselves, till they saw in front
of them a tall hat, and the skirts of a frockcoat, flapping
like two black wings.   The last to hear the news, Dr
Bonnefille was hurrying up, glass in hand like Dr Latonne.
He stopped to speak to the Marquis.

"What is it, Marquis? A spring? A mineral spring?"

"Yes."

"Flowing freely?"

"Yes, certainly."

"And ... and ... the others? Are they both there?"

"Oh, yes," said Gontran gravely.   "And Dr Latonne
has actually analysed the water already."

At this Dr Bonnefille broke into a run.   Somewhat
cheered and diverted by this encounter, Christian said:

"Well, no, I think I won't go home yet.   Let us sit
in the park."

Andermatt still lingered by the spring and watched
the water bubbling up.

IIII

THAT evening the dining-room at the Hôtel Splendid was buzzing with animation. Conversation was enlivened by the absorbing topic of the boulder and the spring. There were, however, not more than twenty guests. For the most part these were quiet people, in feeble health and of taciturn habits, who had derived no benefit from any of the well-known health resorts and were now trying the more recently established spas. The Ravenels and Andermatts had for neighbours Monsieur Monécu, a little man with white hair; his daughter, a tall pale girl, who sometimes hurried from the table in the middle of a meal, leaving her plate almost untouched; stout Monsieur Aubry-Pasteur, the retired engineer; Monsieur and Madame Chaufour, who wore mourning and were to be met all day long in the park, wheeling their crippled child in a bath-chair; Madame Paille and her daughter, two portly widows with figures fully developed, front and rear.

"You can see," said Gontran, "that they have eaten their husbands and the meal has disagreed with them."

And it was in fact gastric trouble that had brought the pair to Enval. Beyond them sat a man with a very high colour, almost brick red, who also suffered from indigestion, and then some of the usual silent nonentities, who slink into the hotel dining-room, the wife leading, the husband following, make their bow as soon as they enter, and subside into their seats with a deprecating air. The other end of the table was unoccupied, though places had been laid for prospective guests. Andermatt was talking

41

excitedly. He had spent the afternoon in conversation with Dr Latonne, to whom he had dropped hints of great schemes for developing Enval. The doctor had described with enthusiastic conviction the surprising qualities of the local waters. He declared them far superior to those of Châtel-Guyon, which, however, had attained a definite vogue during the last two years. To the right of Enval lay Royat, an uninteresting hole, though its fortune had been made and its success assured; to the left lay Châtel-Guyon, a poor sort of place too, but already in the swim.

Andermatt turned to the engineer.

"Everything depends on how one sets about it. It's entirely a question of tact, skill, boldness and seizing the right moment. In establishing a spa, a good start is everything, and that implies enlisting the sympathies of the great body of Paris doctors. Personally I always make a success of all my enterprises because I go to the root of the matter and set to work to discover the one and only practical method essential to the success of each particular scheme. I wait patiently till I have found it. It is not enough to have the water; you must get people to drink it, and to make them do this it is not sufficient to proclaim in newspapers and elsewhere one's own personal conviction of its unrivalled merits. You must have your advertising discreetly done for you by the only people with influence over the health-seeking, water-drinking public, whom we want to get at, the credulous people, who are always ready to pay for drugs; that is to say, our advertisers must be the doctors themselves. Never conduct your own lawsuit. Leave it to the barristers, who alone have the ear of the court. And never try to persuade a sick man yourself. Leave it to the doctors; the only people he will listen to."

"It's perfectly true," cried the Marquis, who had a great admiration for his son-in-law's robust common-sense. "You always hit the nail on the head."

"There's a fortune to be made out of this place,"

Andermatt continued excitedly. "The country is beautiful, and the climate perfect. The only point on which I
am doubtful is whether there is sufficient water for an
establishment on the grand scale. Half measures are
doomed to failure. To run it properly we should require
enormous quantities of water, enough to ensure a rapid
and steady supply to two hundred baths simultaneously.
The new spring and the old one together would not
suffice for fifty, whatever Dr Latonne may say."

"Oh, as for water," broke in Monsieur Aubry-Pasteur,
"I will guarantee as much as you want."

"You?" cried Andermatt in amazement.

"Yes, I myself. I see you are surprised. Let me
explain. I was here about the same time last year.
Personally I find these Enval baths beneficial. One morning as I was resting in my room I had a visitor, a portly
person, who turned out to be the President of the Board
of Directors of the Hydropathic. He was much upset
and for this reason. The Bonnefille spring was running
so low that the management was afraid it would peter
out altogether. Hearing that I was a mining engineer,
he came to ask me if I could save the situation.

"So I set to work to study the geological system of the
country. You are aware that all over the world upheavals
of different kinds and varying conditions of the earth's
surface have been produced by primeval convulsions.
The problem was to ascertain from what fissures the
Enval waters sprang, then the general direction of these
fissures, their origin and character. I inspected the
establishment minutely, and in a corner I came upon an
old discarded bath-pipe, which I noticed was almost completely choked with calcareous incrustations. The deposits of solids contained in the water evidently blocked
the pipes in a short time, and, the soil being granite, the
same process would inevitably be repeated in the natural
channels. The Bonnefille spring, therefore, was blocked.
That was the whole trouble.

"It was necessary to locate the channel at another

spot. Most people would have explored at a higher level. But after a month's study, observation and deduction, I looked for it and found it fifty yards lower down. This was my method of reasoning.

" I said just now that the first problem was to discover the origin, character and general direction of the granite fissures along which the water flowed. I had no difficulty in ascertaining that, instead of sloping downwards from the mountain to the plain, these fissures inclined upwards from the plain to the mountain, like a roof. The reason for this was, no doubt, because the plain had subsided and involved in its collapse the outlying spurs of the mountain. Thus the water, instead of flowing downwards, was forced upwards through the faults in the granite strata. At the same time I discovered the cause of this remarkable phenomenon.

"Limagne, that vast tract of land, part sand, part clay, which stretches away almost beyond range of sight, was once on a level with the nearest plateau of the mountain. But owing to the geological composition of its foundations, it subsided, drawing down with it the outer edge of the mountain, as I explained just now. This gigantic mass formed at the dividing line between the soft soil and the granite an immense and tremendously deep barrier of clay, impermeable to liquids.

" Now all this mineralised water originates in the burning centres of old volcanoes. If it comes from a long distance, it cools down on the way and bubbles up, icy cold, like an ordinary spring. Coming from a short distance, it issues still warm, the temperature varying with the length of its journey. Its course is as follows. The water descends to unfathomable depths until it reaches the clay barrier of Limagne, which it cannot penetrate, and is forced by tremendous pressure to seek another outlet. Discovering the sloping fissures in the granite, it flows along them in an upward direction until it reaches a surface outcrop. It then resumes its former direction and flows down to the plain along the natural water courses. I may add that we do not see the hundreth part of the mineralised waters of these valleys. We only discover springs whose outlets are exposed. The others, emerging from their channels beneath a thick layer of vegetation and cultivated land, are absorbed by the soil and disappear.

" Thus I draw the following conclusions :

" Firstly.—To find water you have only to follow the slope and general direction of the granite strata.

" Secondly.—To maintain your supply, you have only to prevent the channels from being blocked by calcareous deposits ; in other words, to look after the artificial wells which would have to be sunk.

" Thirdly.—To tap your neighbour's spring you have only to bore down to his particular granite fissure, but at a lower level, and remembering to select a spot between him and the clay barrier by which the water is forced upwards.

" From this point of view, the spring discovered to-day is admirably situated, being only a few yards away from the barrier. Anyone starting a new Hydropathic should build it there."

After he had spoken, there was a general silence, broken only by Andermatt, who exclaimed enthusiastic- ally :

" There you are. One peep behind the scenes, and there's an end of the mystery. You are simply invaluable, Monsieur Aubry-Pasteur."

Besides Andermatt, only the Marquis and Paul Brétigny had understood the disquisition, while Gontran had distinguished himself by not listening to a single word. The rest of the party had hung with open mouths and open eyes on the engineer's lips, and were struck dumb with amazement. Madame Paille and her daughter, who were very pious, wondered whether an explanation of a phenomenon ordained by God and produced by His own secret methods, had not a touch of irreverence. The elder lady felt bound to observe :

"God moves in a mysterious way," a remark which elicited approving nods from some ladies further down the table, who were likewise disturbed by that incomprehensible discourse.

Monsieur Riquier, the man with the brick-red complexion, exclaimed:

"These Enval waters may come from volcanoes or from the moon, but I have been taking them for ten days without the slightest result."

Monsieur and Madame Chaufour, however, protested that their child could move its right leg a little, which hitherto it had been unable to do, in spite of six years of treatment.

"That only proves that we are not suffering from the same complaint; it doesn't prove that the Enval waters are good for gastric troubles," snapped back Monsieur Riquier, evidently exasperated by the failure of his most recent experiment.

Monsieur Monécu spoke up on behalf of his daughter, who during the last weeks had begun to retain her food without having to leave the table half-way through a meal. The tall young woman blushed and looked down at her plate. Madame Paille and her daughter also professed to be feeling better.

Monsieur Riquier's wrath was roused and he turned on the two widows.

"You are suffering from gastric trouble, ladies?"

"Yes," they replied in the same breath, "we cannot digest anything."

He nearly jumped out of his chair.

"You? You?" he exclaimed. "But one has only to look at you. The trouble with you is that you eat too much."

Madame Paille flared up.

"Your case, sir, is plain enough. You exhibit the bad temper which is always associated with a ruined digestion. People with good digestions, they say, are always good-humoured."

A haggard old lady, whose name none know, remarked authoritatively :

" I am sure the waters would do us all more good, if the hotel cook would only realise that he is catering for invalids. He gives us food which no one could possibly digest."

This united the whole company in a denunciation of a hotel-keeper who served up crayfish, pork, eels with mustard sauce, cabbage, actually cabbage and sausages ! in short all the most indigestible dishes imaginable, to patients who were ordered by the three local doctors to touch nothing but tender, lean, white meat, fresh vegetables and milk puddings.

" Surely in a health resort the doctors ought to super-intend the diet provided," exclaimed Riquier, quivering with indignation, " and not leave this very important matter to the discretion of a fool. Every day the hors d'oeuvre consist of hard-boiled eggs, anchovies and ham."

Monsieur Monécu broke in upon him :

" I beg your pardon. Ham is the only thing my daughter finds no difficulty in digesting; it is exactly what Mas-Roussel and Rémusot ordered her to take."

" Ham ! " cried Riquier, " Ham ! Why it's poison, sir."

The table was split into two factions, those who could, and those who could not, eat ham. The interminable daily discussion on the different categories of food was resumed. Even milk provoked a heated argument. Riquier protested that in his case a wine glass of milk at once brought on an attack of indigestion.

Wounded to the quick by these strictures on all his favourite dishes, Aubry-Pasteur made answer :

" But confound it, sir, if you are afflicted with dys-pepsia, while I suffer from gastritis, we naturally require different foods, just as much as short-sighted and long-sighted people require different glasses, though both may be said to be suffering from defective sight. A single glass of red wine is enough to upset me. I believe wine is the worst thing in the world for one's health. All teetotallers live to be a hundred, while we. . . . "

"Personally," Gontran laughingly interrupted, "I should find life pretty dull without wine and . . . women."

Madame Paille and her daughter cast down their eyes. They themselves drank a good brand of claret, undiluted and in considerable quantities, and their double bereavement at an early age seemed to indicate that they had followed a similar policy with their husbands, for the daughter was not more than twenty-two and the mother barely forty.

Contrary to his usual habit, Andermatt remained silent and thoughtful. Suddenly he asked Gontran if he knew where the Oriols lived.

"Yes, I was shown their house just now."

"Will you take me there after dinner?"

"With pleasure. I should rather like to see those two girls again."

Immediately after dinner they left the hotel, while Christian, who was tired, went up to the drawing-room to spend the evening with the Marquis and Paul. At health resorts dinner is usually early, and it was still broad daylight.

"My dear fellow," said Andermatt, taking Gontran's arm, "if the analysis equals Latonne's expectations, and if I can come to terms with old Oriol, I may launch out into something big, and make Enval the queen of watering-places. The idea appeals to me tremendously."

He halted in the middle of the street, and seized his companion by the lapels of his coat.

"Ah, you fellows, you don't realise the fascination of business. I don't mean the sort of business carried on by tradesmen and merchants, but great enterprises such as we financiers conduct. If you thoroughly understand it, business comprises all that man has ever cared for : politics, war, diplomacy—everything, everything. You have to seek and find and create and effect your combinations with the utmost audacity. Nowadays the battle is waged with money. To me, five-franc pieces are little soldiers in red breeches; louis, glittering lieutenants; hundred-franc notes, captains; thousand-franc notes, generals. And I wage war, by Jove; I wage war from morning till night. My enemy is the world, the whole world.

"That is life, a life as spacious as that of the heroes of old. To-day, it is we who are really the mighty men, the only mighty men. Just look at this village, this insignificant village. I shall turn it into a town, a town of dazzling whiteness, of great hotels, equipped with lifts, servants, livery stables. There will be a crowd of rich people, and the poor will flock to serve them. And all this simply because I took it into my head one evening to challenge Royat, over there on the right, Châtel-Guyon, yonder on the left, Mont-Dore, Bourboule, Châteauneuf, St. Nectaire behind us, and Vichy in front there. And I shall succeed, because I have found the key to the situation, the one and only key. I suddenly saw it, as clearly as a great general seizes upon the enemy's weak spot. It is our business to manage men, to lead them on, and to dominate them. How fascinating life can be with such things in one's power! I shall get at least three years' amusement out of my town. What luck it was meeting that engineer, who talked such excellent sense, such really admirable sense, to us at dinner! His method is clear as daylight. Thanks to him, I see my way to ruining the existing company without even having to buy it out."

They had resumed their walk and were now slowly climbing the road on the left, which led to Châtel-Guyon.

"When I am with my brother-in-law," Gontran was wont to remark, "I can hear his head ringing with all the sounds one hears in the rooms at Monte Carlo: the clink of gold, as it is handled, flung down, shovelled out, raked in, lost and won."

Andermatt, in fact, suggested a curious human machine, constructed solely for the purpose of making

D

plans for manipulating money and applying it in various directions. He prided himself on his peculiar flair, and boasted that he could estimate at a glance the precise value of any given object. Wherever he happened to be, at any odd moment, he would pick up a thing, examine it, turn it over and declare its worth in money. His wife and brother-in-law made fun of this obsession and amused themselves by presenting out-of-the-way oddities for him to value. When he was perplexed by their extraordinary finds, they went into fits of laughter. In Paris, Gontran would stop him in the street and invite him to estimate all the exhibits in a shop window, or a lame cabhorse, or a pantechnicon and its entire contents. One evening, at a big dinner party at the Andermatts' house, he challenged his host to estimate respectively the value of the Obélisque, the Solférino Bridge, the Arc de Triomphe, and finally remarked with solemnity :

" What an interesting book you could write on the cash value of the world's principal monuments ! "

Andermatt never took offence, but entered into the fun with the complacency of a man who is perfectly sure of himself.

" And what am I worth? " asked Gontran one day. William declined to answer, but his brother-in-law insisted.

" Now supposing I was captured by brigands, how much would you give for my ransom? "

" Why . . . why . . . I'd give them an I.O.U.," replied Wiliam, with a smile so significant that Gontran desisted, slightly chagrined.

Andermatt, who was a man of keen intelligence, had a fine taste for objects of vertu, understood his subject thoroughly, and in forming his collection exhibited the same unfailing intuition which characterised all his business transactions.

Gontran halted in front of a house of homely aspect.

" Here we are," he said, plying the iron knocker on the solid oak door. A gaunt maid opened to them.

" Monsieur Oriol? " queried Andermatt.

" Please come in, sir."

Through the kitchen, the usual spacious kitchen of farmhouses, where a pot was still hanging over a small fire, they passed into a sitting-room, and found Monsieur Oriol and his family. The old man was asleep, sitting on one chair with his feet upon another. His son, with his elbows on the table, was reading the *Petit Journal*, with the desperate determination of a feeble intelligence unable to concentrate, while the girls sat together in the recess of the window, working at opposite ends of the same piece of embroidery.

Dumbfoundered at the unexpected visit, the two sisters at once sprang to their feet. Then Jacques raised his face, flushed with his mental exertions, and finally old Oriol woke up and deliberately withdrew his long legs, one after the other, from the chair where they reposed.

The bare, white-washed room, with its flagged floor, was furnished with straw-bottomed chairs, a mahogany cupboard, four crude colour-prints from Epinal, and long white window curtains.

The whole party looked at one another, while the maid, her skirts tucked up to the knee, remained standing by the door, spellbound with curiosity.

Andermatt introduced first himself, then his brother-in-law, Count de Ravenel, and he favoured the two girls with a specially deep bow of supreme elegance. Then he calmly subsided into a chair.

" Monsieur Oriol," he began, " I have come to talk business, and I do not propose to beat about the bush, but to go straight to the point. You have just discovered a spring in your vineyard. In a few days we shall have the analysis of the water. If the report is unfavourable, I need hardly say that I shall withdraw at once. But if it comes up to my expectations, my proposal is to buy from you that particular plot of ground and all the ground round about.

" There is this to consider. No one but myself could

possibly afford to make you such an offer. The old
company is on the verge of bankruptcy, and cannot,
therefore, entertain the idea of constructing new buildings. The failure of this venture will discourage other
attempts.

"I don't ask you to give me your answer now. Talk
it over with your family. When we get the analysis, you
can fix your price. If it suits me, I shall accept it; if it
doesn't I shall say no and go my way. I never bargain,
never."

In his own peculiar way the peasant, too, was a man
of business and as cunning as a fox. He replied politely
that he would see, that he was much honoured and would
think it over. He offered his guests a glass of wine,
which Andermatt accepted. As it was growing dark,
Oriol told the girls, whose eyes were bent upon their
work, to bring lights. They rose together, went into the
next room and returned with two lighted candles and
four common tumblers. The candles, which were new
and had frills of pink paper round the sockets, had
doubtless adorned the mantelpiece in the girls' bedrooms.

Colosse got up to go down to the cellar, which was the
masculine prerogative in that household, when an idea
occurred to Andermatt.

"I should very much like to visit your cellar. You
are the chief wine grower in this part of the country;
your cellar ought to be worth seeing."

Andermatt's flattery went straight to old Oriol's heart;
seizing one of the candles, he hastened to lead the way.
They passed again through the kitchen, and thence into
the courtyard below. In the fading light they could
distinguish empty casks standing on end; here enormous
granite millstones with a hole through the middle, like
wheels of some colossal chariot of antiquity; there, a
dismantled wine-press with its screws and sections of
brown wood polished by use and suddenly darting forth
reflections of the candle-light through the gloom; in yet
another corner agricultural implements, the steel bur-

nished by the soil till it shone like armour. One after another, all these different objects emerged from the darkness, as the old man passed by holding the candle in one hand, and shading it with the other.

They came to a door secured by two locks, which Oriol opened, and they were met by the scent of wine, the perfume of crushed, dried grapes. Raising the candle above his head, he afforded his visitors a vague glimpse of a long row of casks, each carrying a smaller one on its bulging side. He pointed out that the cellar plunged straight into the heart of the mountain, and then explained the age, vintage, and qualities of the contents of the different barrels, until he came to the special family brand. Stroking the cask, as if he were patting a favourite horse, he said proudly:

"You shall taste this. There is no wine like this in bottle at Bordeaux or anywhere else."

He had the passionate prejudice of the peasant in favour of wine in the wood. Following behind with a jug, Colosse bent down and turned the tap, while his father held the candle as if he were assisting at some delicate and difficult piece of work. The light fell full upon the two faces, that of the sire, with his look of an old farm grieve, that of the son, with his mingled aspect of trooper and peasant.

"Like a fine Teniers, what?" murmured Andermatt in Gontran's ear.

"Personally I prefer the girls," the young man whispered back.

They returned to the sitting-room, and to please their hosts, the visitors had to drink deep of the wine. The girls had drawn up their chairs to the table and went on with their work as if no strangers were present. Gontran kept glancing at them, wondering if they were twins, because of their close resemblance to each other. He noticed, however, that one sister was shorter and plumper in figure, while the other was more graceful. Their hair, of a rich dark brown, was drawn down over their temples and glinted with each little movement of their heads. Each had the somewhat pronounced Auvergnat jaw and forehead and rather high cheek-bones, but both possessed enchanting mouths, fascinating eyes, with beautiful, delicately pencilled eyebrows and exquisite complexions. It was evident that they had not been brought up at home but at a first-rate school. In the convent, to which all the best families in Auvergne sent their daughters, they had acquired the simple manners of well-bred girls. At last Gontran, who was sick of the sight of the wine, kicked Andermatt under the table as a hint to him to go. Both shook hands warmly with the two men and bowed ceremoniously to the girls, who, without rising, responded with a slight inclination of the head.

" What a curious household ! " Andermatt exclaimed as soon as they were out of the house. " How clearly you can trace the transformation from the plebeian to the well-bred. The boy had to stay at home to work in the vineyards so as to save the wages of a hired man : a stupid piece of economy, but there it is. He therefore remains of the people. The girls, on the other hand, are almost ladies already. If they make suitable marriages they will be quite equal to any of our society women, and better than most of them. It's as interesting to me to come across people like that as it is to a geologist to find an animal of the tertiary period."

" Which do you like best ? " asked Gontran.

" Which do I like best ? Which what ? "

" Which of the girls ? "

" I can't tell you. I never thought of comparing them. But what does it matter to you ? You're not thinking of running off with one of them."

" Of course not," laughed Gontran. " But it's delight-ful for once to meet girls with the bloom still on them. It's always rubbed off women of our own class. I enjoy looking at them, just as you do at a Teniers. In my eyes there's nothing to equal a pretty girl, wherever you meet her, and whatever her social standing. Pretty girls are the only works of art for me. I don't collect them, but I admire them, admire them tremendously, with the sure but dispassionate eye of the connoisseur. It's my hobby. By the way, could you lend me five thousand francs?"

His companion came to a halt.

"Again!" he exclaimed in forcible tones.

"Every time," replied Gontran ingenuously.

They walked on.

"What the devil do you do with the money?"

"Spend it."

"Yes, but you're ridiculously extravagant."

"My dear fellow, I enjoy spending money, as much as you enjoy making it. Don't you see?"

"Perfectly. But you never make any."

"True. I don't know how. You can't have everything. You have the knack of making money, but have no idea how to spend it. Your only use for money is to get interest on it. Now, I don't know in the least how to make it, but I have a perfect genius for spending it. With money I can buy a thousand things of which you hardly know the name. We were cut out to be brothers-in-law. I am your exact complement."

"What a lunatic!" muttered Andermatt. "No, you can't have five thousand francs, but I'll lend you fifteen hundred, because I may want you to do something for me presently."

"Very well," said Gontran coolly, "I'll take fifteen hundred on account."

Andermatt patted him on the shoulder, but made no reply.

They reached the park, which was lighted with Chinese lanterns hanging from the trees. The orchestra was haltingly executing a dreary piece of classical music, punctuated with breaks and sudden pauses. The four musicians were worn out with playing in that solitude, day after day from morning till night, with no one to hear them save trees and brooks; exhausted with trying to produce the effect of twenty instruments, and exasperated by never receiving their full pay at the end of the month. Petrus Martel always paid part of their salaries in hampers of wine and bottles of liqueurs, which the patients never touched. Above the noise of the orchestra could be heard the click of billiard balls, and · voices calling the score :

"Twenty, twenty-one, twenty-two."

Monsieur Aubry-Pasteur and Dr Honorat, sole occupants of the gardens, were taking their coffee alongside of the orchestra. Andermatt and Gontran went up to the billiard room, where Petrus Martel and Lapalme were engaged in their usual desperate contest. The cashier woke up and asked :

"What will you take, gentlemen?"

IV

AFTER the girls had gone to bed, father and son talked
far into the night. Roused and excited by Andermatt's
proposal, they thought out schemes for kindling his enthusiasm without compromising their own interests.
Hard-headed peasants and practical men, they carefully
weighed all possible chances, realising that in a country
where mineral springs gush out along the course of every
stream, it would never do to frighten away with exor-
bitant demands this unique and unexpected purchaser.
At the same time it would be unsound to relinquish their
entire interest in this new spring, which, as they augured
from Royat and Châtel-Guyon, might prove some day a
veritable stream of silver.

They racked their brains for plans wherewith to in-
flame the banker's ardour to fever-heat. They conceived
the idea of mythical rival companies, ready to outbid
him, and a whole series of clumsy stratagems which they
felt to be inadequate, although they could not improve
upon them. They slept badly. The father, who was the
first to awake the next morning, wondered nervously
whether the spring had not disappeared again in the night.
It might conceivably have vanished into the earth as
suddenly as it had come, beyond hope of recovery. With
all a miser's anxiety he rose, shook his son awake, and
confided to him his fears. Colosse dragged himself out
of his grey blankets, dressed, and left the house with his
father. In any case, it was an excellent opportunity to
tidy up the spring and its surroundings, remove the
stones, and make everything clean and presentable, like
an animal prepared for the market. Armed with picks

and shovels, they set out side by side, walking with the same long, deliberate stride. Absorbed in their own concerns, they had no eyes for their surroundings, and replied with monosyllables to the greetings of friends and neighbours. Once on the Riom road, their anxiety increased and they strained their eyes to see if they could catch a glimpse of the water bubbling up and glittering in the morning sun. The road was deserted and white with dust, and alongside of it murmured the brook, fringed by the willows. Oriol saw two feet projecting from the shade of a tree. Two more steps revealed to him Father Clovis, seated by the road with his crutches on the grass beside him. The old man was a paralytic, a well-known character in the neighbourhood, where for the last ten years he had dragged himself slowly and painfully around on what he called his pair of wooden legs. In appearance he resembled one of Callot's beggars. Once a notorious poacher of woods and streams, he had often been caught and sent to jail. But during his long night watches in the wet grass and on nocturnal fishing expeditions, when he used to wade waist deep through the water, he had contracted rheumatism. Nowadays, moaning and groaning, he crept along like a crab which has lost a claw, dragging his left leg after him like a limp rag, while the other was doubled up.

The village lads, however, out after girls or hares at dusk, declared that old Clovis could be seen, swift as a stag and lithe as an adder, darting in and out of thickets and clearings and that his rheumatism was merely a piece of bluff to deceive the police. Colosse, in particular, vowed that he had seen him, not once, but scores of times, setting snares, with his crutches under his arm. Oriol stopped and looked down at the old vagabond. A scheme was shaping itself in his mind, though dim as yet, for ideas were slow to mature in his square Auvergnat skull.

They said good-morning and talked about the weather, the vine, which was then in flower, and other matters. Then Oriol hurried after Colosse, who had gone on.

They found the spring still flowing, while the bottom of the basin was covered with a deep red, derived from a rich deposit of iron below. Exchanging smiles of satisfaction they set to work to clear the ground and to collect the stones into a heap. They found the remains of the dog, and cracked a joke as they buried them. Suddenly old Oriol dropped his spade, and an expression of malicious joy and triumph deepened the lines about his set mouth and crafty eyes.

" I want to show you something," he said to his son, who obediently followed him, as he retraced his steps, till he reached the spot where old Clovis was still sunning himself and his crutches.

" Do you want to earn a hundred francs? " asked Oriol.

The cripple prudently refrained from speech.

" A whole hundred francs," insisted Oriol.

" Well, who wouldn't? " muttered old Clovis at last.

" Well then, my boy, this is what you've got to do."

He explained at great length, with all sorts of sly hints and innuendoes and endless repetitions, that if he would agree to take an hour's bath between ten and eleven every morning, in a hole dug for him by the Oriols close to their spring, and pronounce himself cured at the end of a month, they would give him a hundred francs in silver.

The old fellow listened with an air of dense stupidity.

" All the medicine I've taken has never cured me, so why should that water of yours? "

Colosse broke out angrily :

" None of that, you old humbug. I know all about your rheumatics. What were you doing last Monday in Comberombe wood at eleven o'clock at night? "

" It's a lie," snapped the ancient.

" Didn't I see you jump over Jean Mannezat's sunk fence and slink off by Poulin bottom? "

" That's another lie."

" And I suppose it's a lie that I called to you ' Look out, Clovis. Police ! ' and that you turned off down the Moulinet path? "

" That's another lie."

" A lie, is it?" exclaimed the big fellow furiously, almost menacingly. "All right, old dot-and-carry-one, my legs are longer than yours. Next time I see you at night, either in the wood or by the stream, I'll catch you and tie you to a tree, and in the morning I'll bring the whole village to see you."

Oriol checked his son.

" Listen, Clovis," he said soothingly, "you might as well try it. We'll dig a bath for you, Coloche and I, and you shall come every day for a month. For doing that, I'll give you not one hundred but two hundred francs. And then, listen. If you're cured at the end of the month, you shall have another five hundred. Five hundred francs, all in silver. That with the other two hundred, makes seven hundred. Think of that! Two hundred for the baths, and another five hundred for the cure. And listen! If you get your pains back again in the autumn, it won't be our fault. The water will have produced its effect just the same."

" All right," said the old fellow, placidly. " I'll take on the job. I don't suppose it will do any good. But we'll see anyhow."

They shook hands on the bargain and the Oriols returned to the spring, to dig out a bath for old Clovis.

They had been at work for quarter of an hour, when they heard voices on the road, and caught sight of Andermatt and Dr Latonne. The two men winked at each other and stopped digging.

Dr Latonne and Andermatt came up to them and shook hands and all four gazed at the spring in silence. It was violently agitated like water over a hot fire, throwing up gas and bubbles, and trickling down to the stream by a narrow channel it had already made for itself.

" What about that for iron?" said Oriol, with a triumphant smile on his lips, as he pointed out the red deposit at the bottom. Even the little pebbles in the water were covered with a layer of reddish rust.

" Yes, but that's nothing," replied Dr Latonne. " We have to find out the other constituents."

" Well, Coloche and I drank a whole glass each yesterday evening, and we feel all the fitter for it, don't we, my boy? "

" Yes, rather. All the fitter," said Colosse with conviction.

Andermatt, who was standing on the edge of the hole, made no sign. He turned to the doctor.

" We should require about six times this volume of water for my purpose, shouldn't we, Doctor? "

" About that."

" Do you think we can get it? "

" I know nothing whatever about it."

" This is how it stands. The purchase of the land cannot be definitely concluded until borings have been made. After receiving the analysis we must draw up a contract of sale, but it will not come into effect unless the various soundings prove satisfactory."

Old Oriol began to feel uneasy. He did not understand the situation. Andermatt explained that a single spring was not sufficient, that he could not think of concluding the purchase unless other springs were discovered, nor prospect for springs until the provisional contract was signed. The two peasants at once seemed positive that there were as many springs on their land as there were vines. They had only to dig; they would see, they would see.

" Yes," said Andermatt quietly, " we shall see."

Old Oriol dipped his hand into the water.

" Why it's hot enough to boil an egg, much hotter than that spring of Bonnefille's."

Latonne moistened one finger and admitted that this was possible.

" And then it has more taste and better taste than the other one," the old peasant continued, " and it doesn't smell all wrong. Oh, this is all right, this is. I'll answer for it. I know everything about the waters in these parts; I have had my eye on them for the last fifty years, and I've never seen a better spring, never."

After a moment's silence, he resumed :

"Mind you, I'm not saying this to crack up my property. I'd like to put it to the test, to a proper test, not your chemical analysis, but a test on a real invalid. I bet this spring could cure a paralytic. Just look how hot it is and what a flavour it's got."

He seemed to be racking his brains and then to be searching the neighbouring mountain tops for the requisite subject for his experiment. After this evidently fruitless quest, he glanced down the road. Some two hundred yards away, the old vagabond's crippled legs projected from behind the tree trunk which screened the rest of his body.

Shading his eyes with his hand, Oriol turned to his son :

"That can't be old Clovis still there?"

"That's him all right," laughed Colosse. "You know he can't run like a hare nowadays."

Oriol moved a step nearer to Andermatt.

"Now, sir, listen to me," he said earnestly. "There's an old paralytic over there. The doctor here knows all about him. He's a genuine case. He hasn't walked a step for the last ten years. That's so, Doctor, isn't it?"

"Oh, that fellow! If you cure him, I'll give you a franc a glass for your water! The old chap is a martyr to gouty rheumatism, and suffers from spasmodic contraction of the left leg and complete paralysis of the right. I believe he's incurable."

Oriol heard him out.

"Well, Doctor," he said deliberately, "will you try the experiment for a month? I don't say it will be successful; I don't say anything. All I wish is to try the experiment. Look here. Coloche and I were just digging a hole to bury the stones; well, we'll make it into a hole for Clovis. He shall take an hour's bath every morning. And we shall see what we shall see."

"You can try," muttered the doctor. "It won't be the slightest use."

Fascinated by the idea of an almost miraculous cure, Andermatt welcomed the suggestion with enthusiasm. The four men went along the road till they came upon Clovis, still basking in the sun. The old poacher played up to Oriol; made a pretence of refusing, and held out for a long time, but at last suffered himself to be persuaded, on condition that Andermatt paid him two francs a day for his immersion.

When the bargain had been concluded, it was agreed that that very day, as soon as the hole had been dug, old Clovis should take his first bath. Andermatt was to provide a change of clothes for him to put on afterwards, and the Oriols arranged to bring from their yard an old, disused shepherd's hut, where the invalid could dress.

Andermatt and Latonne returned to the village, where they separated. The doctor went home to his consultations, and Andermatt adjourned to the Baths to wait for his wife, who was due there at half-past nine.

She appeared in a few minutes. From head to foot, her gown, her hat, her sunshade, her cheeks, all one rosy red, she seemed an incarnation of the dawn, as, disdaining the winding road, she tripped down the steep slope from the hotel, lightly as a bird flits from stone to stone with folded wings.

"What a delicious place!" she exclaimed, as soon as she saw her husband. "I simply love it."

One or two visitors, gloomily wandering about the desolate little park, turned to look at her as she went by, and Petrus Martel in his shirt-sleeves, smoking his pipe at the window of the billiard room, called to his crony Lapalme, who was sitting in a corner with a glass of white wine.

"Isn't she a daisy?" he said, smacking his lips.

Christian entered the hall with a smile for the cashier on the left of the door and a pleasant good-morning for the old jailer on the right. Handing her ticket to an attendant in the same uniform as the girl behind the bar, she followed her along a passage, off which opened the various bathrooms. She was ushered into a fair-sized room with bare walls and no furniture except a chair, a looking-glass, a shoehorn, and a large oval trough, lined with cement as yellow as the soil.

The attendant turned a key like that of a street stand-pipe, and the water gushed in through a small round grating at the bottom of the bath, quickly filling it to the brim, while the overflow was carried off by a waste pipe in the wall.

Christian, who had left her maid at the hotel, declined the help of the Auvergnat attendant, and sent her away, saying that she would ring for her towels and for anything else she wanted. She undressed slowly, watching the almost imperceptible flow of the limpid water. When she had thrown off her clothes, she dipped one foot into the bath and was at once suffused with a delightful glow. Then she immersed the other foot and finally sat down in the delicious warmth of that crystal stream, which swirled around her, while little bubbles of gas clustered all over her body, her legs, her arms, her bosom. She marvelled at these innumerable, minute globules of air, clinging about her like a corselet of tiny pearls. They kept rising from her white limbs to evaporate on the surface, and were immediately replaced by new bubbles, continually forming upon her skin, each like a fairy fruit, the exquisite, intangible fruit of that fair, rosy, youthful body, which enriched the water with these gems. Christian felt so utterly content, so luxuriously soothed, so exquisitely caressed and embraced by the rippling, flowing, sparkling water, welling up through the bottom of the bath and escaping through the little hole at the top, that she could have stayed there forever, without movement, almost without thought. With the delightful warmth of the bath, there stole over her a sense of tranquil happiness, in which were mingled peace of mind, a feeling of repose, of comfort, health, sober joy, an inexpressible lightness of heart. Lulled by the gurgle of the water as it escaped, her mind dreamily dallied with plans for the rest of that day and for the morrow; with rambles all over the country, with thoughts about her father, her husband, her brother, and that tall friend of Gontran's, with whom, since his adventure with the dog, she did not feel wholly at ease. She disapproved of headstrong people. As she lay in the bath, she was steeped, body and soul, in a tranquillity, which, save for her vague longing for a child, was vexed by no desire for a different existence, for unknown passions and emotions.

She started, as the door suddenly opened and the attendant entered with towels and a wrapper. Her twenty minutes were already over; it was time to dress. It was almost pain, it was almost grief, to rouse herself. She felt inclined to ask the woman for a few minutes' grace. Then she remembered that this delightful experience would be repeated day after day, and reluctantly she stepped out of the bath and wrapped herself in a dressing-gown which was so well warmed that it almost scorched her.

As she passed the consulting-room, Dr Bonnefille looked out and with a ceremonious bow invited her to enter. He felt her pulse, looked at her tongue, asked her how she slept, and questioned her about her general health, her appetite, her digestion. As he escorted her to the door, he remarked :

" You're getting on splendidly. My regards, if you please, to your father, one of the most distinguished men I have had the honour to meet in my whole career."

Impatient at his officiousness, she made her escape, and at the door of the establishment came upon the Marquis in conversation with the rest of his party. Andermatt, in whose head a new idea would buzz unceasingly, like a bluebottle under a glass, was telling them about the experiment with the paralytic. He wanted to go back to the spring to see if he was really having his bath. To humour him, the others went with him.

Christian quietly fell behind with Gontran.

" I want to talk about your friend," she began, when the others were well ahead. " I don't care for him much. Tell me what he is really like."

Gontran, who had known Paul for some years, described his character as a blend of varying impulses, passionate, violent, loyal and tender by turns.

He was intelligent, he said, but an impetuous soul, always in the grip of new ideas. Carried away by every caprice, unable to master or control his passions, to reason with himself, to order his life according to fixed principles, he obeyed every impulse, good and bad alike, as soon as his overheated mind was stirred by a thought, a desire, or an emotion of any description. He had fought seven duels, and was always as ready to make friends with his adversary as he had been to insult him. He was continually falling violently in love with women of every social grade, all of whom inspired in him the same passionate adoration, from the little working-girl whom he met on the threshold of her shop, to the actress, whom he had carried off, literally carried off, after a First Night, just as she was stepping into her brougham. Seizing her in his arms in the midst of a gaping crowd, he had bundled her into a carriage, which drove away at a gallop, baffling all pursuit.

" That's what he's like," Gontran wound up. " A good fellow, but quite mad. Very rich, into the bargain, and capable of anything, absolutely anything, once he loses his head."

" I like that curious scent he uses. What is it? "

" I don't know. He won't tell me. But I rather think it comes from Russia. That actress of his, of whom I'm busy curing him, gave it to him. Yes, it's very pleasant."

Down the road they saw an excited group of villagers and visitors, for this was a favourite walk before luncheon. Christian and Gontran joined the others.

In the very spot, where but yesterday the boulder had stood, they saw rising out of the ground, as if severed from its trunk and planted there, a grotesque human head, adorned with a long white beard and a tattered felt cap. The vinedressers stood round, mystified but impassive, for Auvergnats do not possess the spirit of mockery. Three fat men from some second-rate hotel, however, looked on laughing and joking. The Oriols, father and son, stood watching old Clovis, who was seated on a stone inside the hole in water up to his chin. He looked like an accused of bygone days, undergoing punishment for some mysterious dabbling in the Black Art. He had not relinquished his crutches, which were soaking in the spring beside him.

"Bravo! Bravo!" cried Andermatt in ecstasy. "There's an example which all sufferers in this part of the world ought to follow."

Leaning over the ancient, he shouted in his ear as if he were deaf :

" Are you comfortable? "

" I'm melting," replied Clovis, who seemed completely stupefied by his immersion in the warm spring. *"Bougrre, how hot it is ! "*

" The hotter the better," remarked old Oriol.

" What's all this? " exclaimed a voice behind the Marquis. It was Monsieur Aubry-Pasteur, who was returning, panting and puffing as usual, from his daily constitutional.

Andermatt explained his experiment in therapeutics.

" *Bougrre,* how hot it is ! " the victim kept moaning.

He wanted to get out of the hole, and clamoured for someone to give him a hand. Andermatt, however, managed to soothe him by promising him an extra franc for each bath. The crowd formed a ring round the trough where the old man sat, with his dingy rags floating about him.

" There's broth for you ! " cried a voice. " I shouldn't care for a spoonful of that."

" I should not fancy the soup meat either," chimed in another.

The Marquis pointed out that in this new spring the bubbles of carbonic acid gas seemed larger, more plentiful, more effervescent, than in the water that supplied the Baths. The old tramp's tatters were thick with them. They rose to the surface in such abundance that the water seemed hung with countless delicate chains, strings of minute diamond drops, all glittering like jewels in the noonday sun.

Aubry-Pasteur burst out laughing.

" Bless you, I'll tell you what they do at the Baths. You know you catch a spring, just as you catch a bird, in a sort of trap, that is to say, a thing known as a sump. This process is called tapping. Well, this is what happened last year to the spring that supplies the Baths. The carbonic acid, being lighter than water, accumulated at the top of the receiver, and the excess was presently forced back into the pipes, and thence into the baths in such quantities that the patients were asphyxiated. There were three casualties in two months. So the management came to me again, and I invented a very simple apparatus consisting of two pipes, which conducted the water and the gas separately from the receiver to a space just below the bath, where they were mixed in the proper proportions, thus eliminating all danger from excess of carbonic acid. But my apparatus would have cost a thousand francs. Well, what do you suppose the old jailer did? I'll give you a thousand guesses. He made a hole in the top of the receiver to get rid of the gas, which naturally escaped. So your carbonic acid baths contain no carbonic acid, or none to speak of! Whereas you have only to look at this."

There was a general feeling of indignation. The bystanders' laughter subsided, and they looked enviously at the paralytic. Everyone, who was taking a course of baths, felt like seizing a pick and digging a hole for himself by the side of the old vagabond.

Andermatt took the engineer by the arm and carried him off for a talk. Now and then Aubry-Pasteur stopped and appeared to be drawing diagrams on the ground and indicating various points with his walking-stick, while Andermatt made entries in his notebook.

Brétigny talked to Christian, describing all that he had seen and felt during his tour in Auvergne. The country appealed to those ardent instincts of his, that forever hinted at the fundamental voluptuousness of his character. He had for nature the passion of the sensualist; it thrilled him in every nerve, in every fibre of his being.

"As for me, Madame Andermatt," he said, "my whole soul lies open to every impression. Everything I see and hear enters into me, passes through me, and moves me to tears of ecstasy or anguish. I have only to look at that hillside yonder, that deep fold of verdure, those ranks of trees climbing up the mountain side, and the whole wood enters through my eyes, takes possession of me, masters me, mingles in my blood. It is as if I fed upon it, absorbed it into my system, until I am one with the forest."

He laughed as he spoke, turning his great round eyes now on the wood, now on the impressionable Christian, who listened to him in amazement, till she felt that she, too, like the wood, was being devoured by that intense and eager gaze.

"If you only knew the pleasure I owe to my sense of smell," he resumed. "I drink in this lovely air; it exhilarates me, puts new life into me, and I can distinguish all its components, every single one of them. Let me explain. To begin with, have you noticed, since your arrival, a delicious scent, unlike any other, a scent so exquisite, so ethereal that it seems—how shall I describe it?—the mere ghost of a perfume? It is everywhere, and yet never to be traced, never to be defined. Nothing more perfectly—more perfectly divine—has ever stirred my heart. Well, it's the scent of the vine in flower. It took me four days to find that out. Isn't it delightful to think that besides its gift of wine, which only the elect can appreciate, the grape bestows upon us the most delicate, the most haunting of all perfumes, only to be detected by the most refined senses. Do you recognise the overpowering scent of the chestnut trees, the sugary sweetness of the acacias, the fragrance of the aromatic herbs on the mountain side and then, the smell of the grass, the delicious, delicious smell of the grass, which no one ever suspects?"

She listened entranced to his conversation. Not that it was in itself very remarkable, but it seemed to her so different from the idle chatter she heard around her all day long, that the impression remained with her, disturbing and stimulating.

He went on talking in his veiled yet ardent voice:

"And then, haven't you noticed along the roads, in the heat of the day, a hint of vanilla in the air? You have? Well, that's . . . no, I don't think I can tell you."

He laughed outright, and pointed with his finger.

"Look!"

Down the road came a string of haycarts, each with its pair of slow-footed cows, plodding along, their heads down, their necks bowed under the yoke, their horns tied to the wooden crossbars, the bones of their legs showing under the tautened skin as they moved. In front of each cart went a man in shirt sleeves, waistcoat, black hat, regulating the pace with a switch he carried. He never struck his animals, but now and then he would turn round and gently touch one of them on shoulder or head, and the cow would blink its great, vacant eyes and obey the hint.

Christian and Paul stood back to let the carts pass.

"Do you notice it?" asked Paul.

"What do you mean? The smell of the byre?"

"Yes, the smell of the byre. There are no horses in this part of the country, and all these cows that wander along the roads diffuse this odour, which mingles with the fine dust, and lends to the air that suggestion of vanilla."

" Oh ! " said Christian, a little repelled.

" Forgive me. I was talking like an analytical chemist. But what does it matter?   Here we are in the most fascinating, charming and peaceful country I have ever seen. It's like a land of the Golden Age. And Limagne ! Ah, Limagne ! I won't try to describe it. I must show it to you. Wait till you see it ! "

The Marquis and Gontran joined them. Taking his daughter's arm, the Marquis turned back with her towards the hotel for luncheon.

" Listen, my young friends," he said. " This concerns all three of you. William, who goes mad over every new idea he gets into his head, can think of nothing but the town he proposes to build here. He is anxious to win over the Oriol family, and he wants Christian to make the acquaintance of the two girls and to see if they are at all possible. But the old father mustn't get wind of our plan. So the idea occurred to me that we might get up a fête for some charity or other. You, my child, will go and see the priest, and consult him as to which of all the girls in his parish should be asked to help you with the collection. You will guide his choice to our two young women, and he will invite them, as if it were his own idea. You two fellows will get up a tombola at the Casino, with the help of Petrus Martel and his troupe of actors and musicians. The two little Oriols are said to have been very nicely brought up in their convent, and if they are really attractive, Christian will soon win their hearts."

V

For a whole week Christian was completely engrossed with preparations for the fête. Out of all his parish, the vicar had found no one but Louise and Charlotte Oriol worthy to assist the Marquis de Ravenel's daughter in taking the collection. Delighted at this opportunity for pushing himself forward, he had conducted all the negotiations, arranged and organised the whole affair, and had himself conveyed the invitation to the two girls, just as if it had been his own idea.

The whole place was bubbling with excitement. Glad of a new topic of conversation, the dejected visitors discussed at every table d'hôte what profits might be expected from the two functions, the sacred and the profane.

The day promised well. It was lovely summer weather, warm and bright. Out in the open, the sun was dazzling, but it was deliciously cool under the trees in the village. At nine o'clock there was to be a short celebration of mass with music. Christian had come before the service to cast a final glance at the decorations, which consisted of garlands of flowers procured from Clermont-Ferrand and Royat. She heard footsteps behind her and the parish priest came up with Louise and Charlotte Oriol, whom he introduced. She promptly asked the girls to luncheon, and blushing and bowing they accepted her invitation. When the congregation began to assemble, the three ladies seated themselves on ceremonial chairs placed for them between the choir and the congregation, exactly opposite other chairs, which were occupied by three young men in their Sunday best, the sons of the mayor, the deputy-mayor and a municipal councillor, who had been chosen, in compliment to the local authorities, to act as escort to the ladies. Everything went off splendidly. The service was short, and the offertory yielded a hundred and ten francs, which Andermatt's five hundred, Paul Brétigny's hundred, and the Marquis's fifty, swelled to a total of seven hundred and sixty francs, an unprecedented sum for the parish of Enval.

After the service Christian took the two girls back to the hotel. At the table d'hôte luncheon they seemed a little shy, but by no means awkward, and if they hardly spoke, this was due to modesty, rather than timidity. All the men without exception were delighted with them. The elder girl, the serious one of the pair, was more refined in the usual sense of the word, while her vivacious younger sister possessed greater charm. At the same time no two sisters were ever more alike.

Immediately after luncheon, the party adjourned to the Casino to see the drawing of the lottery, which was to take place at two o'clock. The park was already overrun by a mixed crowd of summer visitors and peasants, and the scene had the aspect of a country fair. The orchestra in the Chinese kiosk was playing a rural symphony of Saint-Landri's own composition. Paul, who was walking with Christian, halted.

"Why, that's a pretty thing," he exclaimed. "The fellow has talent. It would sound very well with a large orchestra. Do you care for music, Madame Andermatt?"

"Very much."

"It has a devastating effect on me. When I listen to some work I love, it is as if the first notes stripped the skin from my flesh, melting it, dissolving it, consuming it, leaving me exposed, like a man flayed alive, to all the onslaughts of the instruments. And really it's my nerves that the orchestra plays upon, my naked, shuddering nerves, which vibrate with every tone. I absorb the music, not only with my ears, but with every fibre of my body and I quiver from head to foot. It's a delight, or rather an ecstasy, that nothing else can procure."

" You must feel very keenly," she said with a smile.

" Upon my soul, what would be the use of life if one didn't? I don't envy people who have their hearts encased in tortoise shell or hippopotamus hide. The only happy people are those whose sensations are painfully acute, and who take a subtle pleasure in their pangs. We ought to turn to account all our emotions, whether happy or unhappy, steep our souls in them, intoxicate ourselves to a pitch of exquisite bliss or exquisite agony."

She raised her eyes to his with the faint surprise which all his remarks had evoked in her during the past days. All that week this new friend of hers, for friend he had become in spite of her first antipathy, had been troubling her peace of mind, disturbing its tranquillity, as one disturbs a pool by throwing stones into it. He kept dropping stones, large stones, into the slumbering depths of her mind. Like all fathers, Christian's had always treated her as a little girl, to whom one could say nothing of importance. Her brother amused her, but never appealed to her intelligence, and it did not occur to her husband that he could discuss with her other matters beyond the commonplace incidents of everyday life. Hitherto she had existed, placid and content, in complete lethargy of soul. But this newcomer broke into her mind with trenchant ideas that were like the blows of an axe. He was, moreover, one of those men whose peculiar nature, whose quivering sensitiveness, appeals to every woman without exception. He could talk to women, say what he pleased to them, and make them understand anything he chose. Incapable of sustained effort, but remarkably intelligent, hating or loving with equal vehemence, discussing everything with the ingenuous ardour of a violent partisan, as fickle as he was enthusiastic, he possessed to an exaggerated degree the true feminine temperament, combining all a woman's credulity, charm, mobility, and sensitiveness with a man's masterful intelligence, vigorous, frank, and penetrating.

Gontran came running up to them.

"Do turn round and look at the Honorat couple."

They obeyed and caught sight of Dr Honorat escorting a stout elderly lady in blue, with a whole nursery garden upon her head, a hat which displayed every variety of plant and flower.

"Is that his wife?" exclaimed Christian in amazement. "Why, she's fifteen years older than he."

"Yes, she's sixty-five. She's an old mid-wife; he fell in love with her between two cases. Apparently they fight like cat and dog."

A general hubbub attracted their attention and they turned back towards the Casino. The prizes for the raffle were arranged on a long table in front of the building, and Petrus Martel, assisted by Mademoiselle Odelin of the Odéon, a tiny brunette, was drawing the tickets, calling out the winning numbers and amusing his audience with professional patter. The Marquis, with Andermatt and the Oriol girls, joined the rest of his party.

"Shall we go?" he asked. "It's very noisy here."

They decided to take a stroll along the road leading from Enval to La Roche-Pradière. To strike this road, which winds round the hill half way up, they had to follow in single file a narrow path among the vines. Christian led the way, walking with swift elastic step. Ever since her arrival at Enval, a complete change seemed to have come over her existence; life and all its pleasures had a zest she had never known before. Possibly by improving her health and removing the slight physical disorders, which, though indefinable, are depressing and enervating, the baths were responsible for quickening her powers of perception and enjoyment. Perhaps it was that she was roused and stimulated by the mere presence, by the vivid intellect, of this newcomer, who was awakening her understanding. She drew long, deep breaths, while she remembered all he had said about the perfumes wafted upon the breeze.

"He has really taught me to notice the scents in the air," she reflected, as she recognised the different odours, especially the delicate, subtle, elusive fragrance of the vines.

On reaching the road, the party divided up. Andermatt and Louise, the elder Oriol girl, walked on ahead, discussing the yield on land in Auvergne. True daughter of her father, and endowed with hereditary instinct, this maiden of Auvergne had at her fingers' ends all the precise and practical details of agriculture, which she enunciated in her pleasant, well-bred voice, speaking with the cultured accent she had acquired at the convent. As he listened, he stole sidelong glances at her, charmed with this solemn child, who already possessed so much serviceable knowledge.

"What?" he exclaimed, somewhat taken aback. "The land in Limagne is worth twelve thousand francs an acre?"

"Yes, when it's planted with apple-trees, bearing good eating apples. Our part of the world supplies nearly all the fruit in the Paris markets."

He turned round for a respectful survey of Limagne. From the road, the great plain, beneath its eternal haze of faint blue, could be seen stretching away into the far distance.

Christian and Paul, too, stood contemplating that vast, misty landscape, which was so fair to look upon that they could have lingered gazing at it hour after hour. At this point the road was sheltered by great walnut trees, whose dense shade felt cool to the cheeks. The path now meandered along at one and the same level, halfway up the side of the hill, whose lower slopes were covered with vineyards, while the upper slopes were carpeted with short green turf stretching to the top of the ridge, which here reached no great altitude.

"Isn't it beautiful?" murmured Paul. "Isn't it beautiful? Why does that landscape move me so profoundly? Why, oh why? From it emanates a charm so deep, so spacious . . . above all so spacious . . . that it bewitches my very heart. As I gaze upon that plain, the fancy seems to spread its wings, to fly, to soar, to escape, to vanish into the distance yonder, towards those lands of our dreams, which we shall never see. Yes, that is its secret. It is so enchanting because it is more like a scene in a dream than anything we have ever beheld."

Eager, expectant, inexplicably moved, she listened to him, drinking in his every word. She, too, caught a glimpse of those other lands, all rose and azure, those fantastic, wonderful, undiscoverable lands, which we are forever seeking, and for whose sake we despise the lands we know.

"Yes," he continued, "it has a beauty all its own. Other landscapes may be more striking, but they have not the same harmony. Ah, Madame Andermatt, beauty, harmonious beauty, nothing else counts in the world. Nothing exists save beauty. But how few people understand it! The lines of a figure, a statue, a mountain, the colouring of a picture, the colouring of that plain, the elusiveness of the Gioconda, the phrase that penetrates to the soul, the little more, which makes an artist as much a creator as God Himself, who can define it? Let me quote to you two verses of Baudelaire:

" Thy birth, in heaven or hell, I seek not to explore,
Beauty, colossal form, terrific, innocent!
If but thy gaze, thy smile, thy touch fling wide the door
Of some loved Infinite, for me in darkness pent.

From Satan or from God, Angel or Siren thou,
What matter?—so thou dost, soft-eyed enchantress, rise
And—rhythm, fragrance, light, queen of my every
  vow—
Brighten dark hours, make earth less hateful to mine
  eyes!"*

  * By kind permission of Dr Henry Sharman.

Amazed at his dithyrambics, and unable to see anything very remarkable in the poetry, Christian gazed at him. Paul guessed her thoughts and was vexed at his failure to inspire her with his own raptures, especially as he had recited the verses admirably.

"I was a fool," he exclaimed with a hint of contempt, "to try to make you appreciate a poet of such subtle genius. Some day I hope you will feel these things as I do. Women, who are blessed with more intuition than understanding, never grasp the veiled and secret suggestiveness of art, unless a sympathetic appeal has been first addressed to their emotions. I shall endeavour to make such an appeal to you," he added with a bow.

She thought him eccentric, but acquitted him of impertinence, and she made no further effort to understand him, for she was suddenly struck by something that had hitherto eluded her. This was the fact that he was remarkably well turned out, but he was so tall, so broad, so virile, that at first sight his studied attention to his dress was overlooked. His head had something rough-hewn and uncouth about it, which to a superficial observer invested his whole person with a certain heaviness. But once his features were familiar, they revealed a crude but compelling charm, a charm that could achieve a tenderness matching the caressing accents of that husky voice of his.

As she realised for the first time how perfectly he was groomed from head to foot, Christian reflected:

"Evidently he's a man whose qualities dawn upon you one by one."

Gontran came running after them, calling to Christian to wait for him. As soon as he had caught them up, he said, still laughing:

"Oh, you must come and listen to the little Oriol girl. She's too funny for words; she's astonishingly witty. Papa managed to put her at her ease and she has been telling us the most amusing things. Let's wait for them."

The Marquis joined them with Charlotte, the younger of the Oriol sisters. With childlike archness and vivacity she was telling him stories about the village and instances of rustic simplicity and cunning. She imitated the gestures of the peasants, their clumsy movements, their solemn utterances, their unending exclamations of "*fouchtra*" and "*bougrre*," which she pronounced "*bigrrre*," while her mimicry of their grimaces lent charm to her pretty, animated face. Her merry eyes sparkled; her somewhat large mouth revealed fine white teeth; her tip-tilted nose gave her a humorous look, while her bloom, her flowerlike bloom, made the lips tremble with desire.

The Marquis had spent most of his life on his estate, while Gontran and Christian, brought up in the family château, among the independent and substantial Norman farmers, who, according to custom, dined now and then at the Marquis's table, had associated on friendly terms with the farmers' children, and had been their comrades at their First Communion. They knew how to draw out this little country lass, who was already three-quarters a lady, treating her with frank cordiality, with sure and kindly tact, to which she responded with gay confidence.

Andermatt and Louise rejoined them. They had gone as far as the village and then turned back. The whole party sat down on the grass by the wayside under a tree. They lingered there, peacefully chatting of everything and nothing, steeped in a languid torpor of wellbeing. Now and then a cart passed them, with its inevitable pair of cows, their necks cramped and weighed down by the yoke, their driver a flat-chested peasant in the usual big black hat, guiding his team with the end of his switch, which he waved like the conductor of an orchestra. He took his hat off to the Oriols, whose youthful voices replied with a friendly good-day.

It was growing late and they set out for home. As they drew near the park, Charlotte Oriol exclaimed:

"The bourrée! They are dancing the bourrée."

And sure enough the peasants were dancing the bourrée to an old Auvergnat tune. Full of airs and graces, they jigged and walked and turned and bowed, the girls holding their skirts with two fingers of either hand, the boys with their arms hanging down or akimbo. The charming, monotonous melody rose and fell on the freshening breeze of evening. It consisted of a single phrase, pitched high, and played over and over again on the violin, while the other instruments marked the time and added to the liveliness of the rhythm. It was genuine peasant music, simple, artless and gay, well adapted to that homely, rustic minuet. Some of the visitors tried to join in. Petrus Martel skipped up and down opposite little Mademoiselle Odelin, who had all the affectations of a ballet girl. Lapalme, the comedian, gave a grotesque imitation, prancing round the cashier, who seemed distracted by memories of Bullier. Gontran caught sight of Dr Honorat, who was throwing himself into the dance with all his heart and executing a classic bourrée like a true son of Auvergne. Suddenly the orchestra stopped and the dance came to an end. Breathless and wiping his forehead, the doctor came to shake hands with the Marquis.

" It's good to be young now and then," he remarked.

Smiling maliciously, Gontran put his hand on his shoulder.

" You never told me you were married."

The doctor stopped mopping himself.

" Well, I am," he replied solemnly, " and what's more, unhappily."

" I beg your pardon? "

" I say I'm unhappily married. Don't you ever be such a fool, young man."

" Why? "

" Why? Listen to me. I have been married now for twenty years, and I'm not used to it yet. Every evening when I go home I say to myself : 'Dear me, is that old lady still here? Isn't she ever going away?'"

He spoke so seriously and so feelingly that everyone laughed. At that moment the hotel dinner bell was heard. The fête was over. Louise and Charlotte Oriol were escorted to their father's house by their new friends, who afterwards, on the way home, began to discuss them. Everyone was charmed with the pair, but Andermatt preferred the elder.

"Isn't the feminine nature adaptable!" exclaimed the Marquis. "The mere proximity of their father's money bags, though they have no idea what to do with them, has turned these two country lasses into ladies."

"Which do you personally prefer?" asked Christian, turning to Paul Brétigny.

"Oh, I never even looked at them. It's not there that my preference lies."

He spoke very softly and she made no reply.

VI

For Christian, light of heart and glad of soul, there followed days of enchantment. First there was the morning bath, the exquisite, sensuous pleasure of that delicious half-hour in the warm, running water, which disposed her to be happy all the rest of the day. And indeed, all her thoughts and wishes were fraught with happiness. The affection, by which she felt herself surrounded and permeated, the intoxication of youth throbbing in her veins, her new environment, this wonderful dream country, so spacious, so fragrant, which lapped her round in the deep embrace of nature, awoke in her new emotions. Everything that approached her, everything that touched her, served but to prolong the morning's impression, the feeling that she was steeped, body and soul, in a warm deep bath of rapture.

Andermatt, who had arranged to spend every alternate fortnight at Enval, had returned to Paris, after requesting his wife to make sure that the old paralytic did not discontinue his treatment. Every day before luncheon, Christian, her father, her brother and Paul went to supervise what Gontran called " the poor man's broth." Other visitors followed their example, and they all stood round the pothole talking to the old vagabond. There was no improvement in his walking, he assured them, but his legs felt full of ants. He described how they ran up and down from his thighs to his toes, and his toes to his thighs. Even at night he could feel them, the maddening creatures, biting him and disturbing his sleep. The visitors and the peasants, who were divided into two camps, sceptics and believers, all took an interest in the cure.

After luncheon Christian often called for Louise and Charlotte to take them for a walk. They were the only women in the place whose conversation and companionship she could enjoy, and she bestowed upon them a certain confidential friendliness in return for a little feminine affection. She had at once been attracted by the elder sister's serious, smiling good sense, and still more by the younger girl's quaint, arch humour. Even more for her own amusement than for the sake of pleasing her husband, she began to cultivate their friendship.

The whole party went for various excursions, sometimes on foot, sometimes in an old travelling landau with room for six, which they had unearthed at a jobmaster's at Riom. Their favourite haunt was a wild little valley near Châtel-Guyon, which led to the hermitage of Sans-Souci. Two and two, chatting to each other, they strolled along the narrow path under the pines by the side of the brook. The track was continually crossing the rivulet, and on each occasion Paul and Gontran, standing on stones in mid-stream, would jump the girls over by the arm, one after the other. At each crossing they changed partners. But, in spite of these transfers, Christian always managed to keep Paul Brétigny to herself for some moments, either by going on ahead or by falling behind. His manner towards her had changed since the first few days of their acquaintance. Less merry, less abrupt, less familiar, he treated her with more deference and consideration. Their conversation, however, was on a more intimate footing and matters of the heart took an important place. He spoke of love and passion like an expert, a man who has fathomed the devotion of women and derived from his experiences an equal measure of joy and pain. Fascinated and somewhat thrilled, burning with secret curiosity, she encouraged his confidences. The little she knew of him inspired in her a keen desire to learn more, to explore mentally one of those masculine existences, fraught with all the stormy mysteries of love, of which books afford

83

but a glimpse. Thus incited, he confided to her daily a little more of his past, with its adventures and disillusions. He spoke with a fervency which rose to passion as he remembered the flame that had scorched him, while his eagerness to please added an element of diplomatic cunning to his words. He revealed to her an unknown world and found eloquent phrases to express the subtleties of desire and expectation, the pangs of dawning hope, the worship of flowers, scraps of ribbon and a thousand treasured trifles, the agony of sudden doubts, the torture of imaginary fears, the shafts of jealousy, and the indescribable intoxication of the first kiss. All this he managed to convey to her with perfect propriety, in language which was veiled, poetic and beguiling. Like all men, whose minds are obsessed by women, he made discreet allusions to those whom he had loved with a passion that still throbbed. He recalled countless charming details, exquisite incidents, calculated to stir the heart, and bring a tear to the eye : all the enchanting absurdities of dalliance, by virtue of which a love affair between two persons of delicate perceptions and cultured minds becomes the most aesthetic, as well as the most delectable, pastime in the world. All these distracting and intimate conversations, renewed and developed each day, fell on Christian's heart like seed upon the ground. The charm of that spacious country, the balmy air, blue-veiled Limagne itself, which seemed to impart something of its own grandeur to the human soul; the mountain with its extinct craters, those ancient hearths of earth, now serving merely to heat water for invalids; the cool shades of the woods; the purling brooks : these, too, entered into Christian's heart and body, saturating them like soft warm rain, falling on virgin soil and causing flowers to germinate. She was aware that this man was paying a mild court to her; that he thought her pretty and rather more than pretty. Her desire to charm him inspired her with a thousand graces, subtle and at the same time ingenuous, calculated to attract and captivate him.

Whenever she thought she had stirred him, she would leave him abruptly. If she felt some tender allusion trembling on his lips, she would dart at him, before he could speak, one of those swift deep glances, which strike like fire to the heart of man. She had subtle phrases, captivating movements of the head, vague gestures of the hand, melancholy airs swiftly yielding to a smile, to hint to him without speech that his efforts were not in vain.

What was her object? She had none. What did she look for? Nothing at all. The game amused her simply because she was a woman, because she did not realise the danger, because, free from all misgiving, she wanted to see what he would do. But soon that inborn coquetry, which lurks in the blood of all creatures feminine, suddenly developed. She who but yesterday had been a simple child, half asleep, had in a moment come broad awake, clear-sighted and adroit, confronted with this man, who never ceased his talk of love. With the peculiar intuition of a woman who is aware that she is wooed, she divined the ever-increasing tumult her presence fostered in his mind; she recognised the dawning passion in his eyes, and interpreted the varying inflections of his voice. Other men, whom she had met in society, had paid court to her, but had been rewarded with nothing but a merry schoolgirl's mockery. Their commonplace compliments had merely amused her. The faces of her disconsolate suitors had filled her with delight and she had made fun of all their manifestations of emotion. But in this man she discerned a dangerous and seductive adversary and she developed into the huntress, keen-eyed and alert by instinct, equipped with coolness and audacity, who, as long as her own heart remains free, lies in wait for men and enmeshes them in the invisible net of sentiment.

At first he had thought her stupid. Accustomed to the dashing type of woman, as practised in love as an old soldier in the art of war, versed in all the subtleties of gallantry, Paul had considered that simple heart of hers commonplace and had treated it with a faint contempt. Soon, however, her very frankness began to amuse him, then to captivate him, and yielding to the dictates of his impressionable nature, he began to surround her with loverlike attentions. He was aware that the best method for disturbing an innocent soul is to discourse continually of love, while apparently thinking of other women. Skilfully fostering the delicate curiosity he had aroused, he had, while pretending to confide in her, given her a regular course of love-making in the shade of the woods. The game amused him as much as her. He revealed to her, by all the little services a man can render, his increasing liking for her, and he played at love, without dreaming that it would some day become a serious matter. During their leisurely rambles they gave themselves up to it as naturally as one plunges into a river, if one happens to be wandering on its banks some hot afternoon. But the moment the instinct of coquetry had developed in Christian, the moment she discovered the natural arts of women for the seduction of man, the moment she took it into her head to bring this gallant to his knees, much as she might have resolved to win a game of croquet, the ingenuous Lothario was caught in the toils of this innocent and straightway fell in love with her.

Thereupon he grew restless, nervous, constrained, while she played with him like a cat with a mouse. With any other woman, he would have felt no scruples. He would have spoken, swept her off her feet with his irresistible impetuosity. But with Christian he did not dare, so different did he deem her from all the women he had known. In a word, the others were women already seared by life, to whom he could say what he chose, risk the most daring appeals, while murmuring close to their lips thrilling words that fired the blood. He always knew instinctively when he could freely communicate to the heart and soul and senses of the woman he loved the imperious desires that racked him. Christian appeared to him like an unmarried girl, so uninitiated did he believe her, and all his usual methods seemed to him of no avail. Besides, his devotion to her had a different quality; it was like the worship one has for a child or for one's betrothed. He desired her, yet he feared to touch her lest he should mar her bloom. He felt no yearning to crush her in his arms like the other women he had loved. All he wanted was to fall on his knees, to touch with his lips the hem of her gown, to bestow lingering kisses, infinitely chaste and tender, upon the tendrils of hair about her brow, on the corners of her mouth, and on her eyes, her closed eyes, whose enchanting azure he would see dawning beneath the drooping lids. He longed to protect her against the whole world, against every contingency, to keep her from contact with the vulgar throng and from everyone unsightly or unclean. He wished he could sweep the mud and stones from the paths she trod, the brambles and branches from the woods, till everything around her was smooth and pleasant, and carry her in his arms so that she need never set foot on the ground. He chafed at the thought of her talking to her neighbours at the hotel, eating the indifferent food at the table d'hôte and submitting to all the trifling vexations inseparable from life.

His head was so full of her that he could think of nothing to say to her, and his inability to reveal the condition of his heart, to perform one fraction of all that he longed to do, to prove to her his vehement desire to devote himself to her, wrought like a fever in his blood and gave him something of the look of a wild beast on a chain, while at the same time he was conscious of a strange impulse to burst into sobs. Without quite understanding them, she saw all these symptoms with the malicious delight of a coquette. When they dropped behind the others, and his manner warned her that he was going to make some disturbing remark, she would suddenly run to catch up her father and exclaim:

" Let's play puss in the corner."

Their expeditions generally ended with a game of puss in the corner. They would find a clearing or a wide part of the road, and play like a pack of schoolboys out for a walk. Gontran and the Oriol girls thoroughly enjoyed these games; they satisfied the continual craving for violent exercise which possesses all young creatures. Paul, who was obsessed by other thoughts, was the only one to show reluctance, but he would gradually thaw and enter into the fun more furiously than the others, in the hope of catching Christian, touching her, suddenly putting his hand on her shoulder or bodice. The Marquis, whose careless, indolent nature lent itself to any proposal as long as it did not disturb his peace, seated himself at the foot of a tree to watch, as he said, the frolics of his school. He found this placid existence much to his taste and considered the world in general perfectly satisfactory.

Soon, however, Christian began to be alarmed at Paul's manner, and one morning she was really frightened. They had gone with Gontran to explore a curious ravine called the End of the World, the source of the little brook Enval. Becoming ever more tortuous and narrow, the gorge plunges into the heart of the mountain. After scrambling over rocks, crossing the stream by stepping-stones and skirting a boulder more than one hundred and sixty feet high, which blocks the cutting, the wanderer finds himself imprisoned in a gully, closely hemmed in between two great walls, bare to the summit, which is clothed with trees and verdure. In this wild glen, so strange and fantastic, more like a scene in a book than in nature, the stream forms a small round tarn.

Paul scanned the face of the high rock which barred the path and blocked further progress, and he noticed traces which indicated that it had been scaled.

"Why, we can go farther," he cried.

With some difficulty, he clambered up the perpendicular rock.

"Oh, it's charming," he cried. "There's a little grove right in the water. You must come."

He lay down, and, seizing Christian's hands, pulled her up, while Gontran guided her feet, placing them in the little projections jutting out from the rock. The soil which had dropped from the summit on to this ledge, had formed a tiny wild garden of shrubs and bushes with the stream trickling over the roots. A little way along the granite corridor, they came upon a second barrier, over which they climbed. After surmounting a third, however, they were confronted by an insurmountable wall of rock, sixty feet high, down which, sheer and sparkling, a cascade fell into a deep basin it had hollowed out for itself, embowered in creepers and green branches. At this point the gorge was so narrow that the two men, holding hands, could touch the wall on either side. Only a streak of sky was visible and there was no sound but the plashing of the water. It was like one of those secret bowers which the fancy of the Latin poets peopled with nymphs. Christian felt as if she had profaned the domain of some fairy. Paul Brétigny was silent.

"Wouldn't it be delicious," cried Gontran, "to see a woman, all pink and white, bathing in that water?"

They turned back. The descent of the first two ledges was easy enough, but the third was so steep, and its footholds so imperceptible, that Christian was frightened. Brétigny slid down the rock, and held out his arms.

"Jump," he said.

But she did not dare. It was not that she was afraid of falling; she was afraid of Paul, and especially of the look in his eyes. He was gazing at her with the avidity of a famished beast, with a passion that had grown ferocious. His outstretched hands beckoned to her so imperiously that she was seized with a sudden terror, with a wild impulse to scream and run away, to climb to the top of the mountain to escape from that irresistible summons.

"Go on," cried Gontran, who was standing behind her, and he gave her a push.

Feeling herself falling, she closed her eyes and was

caught in an embrace at once strong and tender. Without seeing, she felt Paul's tall form close against her own, and upon her face his warm, panting breath. Then in a moment she was on her feet again and smiling, now that her fears were banished. Gontran in his turn clambered down the rock.

She took warning by her panic, and for some days was careful not to trust herself alone with Paul, who now seemed to be prowling round her, like the wolf of the fairy tale round a lamb.

A long excursion, however, had been planned, in which Louise and Charlotte Oriol were to join. They arranged to take a picnic basket with them, drive in the big six-seated landau to the little lake of Tazenat, known locally as the Gour de Tazenat, dine, and return home by moonlight. They set off accordingly one afternoon of tropical heat under a blazing sun, which baked the granite rocks like the slabs of an oven. Drawn by three panting, steaming horses, the carriage wound slowly up the hill, while the coachman nodded on the box half asleep. Swarms of green lizards darted in and out among the stones by the wayside. The scorching air seemed heavily laden with invisible particles of burning dust. At times it felt as if it were clotted, solid, resistant, as they passed through it; at times it stirred a little and wafted across their faces gusts as hot as fire and impregnated with the scent of simmering resin from the heart of the unending pine woods. No one in the landau spoke. The three women in the back of the carriage closed their dazzled eyes beneath the pink shade of their parasols. The Marquis and Gontran were both asleep with their handkerchiefs over their faces, and Paul was gazing at Christian, who for her part was watching him beneath her downcast eyelids. Leaving in its wake columns of white dust, the landau toiled up the interminable hill.

Once the plateau was reached, the coachman sat up, the horses broke into a trot and they drove through wide, undulating country, wooded and cultivated and dotted

with villages and isolated houses. Far away on the left
the great truncated summits of the volcanoes could be
discerned. The lake of Tazenat, whither they were
bound, was formed by the last of the craters in the
Auvergnat range.

"Look at the lava!" exclaimed Paul suddenly, after
they had been three hours under way.

By the roadside there was an outcrop of brown rocks,
weirdly contorted. To the right a squat mountain came
into view, its broad summit apparently flat and hollow.
The carriage turned into a road which seemed to lead
right into the heart of the mountain by means of a
triangular cutting. Christian, who had sprung to her
feet, suddenly discovered in the depths of a crater a
beautiful little lake, as round and as bright as a silver
coin. Wooded on the left, bare on the right, the steep
sides of the mountain fell sheer down to the tarn, en-
closing it within high regular banks. Smooth and shining
as a sheet of polished metal, the still waters reflected the
trees on the one hand and the barren hillside on the
other with such exquisite clearness that substance and
shadow were blended, and all that could be discovered
within that great funnel, in whose waters the blue sky
was mirrored, was a luminous, bottomless hole, which
seemed to run right through the earth until it reached
another firmament.

The road came to an end. The whole party alighted,
and halfway up the slope on the wooded hillside they
followed a path which wound about the lake, a mere
woodcutter's track and as green as a meadow. Through
the branches they caught glimpses of the opposite slope
and of the water shimmering in the hollow of the mountain. A clearing brought them to the very edge of the
lake, where the bank was carpeted with turf and shaded
by oak trees. They threw themselves down on the sward
with a sensuous thrill of exquisite enjoyment. The men
rolled about and thrust their hands deep into the grass,
while the ladies, lying in graceful attitudes, laid their

cheeks to its caressing coolness. After the hot drive, it was one of those sensations so delicious, so intense, so perfect, that they amount almost to positive bliss.

The Marquis dropped off to sleep again and Gontran speedily followed his example, while Paul chatted to Christian and the girls. Of what did they talk? Nothing in particular. From time to time one of them made a remark and someone would reply after a brief silence. Their languid words seemed half asleep upon their lips, like the thoughts within their minds.

Presently the coachman appeared with the picnic basket. Louise and Charlotte, accustomed to household duties, displayed their industrious domesticity by setting to work to unpack and arrange the al fresco repast on the turf. Paul remained stretched on the grass beside Christian, who was lost in a dream. So low that she could scarcely hear him, so low that the words were wafted to her ears like confused murmurs borne upon the breeze, he whispered:

"These are the happiest moments of my life."

Why did these vague words trouble the very depths of her heart? Why was she suddenly moved as never before?

Through the trees she was gazing at a tiny house, the hut of some hunter or fisherman, so small that it could not consist of more than a single room. Paul's eyes followed hers.

"Has it ever occurred to you," he said, "all that days spent in a tiny hut like that could mean to two people desperately in love? They would be alone in the world, really alone, face to face with each other. And if such bliss were within one's grasp, ought not one to give up everything to secure it, since happiness is so rare, so elusive, and so brief? One's humdrum existence, can you call that life? What more depressing than to rise in the morning with no glowing hopes, to go calmly about one's business, to eat and drink in moderation and fall asleep as placidly as an animal?"

She was still looking at the little house, and her heart swelled within her as if she were on the verge of tears, for suddenly she caught a glimpse of raptures she had never suspected. Truly, she felt, one could be happy with just one other in that tiny dwelling, by that toy lake, that jewel of a lake, that veritable mirror of love. One could be happy with no one else near, no neighbours, no human voice, no sound of life—all alone with the beloved, who would kneel by the hour at the feet of his adored, gazing at her while she watched the blue ripples, and murmuring tender words while he kissed her finger-tips. They would live in that silence beneath the trees, in the depths of that crater which would store up their passion as it stored up those deep, limpid waters within its clear-cut, symmetrical bounds, with no horizon for their gaze, save the rounded rim of the hollow; none for their thoughts save the bliss of mutual love; none for their desires save lingering and unending kisses. Were there really people on this earth who could revel in such days? Doubtless there were. And indeed, why not? How was it that she had hitherto never suspected the possibility of such joys?

The two girls announced that dinner was ready. It was six o'clock. After the Marquis and Gontran had been awakened, the whole party moved on a little and sat down, Turkish fashion, by the plates which slipped about on the grass. The sisters continued to wait on them, and the men accepted their ministrations without demur. They lingered over the meal and threw scraps and chicken bones into the lake. Champagne had been brought, and everyone jumped at the sudden popping of the first cork, so incongruous did it seem in such surroundings.

Day was drawing to a close. The air grew cooler, and with evening a strange melancholy sank down upon the slumbering waters in the depths of the crater. Just as the sun was disappearing, the sky turned a flaming red and the tarn suddenly became a bowl of fire. After the sun had set and the horizon glowed like a brazier of dying embers, the tarn became a bowl of blood. Then, all at once, above the crest of the hill, rose the moon, nearly at the full, all wan in a sky where daylight yet lingered. As darkness stole over the land, the round shining orb climbed the firmament till it hung above the crater, round like the moon itself, as if about to plunge down into those waters. And when the moon was high in the heavens, the tarn became a bowl of silver. Across the surface that had lain so still all day, shot ripples, now swift, now slow, as if spirits hovering just above the waters were trailing invisible wings. These ripples were caused by big fish, carp, centuries old, and ravenous pike, rising from the bottom to sport in the moonlight.

The two girls repacked the basket, which was removed by the coachman, and they all set out for home. They followed the path under the trees, where splashes of light filtered like rain through the leaves on to the grass. Christian, who went last of all, save for Paul, suddenly heard a voice murmuring brokenly, close to her ear:

"I love you. I love you. I love you."

Her heart began to throb so violently that she could scarcely move her limbs, and she all but fell. Nevertheless she walked on. Bewildered as she was, she walked on, though ready to turn to him with eager lips and open arms. He had seized the fringe of the light scarf she wore round her shoulders, and was kissing it frantically. Still she walked on, though she was so faint that she could not feel the ground under her feet. Suddenly she emerged from the overarching trees into bright moonlight and hastily mastered her emotion. But before she entered the landau and lost sight of the lake, she turned half round and blew it a fervent kiss, which certainly included the man who followed her. On the homeward drive, a lethargy possessed her, body and soul; she felt dazed and exhausted as if she had had a fall, and as soon as the hotel was reached she hastily took refuge in her own room. She not only shot the bolt but turned the

key, so strong was her feeling that she was being pursued.
Then she stood trembling in the middle of the empty
room, which was almost in darkness. The candle on the
table threw upon the wall flickering shadows of furniture
and curtains. Christian sank into an armchair. Through
her head her thoughts were racing wildly, so fugitive
that she could not seize them and link them together.
She now felt on the verge of tears, she knew not why,
forlorn and miserable, all alone in that desolate room,
lost in life as in a forest. Whither was she drifting?
What fate lay in store for her? Hardly able to breathe,
she rose, threw open the window and shutter, and leaned
her arms on the sill. The air was cool. Far away in the
depths of that infinite sky, no less desolate than her room,
ascending sad and solitary the misty, blue steeps of
heaven, the moon shed down upon forest and mountain
her cold bleak radiance. The whole countryside was
lapped in slumber. Only now and then the violin of
Saint-Landri, who always practised late at night, broke
the stillness of the valley with its soft complaining.
Christian could just hear it, as the shrill, mournful wail
of the quivering strings rose and fell.

The moon, lost in that dreary sky, those faint strains
dying away in the silence of the night, wrung her heart
with such a sense of loneliness that she burst into sobs.
She trembled and shuddered to the marrow of her bones,
shaken as if with the anguish of some fell disease. And
all at once she realised that she, too, was alone in life.
Never before had this feeling possessed her, but now
her agony of mind brought it home to her so vividly that
she thought she must be going mad. Had she not a
father, a brother, a husband, whom she loved and who
loved her?

Yet all at once she felt herself drifting away from
them; they seemed strangers to her, strangers whom she
hardly knew. Her father's calm affection, her brother's
friendly companionship, her husband's careless kindness,
all counted for nothing, absolutely nothing. Her hus-

band! Was that really her husband, that pink-faced chatterbox, who would say to her casually:

"How are you this morning, my dear?"

On the strength of a contract, she belonged, body and soul, to this man. Was it possible? How lonely and forlorn she felt! She closed her eyes to gaze into her mind, seeking to fathom its depths. She conjured up the faces of all those who shared her life: her father, careless and serene, perfectly happy as long as no one disturbed his peace; her mocking, sceptical brother, her bustling husband, his head full of figures, who would remark to her: "I have just brought off a good thing," when he might have murmured "I love you."

Only an hour ago, another man had whispered to her these very words, which still rang in her ears and in her heart. Him, too, she beheld, devouring her with his persistent gaze, and, if he had been with her at that moment, she would have thrown herself into his arms.

VII

ALTHOUGH Christian had gone to bed very late, she woke
up as soon as the sun streamed in through the open
window, flooding the room with crimson light. She
looked at her watch. It was five o'clock. She lay on
her back, luxuriating in the warmth of bed. Her heart
felt so light and happy, that it seemed to her as if some
joy, some great tremendous joy, had befallen her during
the night. What could it be? What was this new bliss,
she wondered, that had thrilled her so rapturously? All
the depression of the previous evening had vanished, had
melted away in her sleep.

So Paul Brétigny was in love with her. How different
he seemed now from her original idea of him. Despite
her efforts of memory, she could not recall him as he
was the first time she had seen him and formed her
opinion of him. She could not conjure up even a
semblance of the man her brother had introduced to her.
The new Paul retained nothing of his old self, either in
looks or ways. Little by little, day by day, that first
impression had been subjected to the gradual transformation a man undergoes in the mind of a woman, as their
relationship passes through all the stages from casual
acquaintance to friendship and from friendship to love.
Unconsciously, hour by hour, she acquires a fuller knowledge of him, his features, his actions, his attitudes, his
whole person, physical and moral. He makes his way
into her eyes, into her heart, with voice and gesture, with
everything he says, everything he thinks. She absorbs
him, she understands him, she interprets all that his
smiles, his words imply, until at last he seems to be all

her own, because of her unreasoning love for everything that is his, for everything that emanates from him. In the end it becomes impossible to recall him as he appeared to her indifferent eyes, the first time she saw him.

So Paul Brétigny was in love with her. Christian felt neither fear nor distress. She was conscious only of deep emotion, and an immense, exquisite new joy, the joy of knowing herself beloved. She wondered, however, a little uneasily what attitude they should adopt towards each other. From the point of view of conscience, this was a delicate matter, and so, trusting to her own tact and adroitness for guidance, she dismissed it from her mind. She left her room at her usual hour, and came upon Paul smoking a cigarette outside the door of the hotel.

"Good-morning, Madame Andermatt," he said, with a deferential bow. "How are you to-day?"

"Very well, thank you. I slept splendidly."

She gave him her hand, fearing that he would hold it too long, but he scarcely pressed it, and they began to talk to each other as calmly as if neither remembered. All that morning Paul did nothing to recall his passionate declaration of the previous evening. During the days that followed he showed himself equally calm and discreet, until she felt that she could trust him. He had realised, she supposed, that further liberties would only wound her, and she hoped, she firmly believed, that they had stopped short at that delightful stage of intimacy, when two lovers can gaze into the depths of each other's eyes without remorse, in stainless innocence. At the same time she was careful not to remain alone with him.

One evening, however, about ten o'clock, the Saturday after their picnic by the lake of Tazenat, the Marquis, Christian and Paul were returning home from the Casino, where they had left Gontran playing écarté in the great hall with Aubry-Pasteur, Riquier and Dr Honorat. Brétigny looked up at the moon shining through the trees.

" Wouldn't it be delightful," he said, " to visit the ruins of Tournoël on a night like this? "

Christian was enchanted by the idea, for, like most women, she could never resist the appeal of ruins combined with moonlight.

She pressed her father's hand :

" Oh, father dear, you will, won't you? "

He was longing for his bed, and hesitated.

" Just think how beautiful Tournoël is even by day." she urged him. " You said yourself that you had never seen such picturesque ruins, with that great tower looking down on the castle. What must it be like by night? "

In the end he gave in.

" Very well, we'll go. But we will only look at it for five minutes and then come home. Personally I like to be in bed by eleven."

" Yes, we will come back at once. It's only twenty minutes' walk."

The three set out, Christian leaning on her father's arm, while Paul walked beside her. He talked about his travels in Switzerland, Italy and Sicily, and described his various impressions, his raptures on the top of Monte Rosa, when the sun, rising on the horizon above that array of icy peaks, that frozen world of eternal snows, suffused all those giant summits with dazzling white radiance, kindling them like ghostly lighthouses, destined to illumine the kingdoms of the dead. He spoke of his emotions on the edge of the monstrous crater of Etna, among the clouds, ten thousand feet up, with nothing but sea and sky around him, how he felt like an insignificant insect as he leaned, half-suffocated by its breath, over that gaping orifice. He enlarged upon these scenes, hoping to stir Christian's emotions, and she thrilled as she listened to him, and in a transport of imagination caught a glimpse of all the wonders he had seen.

Suddenly round a corner of the road, Tournoël came in sight. Aloft on its peak, dominated by its tall slender tower, breached by time, scarred by wars of long ago, the ancient castle loomed against the background of the ghostly sky like the silhouette of some spectral manor.

All three stood spellbound.

"It's really very pretty," observed the Marquis at last, "quite like one of Gustave Doré's visions come true. We'll sit down for five minutes."

He seated himself on the grass by the wayside.

"Oh, father, let us go on," exclaimed Christian. "It's too beautiful, too beautiful. Do let us go as far as the foot, I implore you."

But this time the Marquis was firm.

"No, my pet, I have walked enough. I'm tired. If you want a closer view, Monsieur Brétigny will take you. I will wait for you here."

"Would you care to, Madame Andermatt?" asked Paul.

She was divided between her dread of being alone with him and her reluctance to hurt the feelings of a man of honour by seeming to distrust him.

"Off you go!" said the Marquis, "and I'll wait for you here."

She reflected that her father would remain within earshot, and she said, firmly:

"Come along, then, Monsieur Brétigny," and they set off, side by side.

But in a few moments she felt herself in the grip of some poignant emotion, some vague, mysterious terror, begotten by the ruins, by the night, by the man at her side. As on that other evening by the lake of Tazenat, her limbs betrayed her and refused their support. They bent under her and seemed to be sinking through the ground, and it was only with an effort that she was able to lift her feet. By the wayside stood a lofty chestnut tree, shading the border of a meadow. Breathless, as if she had been running, Christian collapsed against the trunk.

"Let us stop here," she faltered. "We get a splendid view."

As Paul threw himself on the grass beside her, she could hear the fierce, rapid throbbing of her heart.

"Do you believe in a previous existence?" he asked her, after a brief silence.

In her agitation she scarcely grasped what he had said.

"I hardly know," she faltered, "I have never thought about it."

"Personally I do," he continued, "or, rather, I have a feeling. A human being consists of a spirit and a body, which, though seemingly distinct, are without doubt one homogeneous whole. It is, therefore, obvious that when the same elements that once composed a man are combined a second time, that man's existence is renewed. Although he may not be the same individual, it is undoubtedly the same person who reappears, when a replica of an earlier form is tenanted by a soul such as animated it in the past. Well, this evening, Madame Andermatt, I am convinced that I once lived in that castle. I owned it. It was mine, I know it. And I know, too, that within its walls dwelt a lady whom I loved, who was like you, and whose name was Christian like your own. I am so sure of it that I still seem to see you, calling to me from the top of yonder tower. Try to remember! Behind the castle lies a wood, which slopes down to a deep valley. We have often wandered there, you and I. You used to wear light gowns on summer evenings, while my heavy armour rang out beneath the trees. Think, Christian, think! Why, your name is as familiar to me as the names one has known from childhood. If you were to search the stones of that fortress, you would find it there, carved by my hand long ago. I tell you I recognise my home, my domain, just as I recognised you yourself the first time I saw you."

There was a thrill of conviction in his words, for Christian's presence, the moon, the night, the ruins, all inspired him with romantic ecstasy.

Suddenly he threw himself on his knees at Christian's feet.

"Let me still adore you," he murmured brokenly, "now that I have found you again. All these years I have been seeking you."

She tried to rise to her feet and to run to her father for refuge, but she had neither the strength nor the courage. She remained where she was, fascinated by a burning desire to go on listening to him, to hear those enchanting words stealing into her heart. She felt herself wafted away into a dream, an exquisite dream, long desired, fraught with romance, with moonbeams, with poetry.

He had seized her hands and was kissing her fingertips, and murmuring:

"Christian . . . Christian . . . take me . . . kill me . . . I love you . . . Christian."

She could feel him trembling, quivering at her feet. And now, shaken with deep sobs, he was kissing her knees. She feared for his reason, and sprang up to run away. But he was too quick for her. Clasping her in his arms he swooped down upon her lips. At this, without a cry, without a protest, without a struggle, as if his kiss had broken down all resistance, physical and mental, she sank down on the grass, and into his embrace.

Released from his clasp, she jumped to her feet and began to run away, distraught and shivering with cold, like a person who has fallen into the water. With a few strides, he caught her up and seized her by the arm.

"Christian, Christian," he whispered. "Your father! Take care."

Without answering or turning her head, she walked straight on with a stiff, jerky step. Not daring to speak again, he followed her.

As soon as he saw them, the Marquis rose to his feet.

"Let us walk home quickly," he said, "I was just beginning to feel chilly. It's all very fine, this sort of thing, but it doesn't go with my treatment."

As soon as Christian reached her room, she hastily

undressed, plunged into bed, hid her head under the clothes and burst into tears. Motionless, prostrate, her face deep in the pillow, she wept for a long, long time. Her mind was a blank. She was not unhappy; she felt no remorse. Although she wept, she did so without thinking, without reasoning, without knowing why, instinctively, just as one sings, when one is happy. At last, exhausted with tears, worn out with sobbing, she fell asleep from utter weariness.

She was awakened by a soft tapping at the door of her room, which opened on to the drawing-room.

"Come in," she cried.

Her husband entered, brisk and cheerful with a travelling cap on his head, and by his side the little money bag which he always wore on a journey.

"What, were you still asleep, my dear?" he cried. "Did I wake you up? I didn't let you know I was coming. I hope you are well. It was lovely weather in Paris."

He took off his cap and went to kiss her. Seized with a morbid dread, a nervous horror of the little cheerful, pink-faced man, whose eyes were seeking her own, she shrank closer to the wall. Then, suddenly, she closed her eyes and offered him her forehead, which he calmly kissed.

"Do you mind if I wash in your dressing-room?" he asked. "As I wasn't expected, my room isn't ready."

"Yes, do," she stammered.

He vanished through a door at the foot of the bed, and she could hear him, moving about, splashing and whistling.

"Anything happened here?" he called out. "I have brought excellent news. The analysis of the water has surpassed all our hopes. We can cure at least three more diseases at Enval than at Royat. Splendid, isn't it?"

Gasping, she sat up in bed, her head in a whirl at this unexpected return, which hurt her like a blow, oppressed her like a pang of remorse. Diffusing a strong scent of verbena, he came back gaily, and seated himself unceremoniously on the end of the bed.

"What about the paralytic? How is he? Is he beginning to walk again? He can't help being cured, considering all we have discovered in the water."

During the last few days she had forgotten him entirely.

"Why," she stammered, "I . . . I think he's beginning to improve. As a matter of fact I haven't seen him this week. I . . . I have not been feeling very well."

He looked at her attentively.

"You really are a trifle pale. . . . But it suits you. You are looking charming . . . perfectly charming."

He came close to her again and tried to put one arm round her in bed. But she shrank back with such a start of terror that he remained dumbfounded, with outstretched hands, and lips ready to kiss her

"What is the matter?" he asked. "Can't one touch you? I assure you I'm not going to hurt you."

He came nearer, importunate, his eyes aflame with sudden desire.

"No, no," she faltered, "let me alone, I . . . I believe . . . I believe . . . I'm going to have a child."

She spoke without reflection, in an access of panic, merely in order to avoid his touch, much as she would have cried out that she had leprosy or plague.

It was her husband's turn to grow pale, but his emotion was due to profound joy. The only words he uttered were :

"So soon !"

He yearned now to clasp her in a long tender embrace, full of the happiness and gratitude of paternity. Then an anxious thought occurred to him.

"Is it possible? . . . How. . . . You really believe. . . . So soon?"

"Yes," she replied. "It is possible."

At this he skipped about the room, rubbing his hands together, exclaiming :

"Good heavens ! What a lucky day this is !"

Then came another knock at the door. Andermatt opened it, and a chambermaid announced that Dr Latonne wanted to speak to him at once.

"Very well. Show him into the drawing-room. I'm coming."

He went into the drawing-room, where the doctor joined him immediately. The latter's expression of face was solemn; his demeanour formal and cold. He bowed, barely touched the hand which Andermatt, somewhat astonished, extended to him, and took a seat. He then entered into an explanation in the tone of one of the seconds in an affair of honour.

"I find myself, Monsieur Andermatt, in an extremely disagreeable predicament. I feel that I must explain it in full to you, so that you may understand my conduct. When you did me the honour of calling me in to see your wife, I went to her with all possible speed It seems, however, that my colleague, Dr Bonnefille, who occupies an official position and doubtless inspires Madame Andermatt with greater confidence, had already been summoned, through the agency of the Marquis de Ravenel. The result was that I arrived after Dr Bonnefille, and now it looks as if I had tricked my colleague out of a patient. To all appearance, I have been guilty of a discourteous and improper action, such as is not permissible between members of the same profession. You will appreciate, Monsieur Andermatt, that in the exercise of our art, we are obliged to observe the most meticulous tact and caution in order to avoid the grave consequences which friction among ourselves might provoke. Dr Bonnefille has learnt of my visit to your wife and believes that I have committed a breach of etiquette. I confess that the appearances are against me. Be that as it may, he has spoken of me in such terms as, were it not for his age, would compel me to exact satisfaction from him. To clear myself in his eyes and in the opinion of the medical faculty at large, there is only one thing for me to do, and that is, to my great regret, to cease attending your wife and to publish abroad the whole truth of the matter. I would therefore beg you to accept my withdrawal, with the reasons I have given."

Andermatt replied in some embarrassment :

" I understand perfectly the difficult situation in which you find yourself. The fault is neither mine nor my wife's, but my father-in-law's, who called in Dr Bonnefille without letting us know. Couldn't I go to Dr Bonnefille and explain that. . . ."

" Quite useless, my dear sir," Dr Latonne interrupted. " Here we have a question of professional dignity and honour, which I am bound to respect before any other consideration. Keenly as I deplore . . ."

It was now Andermatt's turn to interrupt. He was the rich man, the man who paid, the man to whom the cost of a prescription at five, ten, twenty, or forty francs was no more than the price of a box of matches. All things were rightfully his by the power of the purse. His standard of value for all objects, animate or inanimate, regulated itself solely in terms of money. His appreciation of everything in the world was swiftly and directly brought to the test of a pecuniary valuation. He was accordingly annoyed by the presumption of this vendor of remedies on paper.

" Very well, Doctor. Let it rest at that. I can only trust for your sake that the course you have adopted may not have a detrimental effect on your prospects. We shall certainly see which of us two is likely to suffer most from this resolution of yours."

Dr Latonne took his departure with marked and chilling politeness.

" That I shall be the sufferer, I have no doubt. I have every reason to regret my action. But I can never hesitate between interest and conscience."

He turned to go, and as he left the room, he ran into the Marquis who was coming in, with a letter in his hand. As soon as the Marquis was alone with his son-in-law, he exclaimed :

"Look here, Will. Here is a most annoying thing, and it's entirely your fault. Dr Bonnefille is much hurt at your having called in Latonne for Christian and he has sent me this very dry intimation that I am no longer to have the benefit of his experience."

At this Andermatt let himself go. He walked up and down gesticulating, becoming more and more excited. He was full of that innocuous and factitious anger, which no one takes seriously. He shouted out his grievances. Whose fault was it, after all? The Marquis's, and his only. Had he not called in that jackass Bonnefille without even warning him, Andermatt, who had full information from his Paris doctor as to the respective merits of these three Enval quacks? In any case, what business had the Marquis to meddle in the affair, calling in advice behind the back of the husband, who was the only responsible judge of his wife's state of health? Really, it was the same thing always in everything. None of his family ever did anything that was not rank folly. He had said it before and would say it again. He was a voice crying in the wilderness; nobody understood, not a soul would put any trust in his experiences until it was too late. He spoke of *his* physician, *his* experience, with the authority of a man claiming a monopoly of these things. The possessive pronouns boomed on his lips like the clang of metals. When he said the words, "My wife," it was quite evident that the Marquis had forfeited all rights over his daughter, inasmuch as Andermatt had married her, marriage and purchase being in his mind synonymous expressions.

Gontran entered while the dispute was at its liveliest, and threw himself into an armchair. Immensely amused, he sat there in silence with a smile of merriment on his lips. When Andermatt's breath gave out, Gontran held up his hand and exclaimed :

"It is my turn to speak. There you are, the two of you, without a doctor. Well, then, I propose my candidate, Dr Honorat. He is the only one who has a definite and unalterable opinion about the Enval waters. He makes his patients drink them, but he would not drink them himself for anything in the world. Would you like me to go and fetch him? I will undertake all the negotiations."

As it was the only thing to do, Gontran was requested to go and fetch him immediately. Distressed on his own account at the idea of a change of regimen and attendance, the Marquis was anxious to obtain this new doctor's advice as quickly as possible, while Andermatt's desire to consult him on behalf of his wife was no less keen. Christian heard them through the door, but she made no effort to understand their conversation. The moment her husband left her she fled from her bed as from a place of peril, and, without summoning her maid, dressed herself hurriedly. Her head was whirling with this succession of events. Life to-day was not as yesterday, the world around her had undergone a change; even the people in it were altered.

Again she heard Andermatt's loud voice:

"Hallo, Brétigny, how are you?"

He no longer called him "Monsieur."

Another voice replied:

"Very well indeed, Andermatt. So you got here this morning?"

Christian, who was putting up her hair, stopped, with her hands still raised to her head. Through the partition she seemed to see the two men shaking hands. She felt as if she were choking. Her limbs failed her and she collapsed into a chair, while her uncoiled hair fell loose upon her shoulders.

Now it was Paul who was speaking. At every word that escaped his lips she quivered from head to foot. Although she could not distinguish the meaning of what he said, his every utterance resounded within her heart like the clanging of a hammer on a bell. And suddenly, almost out loud, she exclaimed:

"I love him. . . . I love him."

It was as if she had received some new and surprising assurance which redeemed her, comforted her, acquitted her before the tribunal of her conscience. Impulsively, she sprang to her feet again; in a single moment she had accepted the situation. As she once more began to put up her hair, she murmured :

"I have a lover. That is all. I have a lover."

To strengthen her resolution, to secure herself from all remorse, she suddenly determined with ardent sincerity, to love him frantically, to give her life, her happiness into his keeping, to sacrifice everything to him, with the fantastic morality of one, who, though fallen, yet preserves her delicacy of conscience, and holds herself justified by the intensity of her devotion. And towards her lover, who was on the other side of that dividing wall, she threw kiss after kiss. The struggle was at an end. She surrendered herself to him without reserve, as a devotee offers herself to a god. The child in her, still timid and shy for all her arch, roguish ways, was of a sudden extinct; and the woman had come to life, passionate, resolute, tenacious, of whom there had been no revealing hint, save the energy dormant in her blue eyes, which had lent an air of courage, almost of bravado, to her charming pink and white face.

She heard the door open, but did not turn her head. As if a new sense, a new instinct, had just developed in her, she was aware that it was her husband.

"Will you be ready soon?" he asked. "We are going immediately to see Clovis in his bath, to find out whether he is really better."

"Yes, Will dear, in five minutes," she replied calmly.

Gontran, who had returned, called Andermatt back into the drawing-room.

"Would you believe it," he said. "I met that idiot Honorat in the park, and he also refuses to come and attend you. He is afraid of the others. He speaks of procedure, etiquette, custom. You would think . . . he looks like. . . . In short, he's as big a fool as the other two. Really, I couldn't have believed he was such an absolute ape."

The Marquis was dumbfoundered. He believed that Nature, when she made these healing waters flow, had passed a law by which the doses were regulated, the hours and stages of treatment specifically prescribed. The mysterious secrets of Nature were known only to the doctors, who were Nature's seers and sages. The idea of taking the waters without medical advice, of staying five minutes too long in his bath, of drinking a glass too much, filled him with dismay.

" It comes to this," he cried. " A man might die here, die like a dog, and not one of these fellows would put himself out in the slightest ! "

He was furious. He was seized with the egotistic rage of a valetudinarian threatened in his health.

" Have they any right to behave like that? " he went on. " They pay for their licenses just the same as grocers. The scoundrels ! They ought to be compelled to attend people, just as railway trains are compelled to accommodate passengers. I shall write to the newspapers. The whole world shall know of it."

In a great state of excitement he paced up and down. Then, turning to his son, he resumed :

" Look here. We must get a doctor from Royat or Clermont. We can't stay like this. . . ."

Gontran replied, laughing :

" Unfortunately the Clermont and Royat doctors don't understand the Enval waters. Their action on the digestive organs and the circulation is different from that of their own springs. And in any case you may be sure that those doctors won't come either. They will never run the risk of being accused of poaching on another man's preserves."

" Then what is to become of us? " stammered the Marquis in dismay.

"Leave it to me," said Andermatt, seizing his hat. " I guarantee that you will have all three of them here to-night. Mark my words, all three of them, on their knees. Now let us go and see old Clovis. Are you ready, Christian?"

Pale but resolute, she appeared in the doorway. After kissing her father and brother, she turned to Paul and held out her hand to him; he took it, with downcast eyes and trembling with agitation. Her father, husband, and brother moved away, talking, and paying no heed to her and Paul. Casting upon her lover a glance in which affection and determination were mingled, she said in a firm voice:

"I am yours, body and soul. Henceforth you may do as you please with me."

And without giving him time to reply, she left the room.

As they drew near to the Oriols' spring, they caught sight of old Clovis's hat, like an enormous mushroom. The cripple was dozing in the sunshine, lying in his pit, immersed in the hot water. He now passed his whole mornings in this fashion. He had become used to the boiling bath, which, according to him, made him as spry as a young bridegroom.

Andermatt roused him.

"Well, my good fellow, how goes it? Better?"

Clovis, recognizing his patron, made a grimace of satisfaction.

"Yes, yes. It's working. It's working properly."

"You are beginning to get about?"

"Like a rabbit, sir, like a rabbit. I shall be dancing the bourrée with my sweetheart on the first Sunday of the month."

"Honestly, are you able to walk?"

Clovis became serious:

"Oh, well, it doesn't amount to much. But never mind. It'll come."

Nothing would satisfy Andermatt but to see the old vagabond walking. He revolved round the hole in great excitement, issuing orders as if he were refloating a sunken ship.

" Now, Gontran, you take his right arm. Brétigny, you his left. I'll hold him round the body. Now, all together, one, two, three. Marquis, you take his leg. No, the other one, the one in the water. Quick, please, I'm fairly done. That's it. One ... two ... three, there we are. . . . Ouf ! "

The old man made no attempt to help them, but submitted with an ironical air to their efforts. Having placed him in a sitting posture on the ground, they renewed their exertions and hoisted him to his feet. Then they handed him the crutches, which he used as walking-sticks, and he began to walk. Doubled up, groaning and puffing, and dragging his feet, he crawled along like a slug, leaving behind him a long trail of water on the white dust of the road.

Full of enthusiasm, Andermatt clapped his hands and shouted, " Bravo, bravo ! Splendid ! " as if applauding an actor at the play. When the patient seemed exhausted, Andermatt sprang to support him, and though the old man's clothes were dripping with water, seized him in his arms :

" That will do. You mustn't overtire yourself. Now we will put you back into your bath."

Clovis was according replaced in his bath by the four men, who each took him by a limb and transported him as cautiously as if he had been some precious and fragile object. The paralytic then declared in tones of conviction :

" It's wonderful water. There's nothing like it anywhere. Water like that is worth a gold-mine."

Andermatt turned sharply to the Marquis :

" Don't wait luncheon for me. I'm off to see the Oriols. I don't know when I shall get away from them. One can't afford to dilly-dally in an affair like this."

He made off in great haste, almost at a run, and twirling his cane like a man in the height of joy. The others sat down under the willows on the edge of the wood, opposite to old Clovis's hole.

With Paul beside her, Christian sat gazing at the knoll from which she had witnessed the blasting of the rock. Hardly a month had elapsed since the memorable day when she had reclined there, on that sun-scorched grass. One month. Only one month. She recalled every little detail : the tricolor umbrellas, the cooks and their underlings, and all the trivial chatter. And the dog, the wretched dog that had been blown to pieces by the explosion. And the tall stranger, who at a word from her had sprung to save the poor little creature. To-day that stranger was her lover! Her lover! Yes, she had a lover. She was his mistress . . . his mistress! In the dark recesses of her mind, she repeated the words . . . his mistress. How odd it sounded! That man, who sat beside her, his hand plucking the blades of grass one by one close to her dress, which he was longing to touch, that man was now bound to her, heart and body, by that chain, mysterious, unavowable, shameful, with which Nature has linked man and woman together. With the voice of thought, the dumb voice that speaks loudest in the silence of perturbed souls, she repeated over and over again : " I am his mistress, his mistress." How strange it was, how utterly unforeseen.

" Do I love him ? " she wondered. She sped a swift glance at him, and their eyes met. The ardent gaze with which he enveloped her affected her like a passionate caress, and she quivered from head to foot.

She now felt a mad, irresistible desire to seize the hand that was playing in the grass, and to press it so hard, that it would express as much as a complete embrace. Her own hand glided along her dress until it touched the turf, and there it lay, motionless, with outspread fingers. Then she saw his hand stealing very gently towards hers, like some small animal in love, seeking its mate. Nearer it came, and nearer; till it was quite close. Their fingers touched. Lightly, hardly perceptibly, the tips brushed, withdrew, met again, like lips that kiss. But this imperceptible caress, this slight contact of their finger-tips, thrilled her so violently that she felt as faint as if he had again crushed her in his arms. And of a sudden she understood how entirely a woman may belong to her lover, how completely she may lose her personality under the influence of the passion that possesses her, how another human being may seize her, body and soul, flesh, blood, thoughts, will, nerves, all, all that is hers, like a great wide-winged bird of prey swooping down on a wren.

Carried away by Andermatt's enthusiasm, Gontran and the Marquis were discussing the future health resort. They enumerated Andermatt's good qualities, his clearness of mind, his sureness of judgment, the safety of his speculative methods, the boldness of his tactics, and his steadiness of character. In this atmosphere of probable, nay, to their minds, sure success, both men with one accord, congratulated each other on their connection with him.

Completely absorbed in themselves, Christian and Paul hardly seemed to be listening.

"Well, darling," said the Marquis to his daughter, "some day you may well be one of the richest women in France. People will talk of the Andermatts as they talk of the Rothschilds. Will is really a remarkable man, a very remarkable man, a man of great intelligence."

At these words, Paul was suddenly seized by a curious pang of jealousy.

"What nonsense!" he exclaimed. "I know the sort of intelligence these jobbers have. They have only one idea in their heads: money. All the thoughts we give to beautiful things, all the actions we fail in through our caprices, all the hours we throw away on our distractions, all the energy we waste on our pleasures, all the ardour and power that love, divine love, exacts from us, they devote to seeking gold, dreaming about gold, piling up gold. Man, intelligent man, lives for all the great disinterested emotions, for the arts, for science, love, travelling, literature. If he tries to make money, it is because money helps him to obtain the true joys of the mind and the happiness of the heart. But these money-grubbers have not a thing in their heads except the ignoble lust for a deal. They are parasites on life; they bear the same relation to men of real worth as the picture-dealer does to the artist, the editor to the writer, the theatrical manager to the dramatist."

Feeling that he was letting himself be carried away, he suddenly checked himself. In calmer tones he resumed :

" I don't say that that applies to Andermatt. I think he is a charming fellow. I am very fond of him. He is worth a hundred of the others."

Christian withdrew her hand, and Paul again fell silent. Gontran began to laugh. In that mischievous tone in which he was capable of any audacity, in his moments of semi-serious chaffing :

" In any case, my friend, these men have one rare merit. Some of them marry our sisters; and some of them beget rich daughters for us to marry."

The Marquis was annoyed, and rose to his feet.

" Gontran, there are times when you are positively revolting."

Paul turned to Christian.

" Are such men capable of dying for a woman, or even giving her every penny, all that they possess, without keeping back a single thing? "

This remark had an obvious significance. It meant : " All that I have is yours, even life itself." Thrilled with emotion, she thought of an excuse for holding his hands.

" Help me up," she said. " I'm so stiff I can hardly move."

Standing by the side of the road, he caught hold of her wrists and drew her up, till she was close to his heart. She saw his lips shape the words, " I love you," and she turned away quickly to avoid echoing this utterance, which sprang in spite of herself to her lips in an impulse which thrust her towards him.

When they returned to the hotel, the bath hour was past and luncheon time was approaching. Christian rang the bell, but as there was no sign of Andermatt, they took another turn in the park and then decided to go in. The meal was protracted, but it was over long before Andermatt made his appearance. Returning to the park, they seated themselves under the trees. Hour after hour slipped past; the sun began to set above the mountains, and its light crept over the foliage. Day was drawing to a close, and Will had not yet come back. Suddenly they caught sight of him. He was walking quickly. His hat was in his hand, and he was mopping his forehead. His tie was askew, his waistcoat half open, as if he had come from a long journey, or a wrestling match, or some terrible and protracted struggle. As soon as he saw the Marquis, he cried out :

"Victory! The battle is ours. But what a day I've had, my friends. Ah, the old fox, what a time he gave me ! "

He at once proceeded to an account of his troublesome negotiations. Old Oriol had at first shown himself so unreasonable that Andermatt broke off the discussion and went away. He was, however, called back. Old Oriol's notion was not to sell his vineyards outright, but to convey them to the Company, with right of resumption in case the scheme was a failure. In the event of the scheme succeeding, he claimed half-profits.

Andermatt had had to demonstrate to him by means of written calculations and by diagrams, that the total value of the fields was not more than eighty thousand francs at the present date, whereas the expenses of the Company would touch a million at the very outset. To this Oriol had retorted that he meant to base his profits on the enormous increment which would accrue to the value of his property in virtue of the prospective construction of Baths and hotels. He proposed to proportion his gains to the acquired value, not to the present value. Andermatt had then to point out to him that the risks must be in proportion to the possible gains; thus inspiring in him the fear of total loss. The final arrangement was as follows. Oriol was to convey to the Company all the land on the banks of the stream—that is to say, all the ground which seemed to offer a possibility of mineral springs. In addition, the Company was to have the knoll on which to build a casino and a hotel, as well as certain vineyards on the hillside, which were to be divided up into lots and offered to leading physicians from Paris. In consideration of this conveyance, reckoned at two hundred and fifty thousand francs, or about four times its true value, Oriol was to take one-quarter share of the Company's profits. He retained ten times as much land round the proposed establishment as he had made over, and was therefore sure in the event of the project succeeding, to realize a fortune, by the discreet sale of these lots, which would, as he said, constitute his daughters' dowries. As soon as these terms had been arranged, Will had to take father and son straight to the notary in order to draw up a promise of sale, annullable in the event of the requisite springs not being discovered. The drawing up of these articles, the disputes over every point, the endless repetition of the same arguments, the eternal recapitulation of the same reasons, had taken the whole afternoon. But at last the end had been reached. The banker had held his ground, though a lingering regret still troubled him.

" I shall have to limit my activities to the water question," he said. " I can't touch the land business. That old monkey was as sharp as a needle."

Presently he said :

" Pooh, no matter. I shall buy up the old Company. That's where my speculations will come in. . . . I must be off to Paris to-night.'

" To-night? Why? " asked the Marquis in amazement.

" I have to prepare the final document. Meanwhile Aubry-Pasteur will be boring for springs. I must arrange for the work to be put in hand within a fortnight. I haven't a moment to waste. By the way, I give you notice that you are a member of my Board of Directors.

I must have a strong majority on it. I give you ten shares. You, too, Gontran. You shall have ten shares."

Gontran began to laugh.

" Thanks, old man. I hereby sell them back to you. That makes five thousand francs you owe me."

Andermatt, who was in no mood for joking over such grave matters of business, rejoined drily :

" If you can't take it seriously I shall go elsewhere."

" Not on any account, my dear fellow," said Gontran, who at once stopped laughing. " I am entirely at your service, as you know."

Andermatt then turned to Paul.

" Will you do me a friendly service and accept ten shares and a directorship? "

Paul bowed and replied :

" With your permission, Monsieur Andermatt, I beg to decline your generous offer. But if you will allow me to put a hundred thousand francs into your scheme, which I consider a magnificent one, you will be conferring a favour on me."

William was in ecstasies. He grasped Paul's hands. Such a mark of confidence was irresistible. He was always seized with an overpowering desire to embrace anybody who would finance his enterprises.

Christian, however, was hurt and affronted, and blushed to the roots of her hair. She felt as if she had been bought and sold. Would Paul ever have offered her husband his hundred thousand francs if he had not loved her? Certainly not. At least he might have avoided carrying out such a transaction in her presence.

The bell rang for dinner and they went back to the hotel. As soon as they were seated at table, Madame Paille said to Andermatt :

" I hear you are going to found another Hydropathic Establishment at Enval."

The news had already spread through the whole countryside and had become common property, to the great excitement of all the visitors.

" Quite correct," William replied. " The present establishment is inadequate."

He turned to Aubry-Pasteur.

" You will excuse me for mentioning at table a request which I intended to make to you. I am leaving to-night for Paris, and haven't a moment to spare. Would you be willing to supervise the work of excavation, with a view to discovering a larger volume of water? "

Flattered by the proposal, the engineer consented, and, amid a general silence, the essential features of these investigations, which were to be put in hand at once, were settled. The whole procedure was thrashed out and arranged in a few minutes with the lucidity and precision which Andermatt always contributed to business affairs. Conversation next turned on the paralytic, who had been seen that afternoon crossing the park with the aid of a single crutch, whereas on the morning of that same day he had still been using two.

" It is a miracle, a real miracle ! His cure is progressing by leaps and bounds," said Andermatt.

To please him, as Christian's husband, Paul remarked :

" Old Clovis himself is making the leaps and bounds."

There was a laugh of approval from the whole table. Every eye was turned on Will; everyone was showering compliments on him. The waiters served him before the rest, with a respectful deference which vanished from their demeanour as soon as they proceeded to offer the dishes to the other guests. One of them handed Andermatt a visiting-card on a plate. Taking it, he read out, half-aloud :

" Dr Latonne, of Paris, would be obliged if Monsieur Andermatt would be so kind as to grant him a brief interview before his departure."

" Tell him I have no time," said Andermatt. " But I shall be back here again in a week or so."

At the same moment a bouquet of flowers from Dr Honorat was brought to Christian.

" Dr Bonnefille is a bad third," laughed Gontran.

The dinner approached its close, and Andermatt was informed that the landau was ready. He went upstairs to fetch his handbag, and on his return found half the village assembled outside the door of the hotel. Petrus Martel came and shook his hand with over-acted effusiveness.

Whispering in Andermatt's ear, he said :

" I have a proposal to make to you, something tremendous, which will do the trick for you."

Suddenly Dr Bonnefille came in sight, with his customary appearance of haste. He passed close by Will, and, honouring him with the low bow he usually reserved for the Marquis, said :

" Bon voyage, Baron."

" A palpable hit," said Gontran.

Swelling with triumph, joy and pride, Andermatt shook hands all round, thanking everybody, and exclaiming repeatedly, " Au revoir, au revoir ! " His mind was so engrossed with his own thoughts that he almost forgot to kiss his wife. This mark of indifference was a comfort to her. When she saw the landau drive away, drawn by the horses at full trot, along the darkening road, she felt that henceforth, for the rest of her life, she had nothing to fear from anyone. She passed the whole evening in front of the hotel, seated between her father and Paul. Gontran had, as usual, gone to the Casino. She had no desire either to walk or speak, but remained motionless, with her hands clasped upon her knee, and her eyes gazing into the darkness. She felt languid and weak; a little perturbed yet happy; she hardly thought, she hardly even dreamed. From time to time she struggled against a pang of vague remorse, which she repelled by saying over and over again to herself : " I love him, I love him, I love him."

She went up to her room early, anxious to be alone with her thoughts. Enveloped in a loose dressing-gown, and sunk in the depths of an armchair, she looked out through the open window at the stars, and in the frame of the window her fancy ever conjured up the image of the man who had won her love. Kind, gentle, impetuous, very strong and yet, in her presence, very humble—thus she pictured him. He had made her his own, she felt, his own forever. No longer was she alone in the world. Henceforth the hearts of these twain would beat as one, their two souls would be merged into one. She knew not where he was; but of one thing she was sure, he was dreaming of her, as she of him. At every beat of her heart, she seemed to hear an answering echo. Hovering around her, brushing her lightly as a bird's wing, was desire, ardent desire, emanating from her lover, stealing in through the open windows, seeking her, pleading with her in the silence of the night! How sweet, how exquisite this new sense that she was loved! What bliss to feel tears of tenderness rise to her eyes at the thought of him! How rapturous this yearning to open her arms to him from afar, to summon him, to stretch out her hands to the vision she evoked, to welcome the kisses forever wafted towards her by her lover in an ecstasy of longing. She flung up her white arms towards the stars. Then suddenly she uttered a cry. A tall dark shadow strode across her balcony, loomed in the frame of the window. She leaped to her feet in wild surprise. It was he. Reckless of the danger of being seen, she threw herself upon his breast.

VIII

ANDERMATT'S absence was protracted. Aubry-Pasteur went on with his excavations. He found four more springs, which yielded twice as much water as the new Company required. The whole countryside was agog with these investigations and discoveries, and went wild with excitement and enthusiasm at the prospects of a glorious future. Nothing else was thought of or discussed. Even the Marquis and Gontran passed their days among the workmen, who were tapping and sounding in the veins of granite, and listened with growing interest to the engineer's instructive dissertations on the geology of Auvergne. Thus Paul and Christian were left in absolute peace and security to the free enjoyment of their love. No one troubled his head about them, no one suspected, no one even thought of spying on them. Everybody's attention and curiosity were passionately concentrated on the prospects of the future health resort.

Christian was like a youth in his first inebriation. The first glass, the first kiss, had set her on fire, had bewildered her. The second glass she had drunk very quickly and had liked it better than the first; and now she was intoxicating herself with deep draughts.

Since the night on which Paul had come to her room, she was no longer conscious of what was passing in the outer world. Time, events, human beings, no longer had for her any reality : all that existed for her on earth or in heaven, was one man, one man only, he whom she loved. Her eyes saw only him, her spirit dwelt on him alone; she had no other foundation for her hopes. She lived, moved, ate, dressed, went through a form of listening and answering, without understanding or knowing what she was doing. Her mind was at peace, for she was beyond the reach of misfortune. Her senses were closed to all beside; physical pain would have had no effect upon a body that vibrated to love and love alone. Mental pain could not touch a soul that was drugged with happiness.

Paul for his part, adoring her with the transport which characterized all his passions, excited Christian's love almost to frenzy. Often, towards the close of day, when he knew that the Marquis and Gontran had gone to see the springs, he would say:

"Let us go and look at our heaven."

What he called their heaven was a clump of pine-trees which had sprung up on the slopes that lay above the gorges. They would climb up through a little wood, by means of a steep path, which made Christian pant for breath. As time was short, they walked quickly, he with his arm around her waist to help her up the hill. She would put her hand on his shoulder and let him support her. Sometimes she would throw her arms round his neck and kiss him on the mouth. The higher they climbed, the keener became the atmosphere, and when they reached the pine clump, the resinous odour refreshed them like a breeze from the sea.

They seated themselves under the dark boughs, she on a grassy mound, he at her feet. The wind blowing through the branches sang the gentle, plaintive song of the pine trees, and the great plain of Limagne, stretching out before them into the dim distance, seemed to them like the ocean itself. Yes, there was the sea, yonder, far below them; how could they doubt it, with its breath upon their faces?

He charmed her with playful, childish prattle.

"Give me your fingers to eat. They are my sugar plums."

He took each one in turn between his lips and pretended to bite them with thrills of epicurean enjoyment.

"Oh, how delicious they are! Especially the little finger. I never enjoyed anything so much as that little finger."

Then he threw himself on his knees with his arms in Christian's lap.

"Ivy, look at me," he murmured. "Look at me. I want to sink into your soul."

He called her Ivy because she clung so close to him when they embraced, like a creeper clinging to a tree. They gazed into each other's eyes with that prolonged, unmoving contemplation which seems indeed to mingle soul with soul.

"Possession such as ours is the only way of love," he said. "The rest is mere degradation."

Face to face, their breath mingling, they sought passionately to fathom the crystal depths of each other's eyes.

"I see you, my Ivy," he murmured. "I see your adorable heart."

"I see yours, too, Paul," she replied.

It was true enough; they could indeed see to the very bottom of each other's heart and soul, for all that was there was the violent ecstasy of their mutual love.

"Ivy," he said, "your eyes are like heaven. They are so blue. So full of light and shadow. Surely I can see the swallows flitting across them. Are they your thoughts?"

After gazing at each other long and lingeringly, they came close and embraced with swift light kisses, and between the kisses they renewed their contemplation of each other. Sometimes he caught her up in his arms and ran with her along the banks of the stream that glided on its way to precipitate itself into the gorges of Enval. It was a narrow upland valley of fields and woods. Paul would bound along the turf and every now and then would lift Christian high up in his powerful arms and cry:

"Ivy, let us take to our wings."

This yearning for wings was inspired in them by love,

by that rapturous love of theirs, harassing, torturing, unceasing, which was forever stimulated by their surroundings, by the rarefied air, an atmosphere for birds, as he called it, the wide blue depths through which it would have been ecstasy to swoop, hand-in-hand, vanishing, when the dusk sank down upon the great plain, into its dark immensity. Forth they would have fared across the shadowy sky of night, never to return. Where to alight? They knew not, but it was a glorious dream.

Out of breath, after having run with her in his arms, he would set her down on a rock, kneel to her, and, kissing her ankles, murmur his adoration in words of loving baby-talk.

Had they been living in a city when their love overtook them, their passion would doubtless have been more restrained, but at the same time more sensual, less ethereal, less romantic. But in that country of verdure and wide vistas, the distant horizon gave scope to their flights of soul. There was nothing to distract them, nothing to attenuate the force of their newly awakened love. They had plunged forthwith into passion, rapturous, poetical, part ecstasy, part frenzy. The surrounding landscapes, the warm breezes, the woods, the balmy air, were, every moment of the day and night, as music to their love. As the spinning dervish, his mind set ever on one idea, is impelled to acts of delirious savagery by the beat of the tambourine and the shrill notes of the flute, so did this music of nature kindle these two to a pitch of mad ecstasy.

One evening, however, when they came home to dinner, the Marquis announced that Andermatt had settled his business affairs and would be back in four days.

" The rest of us will leave the following morning. We have been here long enough. It doesn't do to spend too much time over these cures."

Paul and Christian were as utterly dismayed as if he had announced the end of the world. Their minds were full of consternation at this prospective parting and neither of them spoke one word during dinner. Then they were really to be separated within the next few days, and would never again meet in such freedom? The idea was so incredible, so absurd, that they could hardly grasp it.

Andermatt came, as announced, at the end of the week. He had telegraphed for a couple of landaus to meet the early train. Christian was in the grip of new and strange emotions : an indefinable fear of her husband, mingled with resentment and a curious contempt and defiance. She did not sleep at all that night, and rising at daybreak, she awaited his arrival. He was in the first landau, and with him were three well-dressed men of unassuming aspect. In the second landau followed four other men, evidently of slightly inferior status to the first three. The Marquis and Gontran regarded them with astonishment.

" Who are these people? "

" My shareholders," replied Andermatt. " We are going to form our Company this very day. We proceed at once to the election of the Board of Directors."

Andermatt's preoccupation was so great, that although he kissed his wife he did not speak to her and hardly seemed even to see her. He turned to the seven men who stood behind him in respectful silence.

" Get your breakfast," he ordered, " and go for a walk. Meet me again here at twelve o'clock."

They marched off in silence like soldiers obeying a word of command, and disappeared by the outer steps into the hotel. Gontran watched them moving away and asked with an air of extreme gravity :

" Where did you pick up your corps-de-ballet? "

" They are good, sound men," replied Andermatt with a smile. " Stock Exchange men. Capitalists."

Presently, with a smile that was more marked, he added :

" They are so good as to interest themselves in my little affairs."

After that he went to the notary-public to run through

the deeds which he had sent on a few days before, all ready to be fair-copied. At the notary's he met Dr Latonne, with whom he had been corresponding during his absence, and he had a long and confidential talk with him in a corner of the lawyer's room, while the clerk's pen coursed over the paper, scratch, scratch, like the noise of so many insects. The meeting at which the Company was to be formally constituted had been fixed for two o'clock. The notary's office-room had been arranged as for a concert. Maître Alain was to take his seat, with his head clerk beside him, on one side of the table, and facing him on the opposite side were two rows of chairs for the subscribers. In view of the importance of the affair, Maître Alain was wearing his coat. He was a tiny, pot-bellied man, with a stammer.

On the stroke of two, Andermatt entered with the Marquis, Gontran, and Paul. Next followed the seven gentlemen whom Gontran had described as the corps-de-ballet. Andermatt had the authoritative air of a general. Old Oriol turned up in good time, accompanied by Colosse. Both of them had a look of that distrust and uneasiness which affects all yokels when there is a document to be signed. Dr Latonne was the last to arrive. He had made his peace with Andermatt by dint of complete submission, after paving the way by cleverly turned excuses, which he followed up by offers of unreserved and whole-hearted service. Being now sure of him, Andermatt had promised him the coveted post of inspecting medical officer to the new Baths.

When the whole party was assembled, there was complete silence, which the notary broke by asking them to be seated, adding some words which were drowned by the commotion caused by moving the chairs. Andermatt placed himself so as to face his army and thus keep it under his eye. When all were seated, he began his speech.

"Gentlemen, it is unnecessary for me to dilate upon the object with which we are here assembled. Our first business is to constitute in due form the Company in which it is your desire to be shareholders. I feel bound, however, to acquaint you with certain details which have caused us a little embarrassment. Before committing myself to anything definite, I had to make sure of obtaining the authorisation necessary for the founding of a new establishment of public utility. I have received that authorisation. Anything that remains to be done in regard to this, will be done by me. I have the word of the Minister of State concerned. There was a second check to my plans. We are about, gentlemen, to undertake a struggle with the already existing Company. That we shall emerge victorious from the struggle, victorious and rich, we can rest assured. But the warriors of ancient days had to have a battle-cry, and similarly we, who are combatants in modern warfare, must have a name for our health resort. It must be sonorous, attractive, and well-suited for advertising purposes. It must strike the ear like a bugle-note and arrest the eye like a flash of lightning. The fact remains, however, that we are at Enval and that we cannot rebaptise the whole district. But there is one resource open to us; to designate our establishment by a new appellation exclusive to itself. This is my proposal. If our Baths are to be at the foot of the knoll of which Monsieur Oriol, who is now present with us, is the proprietor, then our future Casino will be built on the summit of the same knoll. We are justified therefore in saying that this knoll, this mountain, for it is a mountain, a small mountain, constitutes our Hydropathic Establishment, inasmuch as we possess it all from base to roof-ridge. What more natural than that our Baths should henceforward bear the name of Mont-Oriol? This health resort will become one of the most important in the whole world. Ought it not therefore to bear the name of the original proprietor? Let us render unto Cæsar the things that are Cæsar's. Note, too, gentlemen, how admirably it sounds. People will say Mont-Oriol as easily as they say Mont-Dore. It catches the eye, it dwells in the ear; it looks well, it sounds well, it is a name that sticks in the mind. Mont-Oriol . . . Mont-Oriol . . . The Mont-Oriol Baths."

On Andermatt's lips the word rang out; it shot forth like a bullet. He listened to the reverberation.

Resuming, he pretended to be conducting a conversation.

" ' You are going to the Mont-Oriol Baths, are you not?'

" ' Yes, Madam. They are said to be perfect, the Mont-Oriol waters.'

" ' They really are excellent, I assure you. And the country round Mont-Oriol is exquisite.' "

He simpered and modulated his voice when he was imitating the lady, and made as if to take his hat off politely when representing the gentleman.

Then in his natural tones, he asked :

" Does anyone present raise any objection? "

The shareholders replied as one man :

" No objection."

Three of the corps-de-ballet applauded.

Raised to the skies by this flattery, old Oriol was completely won over by this appeal to the inward pride of the peasant-parvenu. Twisting his hat in his hands, he smiled and nodded, revealing in spite of himself a joy which Andermatt noted without appearing to look at him. Colosse was no less gratified than his father, but his face remained impassive.

Andermatt next addressed the notary.

" Maître Alain, will you be so good as to read aloud the Company's deed of constitution? "

So saying, he resumed his seat. The notary passed on the order to his clerk Marinet.

Marinet, a wretched consumptive creature, cleared his throat and began. He intoned like a preacher and tried for oratorical effects. He enumerated the statutes at law bearing upon the constitution of a joint-stock company, to wit, the Mont-Oriol Hydropathic Establishment, at

I

Enval, with a capital of two million francs. But old Oriol interrupted him.

"One moment, one moment," he said, drawing from his pocket a greasy notebook which for the last week he had been taking round to every notary and business-man in the department. It contained copies of statutes, which, by this time, he and his son were beginning to know by heart. He fitted his spectacles slowly on his nose, raised his head, found the exact range of vision at which he could best make out the letters, and said:

"Fire ahead, Marinet."

Colosse drew his chair closer and read from the paper his father was holding. Marinet began again.

Old Oriol was soon thrown out of his stride by his double task of listening and reading simultaneously. He was in an agony of apprehension lest a single word should have been changed, but was also obsessed by a wish to see whether Andermatt was not making signs to the notary. He could not let a line pass without a dozen times interrupting the clerk, whose fine oratorical effects were thereby ruined.

"What's that, what's that?" the old man kept exclaiming. "What's that you are saying? I didn't hear. Not so quickly."

Then he would turn to his son:

"Was that right, Colosse?"

"All right, father," replied Colosse, who was more self-possessed; "let them get on with it. It's all right."

But the old peasant was consumed with suspicion. He traced the lines on the document with his crooked finger, at the same time muttering the words to himself. But his attention could not be directed to two places at once. When he was listening, he could not read, and when he was reading, he could not listen. He puffed as if he were climbing a mountain; he sweated as if he had been digging his vineyards in a hot sun, and every now and then he asked for a few minutes' respite to mop his forehead and recover his breath, like a man hard pressed in a duel.

Andermatt lost patience and tapped the floor with his foot.   Seeing the Puy-de-Dôme Monitor on a table, Gontran picked it up and glanced through its pages.   Paul, straddling his chair, looked down at the floor.   His heart was wrung by the thought that to-morrow this pink-faced, corpulent man in front of him would carry away the woman he loved with all his soul, Christian, his Christian, his blue-eyed Christian, who was his, all his, and his alone.   He kept wondering whether he would not elope with her that very evening.

Meanwhile the seven strangers remained grave and sedate.   It took an hour to get to the end of the business.   After the signing of the documents, the notary made a note of the disbursements.   The treasurer, Monsieur Abraham Levy, on being duly called on by name, made a formal declaration of having received the funds.   The Company, thus legally constituted, was then declared to be convened in a General Meeting, all the shareholders being present, for the purpose of electing directors and chairman.   There were only two dissenting voices when Andermatt was proclaimed chairman.   They were those of Oriol and his son, who voted for the old peasant.   Paul was appointed trustee.

The Board of Directors, which consisted of Andermatt, the Marquis, Gontran, Paul, the two Oriols, Dr Latonne, Abraham Levy and Simon Zidler, asked the other shareholders, with the notary and his clerk, to retire, in order that they might deliberate on their first resolutions and agree upon the most important points.

Andermatt again rose to his feet.

" Gentlemen, we now embark upon the live issue, that of success.   Success we must attain at all costs.   Mineral springs are like any other commodity; unless we talk about them a great deal and on every possible occasion, no one will drink them.   The outstanding feature of modern life is advertisement.   Advertisement is the god of contemporary commerce and industry.   Without advertising there is no salvation.   The art of advertising, moreover, is difficult and complicated. It requires the exercise of the greatest tact. The first advertisers were brutal in their methods; they attracted attention by making tremendous noises; they banged the big drum and let off cannon. Mangin was merely a pioneer. Nowadays mere clamour is suspected; startling posters make people smile; names that are shouted on the highway arouse more distrust than interest. None the less, it remains necessary that public attention should be attracted, and, once aroused, that it should be held. Given that you have something for sale, true art lies in discovering the means, the only successful means, of selling it. What we want to sell, gentlemen, is water. We must get at the invalids through the doctors.

" The most distinguished doctors, gentlemen, are men, as we are, and have the same weaknesses as ourselves. I am not suggesting that they are open to corruption. The reputation of the illustrious specialists, whose services we require, sets them far above any suspicion of venality. But where is the man who cannot be won over, if one goes the right way about it, just as there are women who are not to be bought, and who have to be beguiled by other means?

" I now present to you the proposal I have to make, and which I have discussed thoroughly with Dr Latonne. We have classified in three principal groups the maladies that come within our purview. These groups are, first, rheumatism in all its forms, such as herpes, arthritis, gout, etc., etc.; secondly, affections of the stomach, the liver and the intestines, and thirdly, all the disorders arising out of disturbances of the circulatory system. It is undeniable that our carbonic acid baths have a most notable effect on the circulation. And to be sure, gentlemen, the miraculous cure of old Clovis is a guarantee of further miracles. Well, then. Now that we have established the nature of the various maladies curable by these waters, we shall make the following proposal to the leading physicians who treat these maladies. We shall say to them : ' Gentlemen, come and see. Come and see with your own eyes. Come with your patients. We offer you hospitality in a superb district. You want a rest after your hard winter's work. So come to us. Not to stay in our houses, gentlemen, but in homes of your own, for we offer you châlets which will, if you choose, become your own property, on exceptional terms.' "

After a short breathing-space, Andermatt resumed in calmer tones :

" I shall now tell you my plan for translating my idea into actual facts. We have selected six house sites of about a quarter of an acre each. On each of these six sites the Bernese Portable Châlet Company engages to plant one of its model buildings. These dwellings combine elegance with comfort. We shall place them gratuitously at the disposal of our doctors. They can, if they like, buy the house from the Bernese Company. As for the ground-site, we make them a present of it, and they will pay us in . . . invalids. Thus, gentlemen, we gain multiple advantages. We cover our territory with charming villas which cost us nothing. We attract the first physicians in the world, and with them their hosts of patients. Most important of all, these doctors, who will quickly acquire a vested interest in this locality, will be convinced of the curative properties of our springs. As regards all the negotiations preliminary to these results, I make myself responsible for them, and I shall carry them out in no speculative spirit but as a man of the world."

Old Oriol interrupted him, his Auvergnat parsimony aroused at this gift of land. At this, Andermatt was moved to eloquence. He contrasted the generous cultivator who casts the seed abroad in great handfuls on the fertile soil, with the stingy peasant, who counts every grain and in consequence never gets more than a half-crop. Oriol's temper was roused and he stuck to his point, and Andermatt had accordingly to put it to the vote. Six votes to two shut the old man's mouth.

Andermatt's next act was to open a morocco portfolio and draw forth the plans of the Baths, the Hotel and the Casino, as well as the estimates and contracts.

All these had been prepared beforehand in consultation with the contractors, and were ready for approval and immediate signature. The works were to be put in hand at the beginning of the following week. The two Oriols alone wanted to examine and discuss the plans. But Andermatt could stand no more of this.

"Am I asking you for money?" he said. "No, I am not. Then go to the deuce with your objections. If you are not satisfied we will have another vote."

At this they signed with the others, and the meeting broke up.

So intense was the general excitement that the whole countryside had assembled to see them come out, and saluted respectfully. The two Oriols were setting out for home when Andermatt said to them:

"Don't forget that we are all dining together at the Hotel. Bring the girls with you. I have brought them some little presents from Paris."

They agreed to meet at seven o'clock in the salon of the Hôtel Splendid.

The dinner was a grand affair. Andermatt had invited the principal visitors as well as the local officials. Christian sat at the head of the table, with the parish priest on her right hand and the mayor on her left. The sole subject of conversation was the new Hydropathic Establishment, and the future of the spa. Louise and Charlotte Oriol had found under their napkins two jewel cases containing bracelets set with pearls and emeralds. Beside themselves with joy, they chattered away as never before. Louise laughed unrestrainedly at the jokes of Gontran, who was seated between her and Charlotte. Gontran's spirits rose as he talked, and inwardly he was appraising them, with that silent scrutiny, bold and masculine, which is provoked by the presence of any desirable woman.

Paul neither ate nor spoke. . . . He felt as if this evening were the end of his life. He suddenly remembered that it was just a month, to the very day, since they had dined by the lake of Tazenat. His soul was oppressed by that vague sense of suffering, consisting of fears for the future rather than of regrets for the past, which only lovers know; it weighs on the heart; it so works upon the nerves, that one catches one's breath at the slightest sound, and it so afflicts the mind that every word one hears is twisted into some harrowing relationship to the one engrossing idea. The moment they rose from the dinner-table, he joined Christian in the drawing-room.

" I must see you to-night," he said. " Now, immediately. I don't know when we shall ever be able to be alone together again. Do you know that it is exactly a month to-day? . . ."

" Yes, I know," she replied.

"Listen," he resumed. " I will wait for you on the Roche-Pradière road, near the chestnut trees before you come to the village. No one will notice your absence. To-morrow we part. Come quick and bid me farewell."

" I shall be there in a quarter of an hour," she murmured.

He went out at once, anxious to escape from that throng of people, who were getting on his nerves.

He followed the path between the vines they had taken that day, when he and Christian had gazed together for the first time over the plain of Limagne. Soon he came to the highroad. Solitude surrounded him; the sense of it entered his very soul; he was alone in the world. This feeling of isolation was intensified by his consciousness of that illimitable plain, hidden from him in the darkness. He stopped at the spot where they had sat down. It was there that he had recited to her Baudelaire's verses on Beauty. How long ago it seemed! He recalled hour by hour every incident that had occurred since then. Never had he been so happy, never. Never had he been so beside himself with love; and yet, never had he loved so purely, so devotedly. He remembered the evening by the crater of Tazenat, one month ago to the day; the coolness of the forest, steeped in pale radiance, the silvery tarn, its surface rippled by fish rising; the return home, and Christian walking before him through light and shadow, with the moonbeams filtering through the leaves and falling in bright splashes upon her hair, shoulders and arms.

Those were the sweetest hours he had tasted in his life. He turned to look for her, but all that he saw was the moon showing above the horizon. The same moon that had risen upon his first avowal of love was now rising to witness his first good-bye. He felt an icy shiver pass over his skin. Autumn was on its way, autumn the herald of winter. This was the first time he had as yet felt that early touch of cold, and it struck home like the menace of some misfortune.

The white dusty road stretched before him, like a river between steep banks. Suddenly a figure came into sight at the bend of the road. It was she. He stood there, waiting, quivering with mysterious happiness at the consciousness that she was drawing nearer, at the sight of her coming towards him, seeking him. She was walking timidly, not daring to call his name, uneasy because she had not yet caught sight of him, hidden as he was in the shadow of the tree. She felt oppressed by the profound silence, by the moonlit solitude, of earth and sky. As she came down the road, her long, dark shadow crept ahead of her, far ahead, as if hastening to bring him something of herself. When Christian stopped, the shadow stopped with her.

Paul took a few rapid strides to the spot where the rounded shadow of her head fell upon the ground. As if unwilling to lose the least particle of herself, he dropped on his knees and, bending down, put his lips to the edge of the dark silhouette. He was like a thirsty dog crawling on its belly in the spring at which it drinks. Following with his lips the outlines of the shadow of his beloved, he showered ardent kisses on the dust of the road. He came nearer to her, on hands and knees, still tracing her silhouette with his caresses, as though he would gather up with his lips the adorable image projected upon the earth.

Surprised and even a little dismayed, she waited until he was at her feet before she found courage to speak to him. Still on his knees, he raised his head and threw his arms round her passionately.

"What has come over you to-night?" she asked.

"Ivy," he replied, "I am going to lose you."

She plunged her fingers into her lover's thick locks, and, leaning down to him, turned his face so that she could kiss his eyes.

"Lose me?" she asked, in smiling confidence. "Why?"

"Because to-morrow we part."

"Part? But it is for so short a time, my darling."

"Who can tell? We shall never recover the days we have passed here."

"There will be others just as perfect."

She drew him to his feet, led him under the tree where he had been awaiting her, and made him sit down beside her, but on a lower level, so that she could still keep her fingers in his hair. Then she spoke to him seriously. Her attitude was that of a woman who has thought the matter out, a woman ardent and resolute in her love, who has foreseen every contingency and, knowing by instinct what to do, has made up her mind to stop at nothing.

"Listen to me, darling. I can do as I please in Paris. My husband doesn't trouble about me. His business affairs are enough for him. You have no wife, so I shall come to your house. I shall come every day, but at different hours, sometimes before luncheon, sometimes in the evening, so that the servants may not gossip. We can meet just as often as we do here, indeed oftener, because there will be no inquisitive people to be afraid of."

With his head on her lap and his arms round her waist, he repeated:

" Ivy, my Ivy, I shall lose you. I feel I shall lose
you."

She grew exasperated at his irrational despair, at this
infantile repining, in a frame so vigorous.   Fragile
creature as she was compared with him, she was none the
less so sure of herself, so confident that nothing could
come between them.

" If you would, Ivy," he murmured, " we might flee
away together, far away, to some distant land full of
flowers, and love each other there. Shall we go away
to-night? Shall we? "

She shrugged her shoulders. She was a little annoyed,
a little impatient with him for not listening to her. This
was not the moment for amorous nonsense. What was
wanted now was energy, prudence. They must devise
some means whereby they could cherish their passion
without exciting suspicion.

" Listen, my love," she resumed. " It is a question
now of coming to an understanding and of avoiding slips
and indiscretions. In the first place, are you sure of your
servants?   The chief danger is an anonymous letter
betraying us to my husband. William himself would
never suspect a thing. I know William well. . . ."

This name twice repeated suddenly got on Paul's
nerves. He said irritably :

" Oh, don't talk of him this evening."

" Why not? " she asked in surprise.   " It's really
necessary. . . . Oh, I assure you he does not care much
about me," she added, divining his secret thought, the
vague, unconscious jealousy that was stirring within him.
Suddenly he threw himself on his knees, and seized her
hands.

" Listen to me, Ivy," he resumed. " On what terms
are you and he? "

She did not understand.

" Why, we get on very well."

" Yes, I know. But . . . listen. Try to understand.
He is, after all, your husband. . . . You can't imagine

how the idea has haunted me of late, and what agony . . . what torture it is. You understand?"

After a moment's hesitation she grasped the full significance of his words, and in a burst of outraged loyalty exclaimed:

"Oh, my darling, how can you imagine such a thing. Why, I am yours, and yours only, believe me, because I love you. Oh, Paul!"

He buried his head again in her lap and murmured very low:

"But after all, my little Ivy, he is your husband. What can you do? Have you thought of that? There is to-night. There is to-morrow. You cannot always, you cannot always say No."

In a whisper, low as his own, she replied:

"I told him I was going to have a baby. That is enough. Oh, he doesn't care. Never mention the subject again. You can't think how it hurts me. Trust me. I love you."

He did not stir, but kissed her gown, breathing its fragrance, while her hands wandered caressingly over his face.

"It's time to go," she said suddenly. "People will notice our absence."

They threw themselves into each other's arms, and remained crushed in a lingering embrace. Then she broke away, and set off for home at a run. He watched her disappearing into the distance, his heart heavy as if all his happiness, all his hopes had vanished with her.

PART II

II

By the first of July of the following year, Enval had changed almost beyond recognition. On the brow of the hill between the two outlets of the valley, rose a structure of Moorish design, bearing upon its front in letters of gold the word " Casino." On the slope towards Limagne a small wood had been transformed into a tiny park. In front of the building, dominating the wide plain of Auvergne, lay a terrace, buttressed by a wall, which was ornamented throughout its length with enormous urns of imitation marble. Lower down, scattered among the vineyards, six châlets raised their façades of varnished wood. On the southern slope a huge building, dazzlingly white, attracted from afar the attention of travellers approaching from the direction of Riom. This was the great Mont-Oriol Hôtel. Immediately below, just at the foot of the hill, stood a square house, less pretentious, but equally large, in a garden through which flowed the stream that had its sources in the glens. Here patients could profit by the miraculous healing processes set forth in Dr Latonne's pamphlet. The façade of the building bore the inscription " Mont-Oriol Hydropathic Establishment "; its right and left wings respectively, in smaller letters, " Hydrotherapy. Medical Douches " and " Medical Institute of Automatic Gymnastics." The whole place was of a new, crude and dazzling whiteness and, although it had been open a month, there were still plumbers, painters and other workmen about.

From the very first the success of the enterprise had surpassed all the hopes of the promoters. Three eminent doctors, Professors Mas-Roussel, Cloche and Rémusot, had taken the new spa under their wing and had agreed to occupy for a while the villas, which had been erected by the Bernese Portable Châlet Company and placed at their disposal by the Mont-Oriol directors. Their presence had attracted a host of invalids, and the great Mont-Oriol Hôtel was full to overflowing.

Although the Baths had been available since the beginning of June, the formal inauguration had been postponed until the first of July, so as to attract as large a crowd as possible. The ceremony was to begin at three o'clock with the Benediction of the springs. The programme for the evening included a gala performance, followed by fireworks and a ball, and all the visitors to Enval and the neighbouring spas, as well as the principal residents of Clermont-Ferrand and Riom, had been invited.

The Casino on the brow of the hill was completely hidden in bunting. Nothing could be seen but a dense, fluttering curtain of blue, red, white and yellow. From the top of gigantic masts, planted along the paths in the park, floated enormous oriflammes, which writhed like snakes against the azure of the sky. Monsieur Petrus Martel, who had secured the managership of the new Casino, was so much affected by this riot of flags that he believed himself the all-powerful captain of a fantastic ship and issued his commands to the white-aproned waiters in the fierce, reverberating tones of an admiral in action. Borne on the breeze, his ringing words carried as far as the village.

Already out of breath, Andermatt appeared on the terrace. Petrus Martel rushed to meet him and saluted him with a magnificent bow.

" Everything all right? " asked Andermatt.

" Everything, Mr President."

" If anyone wants me, I shall be in the office of the Inspecting Medical Officer. We are holding a meeting this morning."

He hurried off down the hill.

At the door of the Baths, the superintendent and the cashier, both of whom had been detached from the rival Company, now inexorably doomed, sprang forward to receive their master. The jailor honoured him with a military salute, while his companion bowed like a beggar receiving alms.

" Is the Inspector here? " asked Andermatt.

" Yes, sir," replied the superintendent. " All the gentlemen have arrived."

Andermatt passed through the hall between the ranks of deferential bath attendants of both sexes, turned to the right, opened a door, and entered a large, bare room, well stocked with books and with busts of eminent scientists. Here he found a full meeting of the Board of Directors, who had been summoned to Enval. They consisted of Andermatt's father-in-law, the Marquis; Gontran, his brother-in-law; Paul Brétigny, Dr Latonne, and the two Oriols, father and son, who looked almost gentlemen. Their tail coats were so long, and they themselves so tall, that they resembled dummies in a mourning emporium.

After Andermatt had hurriedly shaken hands all round, everyone sat down and Andermatt addressed the meeting.

" One important question remains to be settled, the names to be given to the springs. I do not agree with the Inspector, who suggests calling our three principal springs after the three leading lights of medicine now at Enval. No doubt this flattering distinction would gratify them and ensure their further support. But you may take it from me that it would alienate once and for all, every one of those eminent colleagues of theirs who have not yet responded to our advances and whom we have to convince at all costs, at whatever sacrifice, of the sovereign efficacy of our waters. Human nature, gentlemen, is always the same and it pays to study it and turn it to one's own use. Professors Plantureau, de Larenard and Pascalis, to quote only these three specialists in abdominal diseases, would never dream of sending their patients, their best patients, their most illustrious patients, princes, archdukes, and all the social luminaries to whom they owe fame and fortune—they would never dream of sending them here to be cured by water from a spring called Mas-Roussel, or Cloche, or Rémusot. Their patients and the general public could hardly help assuming that it was these gentlemen, Rémusot, Cloche and Mas-Roussel who had discovered the therapeutic qualities of our waters. It is a fact that giving the name Gubler to the principal spring at Châtel-Guyon, now a flourishing spa, prejudiced at least some of the big doctors, who might otherwise have patronised it from the beginning. I therefore suggest calling the spring first discovered, Christian, after my wife, and the next two Louise and Charlotte, after Monsieur Oriol's daughters. It would be very pretty and very suitable. What do you think? "

All agreed to his proposal, including Dr Latonne, who remarked :

" Professors Mas-Roussel, Cloche and Rémusot might be invited to officiate as godfathers and escort the three godmothers."

" Excellent, excellent," cried Andermatt. " I'll run and see them. They'll be delighted, I'll answer for them; they'll be delighted. We meet at three at the church, where the procession will be formed."

He hurried away and his example was followed almost immediately by the Marquis and Gontran. The Oriols marched off together, two solemn figures in tall hats, patches of black upon the white road.

Dr Latonne turned to Paul, who had arrived for the celebrations only the previous evening.

" I have detained you, my dear sir, because I want to show you something from which I expect wonders—namely, my medical institute of automatic gymnastics."

He took him by the arm and drew him away.

" Let me explain," he said as they entered the gymnasium, " the absolutely rational principles underlying my system of automatic gymnastics, of which I am going to give you a demonstration. You know the theory of my organo-metric system, don't you? My view is that the greater number of our ailments are entirely due to the morbid development of one particular organ, which encroaches upon its neighbours, interferes with their functions, and very soon destroys the general harmony of the body, thus giving rise to serious disorders. Now, combined with douches and thermal treatment, exercise is one of the most effective means for restoring the balance and reducing the encroaching parts to their normal proportions.

" But how induce your man to take exercise? The act of walking, riding, swimming, rowing, involves not only an appreciable physical effort, but a moral effort over and above. It is the will which impels and sustains the body. Naturally energetic men are always active men. Now energy is not an affair of the muscles, but of the mind. The body is obedient to a vigorous will. We cannot hope, my dear sir, to inspire cowards with courage and weaklings with resolution. But there is another thing we can do, something better. We can eliminate the need for courage, mental energy, moral effort, and restrict ourselves to physical activity. Moral effort is replaced, with the happiest results, by extraneous force, which is purely mechanical. You understand? Not quite? Let us go in."

He threw open a door leading into a spacious hall, around which were ranged curious appliances : large armchairs with wooden legs, roughly made deal horses, jointed planks, moveable bars suspended in front of fixed chairs. All these contrivances were equipped with complicated mechanism, worked by hand winches.

" You see," continued the doctor, " there are four principal forms of exercise, which may be called natural—namely, walking, riding, swimming and rowing. Each of these develops different parts of the body and acts in a particular way. Well, here we have all four varieties, artificially produced. You have only to let yourself go, and without troubling to think, you can run, ride, swim, row for an hour on end without your mind taking the smallest share in exertions which are purely muscular."

At that moment Monsieur Aubry-Pasteur, the engineer, came in, followed by an attendant, whose rolled up sleeves revealed well-developed biceps. Monsieur Aubry-Pasteur was stouter than ever. He waddled along, panting and puffing, his legs wide apart and his arms thrust out at an angle from his body by rolls of fat.

" Now for an ocular demonstration," remarked the doctor.

He turned to his patient.

" Well, my dear sir, what are we going to do to-day? Walk or ride? "

Monsieur Aubry-Pasteur shook hands with Paul.

" I should like a little sitz-walking," he replied. " I find it less tiring."

" The patient can take his walking exercise either sitting or standing," explained Dr Latonne. " The latter is more efficacious, but also more exhausting. The patient stands on pedals, which work his legs, while he preserves his equilibrium by hanging on to rings fixed in the wall. Here we have the less strenuous form."

Monsieur Aubry-Pasteur had collapsed into a rocking-chair to which were attached a pair of jointed wooden legs. Into these he inserted his own limbs. His hips, calves and ankles were tightly strapped in, so that no independent movement was possible. The bare-armed attendant then seized the hand-winch and turned it as hard as he could. The armchair began to sway like a hammock, then suddenly the wooden legs started off, flexing and straightening, moving backwards and forwards, with extreme rapidity.

" He's running now," remarked the doctor, and he turned to the attendant.

" Gently, walking pace."

The man relaxed his efforts and put the stout engineer

through slower exercises, which exhibited in absurd detail every movement of his body.

Two more patients, both enormously stout, appeared, followed by two other attendants with bare arms. They were hoisted on to wooden horses, which were set in motion, and, without moving from the spot, began prancing up and down, and jolting their cavaliers in the most atrocious manner.

"Gallop!" ordered the doctor, and the wooden steeds bounded like the ocean, tossed like ships in distress, and exhausted the patients so terribly that with one accord they began to gasp in piteous, breathless tones:

"Enough, enough. I can't stand any more. Enough, enough."

"Halt!" cried the doctor.

"Take a breather," he added. "You will go on again in five minutes."

Choking with suppressed laughter, Paul Brétigny pointed out to the docter that neither cavalier had turned a hair, while the men who worked the hand winches were dripping with perspiration.

"Wouldn't it be better, if they exchanged functions?" he queried.

"Certainly not, my dear fellow," replied the doctor gravely. "You must not confuse exercise with fatigue. The exertions of the men turning the hand winches are injurious, while the motions of riding and walking are excellent."

Paul caught sight of a side-saddle.

"Yes," said the doctor, "the afternoons are reserved for ladies. After twelve o'clock no men are admitted. Now come and watch the dry-swimming."

He showed him an arrangement of flexible boards, screwed together at both ends and in the middle in such a way that they could be elongated into diamonds and expanded into squares, like the child's toy with soldiers in it, thus enabling three swimmers at a time to be alternately contracted and stretched.

"I need hardly point out to you," remarked the doctor, "the advantages of dry-swimming. It does not expose our make-believe swimmer to any moisture, except that of perspiration, and consequently obviates all danger of rheumatism."

An attendant handed the doctor a visiting-card.

"The Duke de Ramas, my dear fellow. I must leave you. Pray excuse me."

When he had gone, Paul turned round and saw the two cavaliers trotting as before. Monsieur Aubry-Pasteur was still walking. And the Auvergnats, with labouring chests, breaking backs, and aching arms, were still toiling away at the task of shaking up their clients, with the motions of men grinding coffee.

On leaving the building, Brétigny met Dr Honorat and his wife, who were looking at the preparations for the fête. As they talked, they gazed up at the flags festooning the hill.

"The procession will fall in at the church?" asked Madame Honorat.

"Yes, at the church."

"At three o'clock?"

"At three."

"Will all the Professors be there?"

"Yes, they're to escort the three godmothers."

Then he stopped to talk to Madame Paille and her daughter, and to Monsieur and Mademoiselle Monécu. He was engaged to a tête-à-tête luncheon with Gontran at the Casino café and he began slowly to climb the hill. He had only arrived the previous evening and had not had his friend to himself for a moment. He was looking forward to regaling him with all the gossip of the boulevards and the demi-monde. They sat talking till half-past two, when Petrus Martel came to tell them that people were going to the church.

"Let us call for Christian," suggested Gontran.

Paul assented.

They found her standing on the perron of the new

hotel. She had the hollow cheeks and sallow complexion of an expectant mother, and her figure indicated a pregnancy of at least six months.

"I was waiting for you," she said. "William has gone on. He had all sorts of things to see to to-day."

She bestowed upon Paul Brétigny a look of deep affection and took his arm. They walked slowly, carefully avoiding loose stones.

"I feel so heavy," she said repeatedly, "so dreadfully heavy. I can hardly walk and I'm terrified of falling."

Paul made no reply, and although he supported her solicitously, he avoided her eyes, which were always wandering towards him.

They found a dense crowd awaiting them outside the church.

"Here you are at last!" cried Andermatt. "Hurry up. Look, this is the order of the procession : two choir boys, two precentors in surplices, the Cross, the Holy Water, the parish priest, then Christian with Professor Cloche, Mademoiselle Louise with Professor Rémusot, and Mademoiselle Charlotte with Professor Mas-Roussel. After them the Board of Directors, the medical staff, and then the public. Is everything clear? Then we'll proceed."

The ecclesiastical participants emerged from the church and fell in at the head of the procession. A tall man, who wore his white hair tossed off his forehead and looked the typical scientist of Academic tradition, came up to Madame Andermatt with a deep bow. Straightening himself again, he strode along by her side. Against his hip he carried his hat, which he had removed to display his beautiful silvery locks, the sage's insignia, and his manner was as impressive as if he had studied at the Comédie Française how to walk and how to impress the populace with his rosette of officer of the Legion of Honour, which was unduly large for a modest man.

"Your husband was just speaking to me about you, Madame Andermatt," he began, "and your condition, with affectionate concern. He mentioned your uncertainty as to the probable date of your delivery."

She blushed to the roots of her hair.

" Yes, I thought I was in that condition long before I really was. And now I haven't an idea . . . I haven't an idea," she stammered in deep embarrassment.

" This spa has a tremendous future," said a voice behind them. " I have already obtained surprising results."

Professor Rémusot was discoursing to his companion, Louise Oriol. He was a small man with untidy yellow hair, a badly cut frock coat and the unwashed appearance of the slovenly type of scientist.

Charlotte Oriol's escort, Professor Mas-Roussel, was, on the other hand, very good-looking, clean-shaven, debonair, plump, well-groomed, with hardly a touch of grey in his hair; his smooth, pleasant face did not, like Dr Latonne's, resemble either that of a priest or an actor.

Next came the Board of Directors, with Andermatt at the head, and the enormous hats of the two Oriols towering above them all.

In their wake followed a further array of tall hats, representing the entire medical corps of Enval, with the exception of Dr Bonnefille, whose place, however, was filled by two new practitioners. One of them, Dr Black, was a little old man, so squat in figure that he was almost a dwarf. His abnormal piety had been the talk of the neighbourhood from the first day of his arrival. The other, a very dashing handsome fellow, who had thought fit to wear a low hat, was an Italian called Mazelli, who was attached to the person of the Duke de Ramas, or, as some said, to that of the Duchess.

Behind them flocked the public; visitors, peasants and residents from the neighbouring towns.

The Benediction of the springs was soon over. The Abbé Litre sprinkled each in turn with holy water, at which Dr Honorat remarked that he would be giving them new properties with this infusion of chloride of sodium. After the ceremony all the specially invited guests adjourned to the large reading-room, where refreshments were provided.

"How pretty the little Oriols have grown," Paul remarked to Gontran.

"They're charming, my dear fellow."

The ex-jailor suddenly broke in upon the two young men.

"Have you seen the President?"

"Yes, he's over there in the corner."

"The trouble is that old Clovis is collecting a crowd in front of the gate."

On the way to the Benediction the whole procession had passed in front of the old cripple, who had been cured the previous year, but had since become more paralytic than before. He would stop strangers on the road, preferably the latest arrivals, and pour out his woes.

"These waters, you know, they're no good. They cure you, it's true, but afterwards you get worse and worse until you're almost dead. It used to be my legs that wouldn't work. But now I'm losing my arms, too. And my legs are like iron. You might cut them, but you couldn't bend them."

In despair Andermatt had endeavoured to get him sent to jail on a charge of spreading damaging reports about the water with a view to blackmail. But he had succeeded neither in obtaining a conviction nor in silencing him.

As soon as he heard that the old man was holding forth outside the Casino gate, he rushed off to stop him. He heard angry voices proceeding from the midst of a crowd, which had gathered by the wayside. People were jostling one another in their eagerness to see and hear.

"What is it?" asked some of the ladies, and one or two men replied:

"It's an unfortunate invalid to whom these waters here have given the finishing touch."

Others supposed that a child had been run over, and

there were rumours that a poor woman had had an epileptic fit.

Andermatt dived through the crowd, fiercely insinuating his little round paunch, after a fashion of his own, past the abdomens of others, thus proving, as Gontran remarked, the superiority of the spherical over the angular.

Seated by the wayside, old Clovis was bemoaning his sufferings and discoursing about his aches and pains, while between him and his audience stood the two exasperated Oriols, uttering threats and abuse at the top of their voices.

" It's not true," cried Colosse. " He's a liar and an impostor. He spends his nights poaching in the woods."

In a thin shrill voice, which rose above the protests of his two assailants, the old man continued imperturbably :

" They have murdered me, kind gentlemen, murdered me with their water. They bathed me by force last year. And look at me now; look at me now."

Andermatt enjoined silence on everyone, and bending over the paralytic he looked him straight in the eyes :

" If you're worse, it's your own fault, you know. But if you will only listen to me, I will personally guarantee to cure you with fifteen or twenty baths at the most. Come and see me at the Baths in an hour's time, after everyone has gone, and we will arrange matters. In the meantime, Father Clovis, hold your tongue."

The ancient grasped the situation. After a moment's silence he replied :

" I'm quite willing to try. We'll see."

Andermatt took the Oriols by the arm and hurried them away, while old Clovis, with his crutches beside him, remained lying on the grass by the road, blinking at the sun.

Much intrigued, the crowd closed around him and some of the men tried to question him. But he now refused to answer and pretended not to hear or not to understand. At last, wearied of a curiosity, which had served its purpose, he began in a piercing voice all out of tune to bawl an interminable ditty in unintelligible patois. Gradually the crowd melted away, till only a few children remained, who hung about for a long time, staring at him with their fingers in their mouths.

Christian, who was very tired, had gone home to rest, and Paul and Gontran mingled with the other visitors, who were wandering about the new park. They caught sight of the theatrical company, which, following the general example, had deserted the old Casino to share in the rising fortunes of the new one.

Mademoiselle Odelin, now dressed in the height of fashion, was leaning on the arm of her mother, who had assumed a new air of importance. Monsieur Petitnivelle of the Vaudeville was evidently dancing attendance on the ladies. Behind them followed Monsieur Lapalme of the Grand-Théâtre, Bordeaux, engaged in a discussion with the members of the orchestra, which still consisted of Saint-Landri, the conductor; Javel, the pianist; Noirot, the flautist, and Nicordi, the double-bass.

As soon as he saw Paul and Gontran, Saint-Landri darted towards them. During the winter a tiny one-act musical play of his had been produced at a freakish minor playhouse. The Press had treated him not too unkindly, and he now looked down on Massenet, Reyer and Gounod.

With a friendly impulse, he held out his hands to Paul and Gontran and at once began to tell them about his discussion with the members of his orchestra.

"Yes, my dear fellow, it's all up, it's all up with the hackneyed composers of the old school. The melody-mongers have had their day. And that's what people won't see. Music is a new art and melody was merely the lisping of infancy. Ritornello has always appealed to the untrained ear and given pleasure, infantile, barbaric pleasure. The ear of the people and of the unsophisticated public, will always have a weakness for little songs, in fact for tunes, just as café concerts will always appeal to their patrons. Let me illustrate my meaning by a parallel. The eye of the peasant delights in crude colours and startling pictures, while the eye of the educated, but inartistic, middle-class man prefers the specious refinement of soft hues and sentimental subjects. But the artistic eye, the trained eye, can appreciate and distinguish the imperceptible variations of one and the same tone of colour, the mysterious harmony that exists between different shades, to which the uninitiated are blind.

" It's the same in literature. Your hall porter cares only for blood-and-thunder stories; the middle-classes read novels that appeal to their emotions, while really cultured people delight in works of genius, which are sealed books to the rest of the world.

" When one of those middle-class Philistines begins to talk music to me, I could kill him. If we happen to be at the Opera, I say :

" ' Can you tell me if the third violin played a wrong note in the overture to the third act? No? Then hold your tongue. You have no ear. The man who cannot hear the ensemble of the orchestra and every separate instrument as well, has no ear at all and is absolutely unmusical. There it is. Good-night.' "

He turned to go, but resumed his discourse :

" To the musician all music is summed up in a single chord. My dear fellow, there are certain chords that intoxicate me, that flood my whole being with indescribable ecstasy. Nowadays, my ear is trained, developed, matured to such a pitch of perfection, that I can actually enjoy certain discords, like a connoisseur whose maturity of taste verges upon depravity. I am becoming a decadent, who aims at the subtlest sensations of hearing. Ah, my friends, certain false notes ! What ecstasy ! What perverse, consummate ecstasy ! How they stir and thrill the nerves, how they titillate the ear . . . titillate . . . titillate the ear ! "

He rubbed his hands together rapturously and chanted :

" Wait till you hear my opera, my opera, my opera. Wait till you hear my opera."

"Are you writing an opera?" asked Gontran.

"Yes. I am just finishing it."

At that moment the commanding accents of Petrus Martel rang out:

"You quite understand? The signal is a yellow rocket. Then you start off."

He was giving directions about the fireworks.

Paul and Gontran joined him and he explained his arrangements, pointing with outstretched arm, as if he were menacing an enemy fleet, to the array of white wooden stakes planted on the mountain side overlooking the glens, just across the valley.

"They will be let off over there. I shall tell my man in charge to be at his post not later than half-past eight. As soon as the theatricals are over, I shall signal from here with a yellow rocket, and he will at once let off the first set piece."

The Marquis came up to them.

"I'm going to have a glass of water," he said.

Paul and Gontran accompanied him down the hill. When they reached the Baths they saw old Clovis, supported by the two Oriols and followed by Andermatt and the doctor, entering the building. He was dragging his legs along the ground, with contortions of agony at every movement.

"Let's go in," said Gontran. "We shall see some fun."

The paralytic was deposited in an armchair, and Andermatt addressed him.

"These are my terms, you old humbug. You are to get cured at once by taking two baths a day. As soon as you can walk, you shall have two hundred francs."

The cripple again began to groan:

"My legs are like iron, kind gentlemen.'

But Andermatt silenced him.

"Listen, will you? You shall have two hundred francs a year, till your dying day—your dying day, mind you, as long as you continue to feel the beneficial effects of our waters."

157

The old man was perplexed. A permanent recovery would be incompatible with his scheme of existence.

"But," he said, doubtfully, "suppose I be taken bad again when your place is shut up, I shan't be able to help it, if your waters are shut up."

Dr Latonne broke in upon him.

"Excellent! Excellent!" he cried, turning to Andermatt. "We'll cure him once a year. That will be better still. It will prove how essential it is to come back and repeat the treatment year after year."

"It won't be so easy this time, kind gentlemen," snuffled the old man. "My legs are like iron, like bars of iron."

A new idea occurred to the doctor.

"Suppose I give him a short course of sitz-walking," he suggested, "it would greatly assist the effect of the baths. It's worth trying."

"Excellent idea," replied Andermatt. "And now, Father Clovis, away with you, and don't forget our agreement."

Still groaning, the old man took himself off.

The afternoon was advancing, and as the theatricals were to begin at half-past seven, the directors of Mont-Oriol adjourned for dinner.

The performance took place in the great hall of the new Casino, which could accommodate a thousand people. Spectators, unprovided with numbered seats, began to arrive as early as seven o'clock, and by half-past seven the hall was crowded. The curtain rose on a two-act vaudeville, which was to be followed by Saint-Landri's operetta, performed by artistes borrowed from Vichy for the occasion. Christian, who was seated in the front row between her husband and brother, was feeling the heat.

"I can't stand it," she kept saying, "I can't stand it."

After the vaudeville was over and the operetta had begun, she nearly fainted.

"My dear Will," she exclaimed, "I shall have to go out. I am being stifled."

Andermatt was in despair. He had set his heart on

the complete success of the fête from beginning to end.

"Do try to sit it out, if you possibly can," he besought her. "If you leave, you will upset the whole performance. You would have to pass right through the hall."

Gontran, who had overheard his remark, leaned over to his sister.

"You're feeling the heat?" he whispered.

"Yes. I'm stifling."

"All right. Wait a minute. I'll give you something to laugh at."

He made for the nearest window, climbed on to a chair and jumped out almost unnoticed. He entered the deserted café, felt under the counter for the rocket, which he had seen Petrus Martel hide there, and ran off with it to a clump of trees. Then he put a match to his prize. A sheet of yellow light shot up in a curve to the clouds, and drew across the sky a long trail of fiery sparks. Immediately a violent detonation replied from the mountain opposite, and clusters of stars were scattered through the night.

A voice rang out above the throbbing chords of Saint-Landri's music.

"They're letting off the fireworks!"

Those of the audience who were near the door, hurriedly rose to make sure, and tiptoed out of the hall. The others all raised their eyes to the windows, but as these faced Limagne, they could see nothing.

"Have they begun?" everyone was asking. "Have they begun?"

The crowd, with its appetite for primitive pleasures, was growing excited and impatient.

"Yes, they're really letting off the fireworks," cried a voice from without.

In a moment the whole audience were on their feet. They made a rush for the doors, jostling one another and shouting to the people who were obstructing the exits:

"Do be quick; do be quick."

Soon everyone was in the park.

Only Saint-Landri remained, furiously conducting his bewildered orchestra, while the valley rang with continuous detonations, as Catherine wheels succeeded to Roman candles.

Suddenly, in a terrible voice, a thrice-repeated cry of rage rang out:

"In God's name, stop. In God's name, stop. In God's name, stop."

A huge Bengal light blazed forth upon the mountain, illuminating the trees and boulders on the right with blue and those on the left with red; it revealed, standing in one of the imitation marble urns that adorned the Casino terrace, Petrus Martel, bareheaded and distracted, waving his arms in the air, shouting and gesticulating. The glare faded away till only the stars of heaven remained. But immediately, another firework was let off and Petrus Martel leapt to the ground, exclaiming:

"What a disaster! Good Lord, what a disaster!"

Shaking his fist in the air, and stamping with rage, he disappeared into the crowd, still muttering with tragic gestures:

"What a disaster! Good Lord, what a disaster!"

Leaning on Paul's arm, Christian had come out into the open air, and was now seated in a chair, delightedly watching the rockets. Her brother joined her.

"Well, that came off. Wasn't it funny?"

"Was it your doing?"

"Yes, of course. Wasn't it a joke?"

She laughed approvingly. But Andermatt came up in great distress. He could not imagine from what quarter the blow had been dealt. The rocket had been stolen from under the counter and the preconcerted signal given. Such a dastardly trick could only have been played by some emissary of the rival Company, some tool of Dr Bonnefille.

"It's deplorable," he kept repeating, "simply deplorable. A display of fireworks which cost two thousand three hundred francs! And all wasted! Absolutely wasted!"

"Not at all, my dear fellow," returned Gontran. "If you reckon it out, the loss hardly amounts to more than a quarter, or, if you like, a third, say seven hundred and sixty-six francs. Your guests will have had the benefit of fifteen hundred and thirty-four francs' worth of fireworks. That really isn't bad."

Andermatt's wrath was diverted to his brother-in-law. He seized him abruptly by the arm.

"You, Gontran, I want to speak to you seriously. As I have caught you, come for a turn in the park. I have only five minutes to spare. I leave you in charge of our friend Brétigny, my dear," he added, addressing Christian. "But don't stay out too long; you might catch cold. Take care of yourself. Take care of yourself."

"Yes, dear," she murmured, "don't worry," and Andermatt drew Gontran away.

"My dear Gontran," he began, "I want to talk to you about your financial situation."

"My financial situation?"

"Yes. Do you know where you stand?"

"No. But if I don't, you ought to, as you have been lending me money."

"Just so. I do know all about it, and that's exactly why I want to talk to you."

"You have hardly chosen the right moment—in the middle of a display of fireworks."

"On the contrary, I have chosen precisely the right moment—not because it's in the middle of the fireworks, but because it's just before a ball."

"Before a ball? I don't understand."

"You will presently. Your situation is as follows. You have nothing but debts and you never will have."

"You're putting it rather crudely," replied Gontran gravely.

"I have to. Listen to me. You have run through

your share of your mother's fortune. We'll say no more about that."

" Agreed," said Gontran.

" Now your father has an income of thirty thousand francs, representing a capital of, say, eight hundred thousand francs; your share of which, later on, will amount to four hundred thousand. Well, you owe me personally, a hundred and ninety thousand. In addition to that you owe the moneylenders. . . ."

" Call them Jews," muttered Gontran insolently.

" The Jews, then, although one of them is a church-warden at St. Sulpice' and made use of a priest as intermediary between himself and you. But I won't quibble. You owe then to various moneylenders, Hebrew and Catholic, almost the same amount—call it a hundred and fifty thousand, to put it at the lowest figure. That makes a total of three hundred and forty thousand, and you have to borrow to pay the interest on all these loans, except mine, which you don't dream of paying."

" True," replied Gontran.

" So you see, you have nothing left."

" Literally nothing . . . except my brother-in-law."

" Except your brother-in-law, who has had enough of lending you money."

" Well? "

" Well, my dear fellow, the poorest peasant, living in one of those huts over there, is better off than you."

" Exactly. And what then? "

" What then? . . . If your father were to die to-morrow you wouldn't know where to turn for your daily bread. You would have to accept a post as clerk in my business. And even that would simply be a pretext for making you an allowance."

" My dear William," said Gontran peevishly, " this sort of thing bores me. I am as much aware of my circumstances as you are, and I must point out to you again that this is not a suitable moment for reminding me of them, with so little . . . so little tact."

" Allow me to finish. Your only hope is in marriage. Now, you're a wretched match, in spite of your name, which sounds well, but is by no means illustrious. Certainly it's not a title for which an heiress, even a Jewish one, would care to exchange a fortune. So the problem is to find you a wife, both rich and presentable, and that is not so easy."

" You may as well name her at once," broke in Gontran.

" Very well. One of the Oriol girls, whichever you prefer. And that's why I wanted to speak to you before the ball."

" And now explain yourself more fully," said Gontran coldly.

" It's quite simple. You see what a success I have made of this spa from the very first. Now if I, or rather we, had at our disposal all the land which that wily old peasant refuses to part with, it would be a perfect gold mine. To mention only the vineyards that lie between the Baths and the Hotel and between the Hotel and the Casino, I would myself give a million francs for them to-morrow. Now these vineyards and the others all round the knoll will constitute his daughters' dowries. Their father told me so again just now, possibly not without intention. Well, now . . . if you were willing . . . we might do extremely well out of it, both of us."

" Possibly," replied Gontran, with a meditative air. " I'll think it over."

" Do, my dear fellow, and don't forget that I never discuss a scheme, until I am perfectly sure of it, after deep consideration and a thorough investigation of all its possible results and its positive advantages."

Just then, as if he had suddenly forgotten all his brother-in-law's remarks, Gontran raised his arm :

" Look ! Isn't that magnificent ? "

It was the grand finale of the fireworks : a flaming palace with a flag waving above it, bearing in crimson letters the words " Mont-Oriol." Opposite, above the plain, rose the moon, red as fire, as if eager to gaze upon the spectacle. After burning for some minutes, the whole palace exploded, like a ship blown up, and scattered all over the sky fairy-like stars, which burst and went out, leaving the orbed moon, serene and solitary upon the horizon.

There was an outburst of frantic applause, mingled with shouts of " Hurrah " and " Bravo."

" Come and open the ball," exclaimed Andermatt. " Will you be my vis-à-vis in the first quadrille? "

" Delighted, my dear fellow."

" Who is to be your partner? Mine is the Duchess de Ramas."

" Oh, I'll ask Charlotte Oriol," replied Gontran carelessly.

As they turned towards the Casino, they saw that Christian and Paul were no longer where they had left them.

" She has taken my advice and gone home," remarked William. " She was very tired to-day."

He wandered away to the ballroom, which had been made ready for dancing during the display of fireworks.

Christian, however, had not gone home to bed as her husband had supposed. As soon as she was alone with Paul, she seized his hand and whispered:

" Here you are at last. I have been expecting you for a whole month. Every morning I said to myself : ' Shall I see him to-day?' and every evening : ' Then surely tomorrow.' Why have you been so long, my love? "

" I had things to see to, matters of business," he replied uneasily.

Leaning towards him, she murmured :

" It wasn't kind of you to leave me all alone with them here, especially in my condition."

He drew his chair a little away.

" Be careful. Someone might see us. Those rockets light up the whole countryside."

But she paid no heed.

" I love you so," she whispered, quivering with joy.

" Oh, I am so happy, so happy, to be with you here again. Think, Paul, what bliss ! We shall love each other more than ever."

In a voice, soft as a sigh, she breathed :

" I'm dying to kiss you, simply dying to kiss you. It's so long since I saw you."

Suddenly, with all the violent energy of an infatuated woman, who will brook no denial, she broke out :

" Listen, you must take me this very minute to that spot on the Roche-Pradière road, where we said Good-bye last year. You simply must. I insist."

" Why, it would be madness," he exclaimed in dismay. " You can't possibly walk so far. You have been on your feèt all day. It would be madness and I won't let you."

" I insist," she repeated, rising from her chair. " If you won't come with me, I shall go alone."

" Look," she said, pointing to the rising moon, " It was on just such a night. Do you remember how you kissed my shadow ? "

He tried to restrain her.

" Christian . . . listen . . . it's absurd. Christian . . ."

But she made no reply, and set off down the slope that led to the vineyards. He knew that calm determination of hers, proof against all persuasion. Those blue eyes, that childlike brow with the golden ringlets, harboured a charming wilfulness, which recognised no obstacles. He took her arm to support her.

" Suppose someone saw us, Christian ? "

" You didn't say that last year. Besides, everyone is at the ball. We shall be back before we are missed."

Soon they came to a steep, rough track. Panting, she lent her whole weight on him.

" How good it is ! " she murmured at each step, " How good it is to suffer so."

He stopped and tried to persuade her to go home, but she would not listen.

" No, no. I am very happy. You don't understand, Paul. Listen . . . I can feel it stirring . . . our child . . .

your child. What bliss! Give me your hand. . . . There.
. . . Can you feel it?"

She did not realise that this man was of the race of
lovers, not of fathers. As soon as he became aware of
her condition, he had shrunk from her, conscious of a
repugnance which he could not control. In the past he
had so often declared that no woman who had performed
the function of reproduction was worthy of love. For
him, the ecstasy of love lay in the transports of two
hearts, striving after an unattainable ideal; in the union
of two ethereal souls; in the unreal and impossible
glamour the poets have shed upon passion. Physically,
he worshipped in woman a Venus, whose sacred form
preserved forever the pure contours of sterility. The
idea of a tiny creature of his own begetting, a human
embryo, stirring within a body which it already sullied
and deformed, inspired him with almost invincible disgust. Maternity had reduced this woman to the level
of an animal. She was no longer the chosen being, the
adorable mistress of his dreams, but a female reproduc-
ing her kind. Actual physical aversion was mingled with
his mental revolt.

But how could she guess, how could she suspect, she,
to whom her lover grew more dear with every movement
of the child for which she yearned? This man, whom
she worshipped, whom she had loved a little better each
day since the moment of her first kiss, had penetrated
not only to the depths of her heart, but had possessed
her whole body and implanted within her the seed of his
own life, a living miniature of himself, soon to be brought
forth. There in her bosom, beneath her folded hands,
she cherished him, her dear, kind, tender lover, her one
and only friend, who would be born again, through the
mysterious workings of nature, of her own flesh and
blood. She loved him with a twofold love, now that he
was hers twice over, the grown man, whom she could see
and touch and kiss, whose voice she could hear, and the
tiny stranger, whom she could only feel stirring within her.

They had reached the road.

" You were waiting for me over there that evening," she said, and offered him her lips, on which, without a word, he bestowed a frigid kiss.

" Do you remember how you kissed my shadow? " she said a second time. " This is how we were standing, you and I. Look."

In the hope that he would repeat his act of homage, she darted away from him into the middle of the road and stood there, breathless and expectant. But the moon, projecting Christian's silhouette on to the ground, threw into relief the unsightliness of her figure. Paul stood motionless, gazing at the ungainly shadow at his feet. His artistic senses were outraged ; he felt exasperated with her for not understanding, for not divining his sentiments, for a lack of that feminine vanity, tact and insight, which should have made clear to her all the little differences that completely alter a situation.

" Oh, Christian," he exclaimed, with a hint of impatience in his voice, " how childish and absurd ! "

Hurt and grieved, she returned to him, and with outstretched arms threw herself on his breast.

" Oh, you don't love me as you did. I feel it. I know it."

Moved with pity, he took her face between his hands and printed upon her eyes two lingering kisses.

Silently they turned home. He could think of nothing to say to her, and as she leaned on him, exhausted and weary, he quickened his step to escape as soon as possible from contact with her ungainly form, which brushed against his side. Near the hotel, they parted and she went up to her room.

When Paul looked in at the ball, the Casino orchestra was playing a waltz. Everyone seemed to be dancing : Dr Latonne with Madame Paille's daughter, Andermatt with Louise Oriol, Mazelli, the handsome doctor, with the Duchess de Ramas, and Gontran with Charlotte Oriol.

Gontran was murmuring in his partner's ear, with that

air of tenderness associated with the early stages of courtship. Charlotte, evidently delighted, was smiling and blushing behind her fan.

"Just look at Monsieur de Ravenel, whispering soft nothings to my young friend," said a voice behind Paul. It was Dr Honorat, who was standing near the door and looking on with amusement.

"It has been going on for quite half-an-hour. Everyone has noticed it. And the little thing doesn't seem to mind. She's a jewel, that girl, a good, happy, simple, affectionate, honest child, worth ten of her sister. I've known them both since they were babies. But the elder one is her father's favourite. There's more of him in her, more of the peasant. She's less open, less confiding, more thrifty, more calculating than Charlotte. Oh, she's a good girl, too; I wouldn't say a word against her. Only I can't help comparing them and drawing my own conclusions, that's all."

When the waltz was over, Gontran joined his friend.

"I say, doctor," he remarked, when he saw Dr Honorat, "the medical faculty at Enval seems to have received some interesting additions. There's a Dr Mazelli, who waltzes divinely, and a little old Monsieur Black, who appears to be on excellent terms with heaven."

But Dr Honorat was discreet. He never expressed an opinion about his colleagues.

III

IT was now the doctors of Enval who had become the burning subject of interest. They had suddenly seized upon the neighbourhood, monopolising the minds and passions of the population. In the old days Dr Bonnefille had been the autocrat of the springs, while bustling Dr Latonne and placid Dr Honorat pursued their mild rivalries.

Things were very different now.

As soon as the success, which Andermatt had been preparing all the winter, was achieved, thanks to the powerful co-operation of Professors Cloche, Mas-Roussel and Rémusot, each of whom had brought with him a contingent of at least two or three hundred patients, Dr Latonne, inspecting medical officer to the new establishment, had become an important personage, under the special patronage of Professor Mas-Roussel, whose pupil he had been, and whose appearance and mannerisms he imitated.

Dr Bonnefille was definitely shelved. Raging and railing against Mont-Oriol, the old physician spent his days in the old establishment with a few old patients, who still remained faithful to him. Some of them actually held that he alone knew the true properties of the waters and possessed their secret, since he had dispensed them officially from the earliest days of the spa.

Dr Honorat's practice was reduced almost entirely to a local clientèle. He acquiesced in his modest lot, remained on friendly terms with everyone, and solaced himself with cards and white wine, both of which he greatly preferred to the exercise of his profession. He did not, however, go so far as to regard his supplanters with affection.

Thus, Dr Latonne would have remained chief augur of Mont-Oriol, save for the sudden appearance one morning of a tiny little man, almost a dwarf, whose large head, sunk between his shoulders, large round eyes and enormous hands, went to make up a very singular figure. Introduced into Enval under the auspices of Professor Rémusot, this new physician, Dr Black, at once attracted attention by his extreme piety. Nearly every morning he would slip into church for a few moments while on his rounds, and nearly every Sunday he went to Communion. The parish priest promptly sent him some patients, a few old maids and impoverished people, whom he treated gratuitously, and pious ladies, who, before calling in a man of science, always consulted their spiritual director as to his principles, his professional propriety and discretion. One day the arrival was announced of the Princess von Maldeburg, an old German lady of high rank and a devout Catholic, who sent for Dr Black her first evening, on the recommendation of a Cardinal of Rome.

From that moment he became the fashion. To be attended by him implied good taste, correct tone, social distinction. He was the only well-bred doctor, it was said, in Enval, the only doctor in whom a woman could repose complete confidence. The little man with the bulldog head could be seen from morning till evening, hurrying from one hotel to the other, whispering in corners with all sorts and conditions of people. He seemed always to be receiving, or imparting, important confidences, for he was continually to be met, deep in mysterious conference with hotel managers and chambermaids, in short with anyone who had anything to do with his patients. As soon as he caught sight of one of his invalids in the street, he made straight for him at his usual quick, short trot, and at once began to whisper in his ear new and precise directions like a priest instructing a penitent.

All the old ladies adored him. He would listen attentively and without interruption to their recitals, and take notes of all their remarks, questions and preferences. His habit of reducing or increasing each day the quantity of water prescribed, convinced his patients that he took a genuine interest in them.

" Yesterday we restricted ourselves to two glasses and three-quarters," he would say. " Very well, to day we won't go beyond two and a half. But three glasses again to-morrow. Don't forget. Three glasses to-morrow. I attach particular importance to it."

And all his patients believed that he really did attach thereto particular importance. Lest he should forget or confuse these figures and fractions, he always entered them in a note book, for what patient will forgive an error of as much as half a glass? With the same meticulous care, obedient to principles known only to himself, he regulated the duration of the daily bath.

Dr Latonne shrugged his shoulders disdainfully in jealous exasperation, and called him a mountebank. His hatred for Dr Black actually moved him at times to traduce the Enval mineral waters.

" As we're practically in the dark about the effects the waters produce, it is perfectly futile to modify the dose day by day with no therapeutical laws whatever to guide us. That sort of procedure does untold harm to the science of medicine."

Dr Honorat merely smiled. He always made a point of forgetting, five minutes after a consultation, how many glasses he had ordered.

" Two more or less," he remarked to Gontran in his hours of ease, " make no difference to anyone but the spring, and even the spring hardly notices."

The only malicious jest he allowed himself at the expense of his pious colleague, was the name, " Dr St. Sitz-Bath," which he conferred upon him. His form of jealousy was underhand, placid and discreet.

" That fellow," he would sometimes add, " knows his

patients inside out, and that's better for us doctors than knowing their diseases."

One morning a pair of Spanish grandees, the Duke and Duchess de Ramas-Aldavarra, arrived at the Mont-Oriol Hôtel. The Duchess was attended by her own doctor, an Italian from Milan, called Mazelli. He was a man of thirty, tall, slim, very good-looking and, except for a moustache, clean-shaven.

The Duke, a melancholy man, colossally obese, had a horror of solitude and preferred to take his meals in the common dining-room. On the very first evening Mazelli won the hearts of everyone at the table d'hôte. He already knew nearly all the visitors by name, and had a pleasant word for every man and a pretty speech for every woman, and even a smile for every servant. Seated on the right of the Duchess, a handsome woman between thirty-five and forty, with pale complexion, black eyes and raven hair, he advised her as to every dish :

" Very little of this," " Don't touch that," " Yes, have some of this."

He himself filled her glass, very carefully mixing the wine and water in proper proportions. He superintended the Duke's diet as well, but with undisguised indifference. For his part the Duke paid not the smallest attention to his advice, but fell upon every dish with savage voracity ; he drank two decanters of undiluted wine at each meal, and afterwards threw himself in a chair in front of the hotel and complained of agonies of indigestion.

After dinner on the first evening, Dr Mazelli, who had taken stock of his fellow guests in the twinkling of an eye, sought out Gontran, as he was smoking a cigar on the terrace of the Casino, and introduced himself. Within an hour they had struck up a friendship. The next day, after the morning bath, he had himself introduced to Christian, who was charmed with him after ten minutes' conversation. Later in the day, he presented her to the Duchess, who shared her husband's dislike for solitude.

Mazelli supervised all the domestic concerns of the ducal household; he bestowed upon the chef excellent hints on cookery, offered the Duchess's maid valuable advice as to the best means of preserving the lustre, luxuriance and raven blackness of her mistress's tresses, and gave the coachman priceless veterinary tips. He had the art of devising new amusements, which made the hours pass swiftly and pleasantly, and of striking up ephemeral friendships with the right people when staying in hotels.

The Duchess said of him to Christian:

" He's a wonder, my dear. There's nothing he doesn't know or can't do. I owe my figure entirely to him."

" Your figure? "

" Yes, I was beginning to lose it, and he saved me with his liqueurs and his system of diet."

He could make even the subject of medicine interesting. He touched upon it airily and gaily, with a laughing scepticism, which impressed his audience with a sense of his superiority.

" It's very simple," he said. " I don't believe in drugs, or hardly at all. The old-fashioned practice of medicine was based on the theory that everything had its remedy. God in His Divine compassion had, it was supposed, created specifics for all diseases, but had playfully left it to man to find them out. Well, man has discovered any number of these drugs, but has never been quite sure to which disease each one applies. The truth is, there are no remedies; there are merely diseases. When a disease manifests itself, some doctors think it best to check its course, others to hasten its development. Each school stands up for its own procedure. Thus you will see the most opposite methods, the most radically different specifics, applied to one and the same case. One man recommends ice; another extreme heat; one man, dieting; another, intensive feeding. I need not mention all the innumerable poisons, chemically derived from minerals and vegetables. They all produce their own

effect, it's true, only nobody knows what it is. Sometimes they are successful; sometimes they prove fatal."

With much spirit, he pointed out the impossibility of
arriving at definite conclusions, and the non-existence of
any scientific basis, until a new school of medicine should
be created on a foundation of organic and biological
chemistry. He illustrated his remarks about the futility
and unsoundness of the science to which they laid claim,
by stories of hideous mistakes made by the most eminent
physicians.

" Get the body to act," he would say, " the skin, the
muscles and all the organs, especially the stomach, which
fosters, nourishes and regulates the whole system and
serves as a storehouse of vitality."

He declared that he could, at will, make people happy
or depressed, capable of physical or of mental exertions,
according to the diet he imposed upon them. He could
even influence the functions of the brain, the memory, the
imagination and all the manifestations of the intelligence.

Laughingly he concluded :

" My own specifics are massage and curaçao."

He waxed eloquent on the subject of massage and
referred to the Dutchman Hamstrang as if he were a
god and could work miracles. He held out his own white
and shapely hands.

" With these one can restore the dead to life."

" He really massages to perfection," commented the
Duchess.

He was in favour of small doses of alcohol adminis-
tered at the right moment, as a fillip to the stomach, and
he carefully concocted short drinks for the Duchess to
take at fixed hours, sometimes before, sometimes after
meals. Every morning, about half-past nine, he could be
seen entering the Casino café and calling for his bottles,
which were brought to him, secured by tiny silver pad-
locks of which he had the key. Slowly he would pour
out a few drops first from one bottle, then another, into
a pretty blue glass, held deferentially by a smart footman.

"There," he said, "take that to the Duchess. She is to drink it, as soon as she has had her bath, before she dresses."

To inquisitive questioners, who wanted to know the ingredients, he replied:

"Only a little fine anisette, pure curaçao, and a dash of excellent bitters."

In a few days the handsome young doctor had become the cynosure of all the invalids, who employed every artifice to elicit his advice. When he wandered through the park, during the hour devoted to exercise, it was one continual cry of "Doctor!" from all the chairs where the pretty young women were resting between the consumption of two glasses of water from the spring named after Christian. If he stopped, with a smile on his lips, he was sure to be caught and carried off for a few minutes' stroll by the river bank.

At first the conversation would turn on this and that, then discreetly, delicately, archly, the subject of health would be broached, with a casual air as if it were the merest small talk. For this particular doctor was not at the beck and call of the public. He did not take fees; and he could not be sent for. He belonged to the Duchess and to the Duchess only. This very fact was in itself an incitement, a stimulant. And when it was whispered that the Duchess was jealous, very jealous indeed, all the other ladies vied with one another to secure the counsels of the handsome Italian. Dr Mazelli proved to be very obliging. Afterwards all the women he had favoured with an opinion, made a pretence of confiding in their friends, just to show them how attentive he had been.

"Oh, my dear, the things he asked me! Such questions!"

"Very indiscreet?"

"Indiscreet isn't the word for it! Terrible! I hardly knew what to say. The things he wanted to know!"

"The same with me. He asked me all sorts of questions about my husband."

" So he did me . . . with such very intimate details. Very embarrassing, questions like that! Still, one realises the necessity."

" Oh, entirely. It's a matter of health. He has promised to give me a course of massage in Paris, to complete the treatment here."

" Tell me, my dear, what are you going to do? One can't offer him a fee."

" Oh well, I thought of giving him a tie-pin. He has two or three pretty ones, so I suppose he likes them."

" What a bore! The same idea had occurred to me. Never mind. I'll give him a ring."

All the ladies tried to captivate him with pleasant little surprises, ingenious gifts, delicate attentions. He had become the central figure, the chief topic of conversation, the one focus of general interest. Then suddenly a rumour arose to the effect that Count Gontran de Ravenel was paying his addresses to Charlotte Oriol with a view to marriage. Soon all Enval was buzzing with excitement.

Ever since he had opened the ball with her at the inauguration of the Casino, Gontran had been dancing attendance on Charlotte. In public he rendered her all the little services a man takes upon himself when he makes no secret of his anxiety to please. Their relations acquired a spirit of playful and natural flirtation which paved the way for sentiment. They met nearly every day. The two sisters had conceived for Christian a tremendous affection, doubtless not without a strong mingling of gratified vanity. And all at once, Christian noticed that Gontran would hardly let her out of his sight. He surprised her and Paul by arranging expeditions for the mornings and games for the evenings. Presently it became obvious that he was interested in Charlotte. He teased her gaily, paid her compliments, with an air of unconcern, and lavished upon her all the little attentions by which bonds of affection are forged 'twixt man and maid. Accustomed to the free and easy ways of this young scapegrace from Paris, Charlotte at first did not take him seriously, and following the bent of her own frank and trustful nature, laughed and played with him as with a brother. One evening, however, as the two girls were walking home together after a merry party at the hotel, in the course of which Gontran had several times tried to kiss Charlotte during a game of forfeits, Louise, who had lately seemed nervous and depressed, suddenly broke out :

"You ought to be more careful. You let Monsieur Gontran take liberties with you."

"Liberties? What has he been saying?"

"You know quite well. Don't pretend to be stupid. At this rate you will very soon find yourself compromised. If you don't know how to behave, it's my business to look after you."

"I really don't understand," faltered Charlotte in shame and confusion. "I haven't noticed anything."

"This mustn't continue, do you hear," her sister retorted with asperity. "If he wants to marry you, it's for papa to think it over and decide. But if he is only amusing himself, it's time to put a stop to it."

At this, without knowing why or wherefore, Charlotte suddenly lost her temper. She resented her sister's interference and censure. In a trembling voice and with tears in her eyes, she told her to mind her own business, and as she faltered the words in indignation, her instinct, vague but sure, warned her of the jealousy aroused in Louise's embittered heart. They went to their rooms without kissing each other good-night. Charlotte lay awake weeping, troubled with ideas that had never before entered her head. But presently she dried her tears and began to think. After all, it was true that Gontran's manner towards her had changed. She had noticed it herself, but without grasping its significance. Now, at last, she understood. He was always making her delicious little speeches and once he had kissed her hand. What did he mean? She knew that she attracted him, but to what extent? Had he, by any possibility, some idea of marrying her? At this, somewhere in the air, in the void of night, where these new dreams of hers were hovering, she seemed to hear a voice that cried : " Countess de Ravenel."

Such was her emotion that she started up in bed. With her bare feet she felt for her slippers under the chair on which she had placed her clothes, and almost mechanically she threw open the window as if to give wider scope to her dreams.

She heard voices in the room below; Colosse was exclaiming :

" Let be. Let be. There's no hurry. Father will see to it. There's no harm done. It's father's business."

On the house opposite she could see the square white reflection of the lighted window on the floor below.

" Whom is he talking to? " she wondered. " And what about? "

A shadow flitted across the lighted wall. Her sister! Why was she not in bed? Just then the lamp was put out and Charlotte was left to meditate on all these new emotions stirring in her breast.

She could not get to sleep. Was he in love with her? Oh, no! Not yet! But since she attracted him, it might some day come to pass. And if he should love her dearly, passionately, after the way of people in society, he would no doubt marry her. Springing from a family of wine-growers, she had, in spite of her education in the convent of the Black Nuns of Clermont, preserved the modesty and humility of a country lass. She had thought, sometimes, that she might perhaps marry a notary, a barrister, even a doctor, but she had never aspired to become a real lady in high society with a handle to her name. Fresh from reading some romantic love story, she had scarcely dallied a moment with such enchanting ideas, before they vanished from her soul like an impossible dream. And now this unlooked for, this incredible thing, had been suddenly conjured up by her sister's words, and seemed to be drawing near her, like a ship sailing before the wind. With every breath she drew, she murmured through her parted lips :

" Countess de Ravenel."

Behind her closed eyelids, dazzling visions flashed in the darkness. She beheld exquisite drawing-rooms, ablaze with lights, lovely ladies who smiled at her, splendid carriages waiting for her at the perron of a château, magnificent footmen in livery, bowing as she passed. She felt hot all over; her heart was beating rapidly. She sprang up again, drank a glass of water, and stood for a few moments barefooted on the cold floor of her room. At last her excitement subsided; she returned to bed and fell asleep.

But her imagination, working like a fever in her blood, woke her at dawn. She felt ashamed of her little room, its walls white-washed by the local house-painter, its cheap muslin curtains, its two rush chairs, each planted in its own corner by the wardrobe. In these primitive surroundings, so eloquent of her origin, she felt countrified and humble, unworthy of the dashing, flippant cavalier whose pink and white, laughing face hovered before her eyes, now fading, now returning, until gradually it took possession of her and stole into her heart. She jumped up, took her mirror, a little hand-glass no bigger than the bottom of a plate, and went back to bed with it. She gazed at her face, framed by her loosened hair, with the whiteness of the pillow for background. Now and then she laid down the tiny glass in which she saw herself, and thought of all the obstacles in the way of this marriage, of the wide gulf that separated them, and a great lump rose in her throat. Then she would turn again to the mirror and smile winningly at herself, and when she saw how attractive she was, the difficulties seemed to vanish.

When she went down to luncheon, her sister said to her with an aggrieved air :

" What do you intend to do to-day? "

"Aren't we going to drive to Royat with Madame Andermatt?" replied Charlotte.

"If you go, you go alone," returned Louise. "After what I said to you, hadn't you better . . ."

"Nobody asked your advice," retorted her sister. "Mind your own business."

Presently old Oriol and Jacques came in and sat down to table.

"What are you children doing to-day?" asked their father.

Without waiting for Louise, Charlotte hurriedly replied :

"Personally I'm going to Royat with Madame Andermatt."

Both men looked at her approvingly.

"That's good, that's good," remarked her father with the insinuating smile which he always wore when conducting a successful transaction. The secret satisfaction, which both men betrayed by their attitude, surprised Charlotte even more than Louise's open hostility. Somewhat taken aback, she wondered if they had all been discussing her affairs together.

Immediately after luncheon, she went up to her room, put on her hat, took her sunshade, threw a light wrap over her arm and walked over to the hotel. The carriage had been ordered for half-past one. Christian was surprised not to see Louise.

"She is a little tired. I think she has a headache," said Charlotte, conscious that she was blushing.

The party set out in the big landau, as usual. The Marquis and his daughter occupied the back seat, while Charlotte sat opposite them between the two young men. They passed Tournoël, then drove along a beautiful avenue of walnut and chestnut trees, which skirted the foot of the mountain. Several times Charlotte was conscious of Gontran pressing close to her, but he did it so discreetly that she could not resent it. He was seated on her right, and spoke almost into her ear, so that she dared not turn her head to answer. Even as it was, she could feel his breath upon her lips and she was afraid of seeing in his eyes an expression that might embarrass her. He chaffed her gently and murmured amusing absurdities and charming little compliments.

Depressed and out of sorts, Christian hardly spoke, while Paul seemed melancholy and preoccupied. The Marquis alone chattered away unconcernedly with the gaiety and merry charm of the self-centred old aristocrat.

At Royat they left the carriage and went to listen to the band in the park. Gontran took Charlotte's arm and walked on ahead with her. Near the bandstand, where the conductor was beating time to his brass instruments and violins, crowds of visitors were sitting about watching the passers-by. Resting their feet on the rung of the chair in front of them, the women showed off their frocks and the pretty summer hats which enhanced their natural charms. Charlotte and Gontran wandered among them, looking for suitable subjects on which to exercise their wit.

"What a pretty girl!" Gontran heard people saying behind them. It gratified his vanity, and he wondered if they took her for his sister, his wife, or his mistress. Christian, who was seated between her father and Paul, caught sight of them now and then, as they passed by. She thought they were behaving rather childishly and called to them, hoping to check them. But they paid no heed and continued to stroll about among the crowd, enjoying themselves thoroughly.

"He will end by compromising her," she murmured to Paul Brétigny. "We must speak to him this evening when we get home."

"I had thought of doing so," replied Paul. "I quite agree with you."

According to the Marquis, who was something of an epicure, not one of the restaurants at Royat was tolerable, so they dined at Clermont-Ferrand and returned home after nightfall. Charlotte was serious now, for as they rose from table, Gontran had pressed her hand ardently when he was giving her her gloves. Her girlish conscience had suddenly taken alarm. A thing like that amounted to a declaration ! It was an advance ! a liberty ! What ought she to have done? Spoken to him? But what could she have said? To have resented it would have been absurd. A case like that demanded so much tact. Yet by doing and saying nothing, she seemed to be accepting his advances, associating herself with his act, and responding to that pressure of his hand. She weighed the situation, and accused herself of having been too gay, too familiar, at Royat. She now agreed with her sister, that she had compromised herself irretrievably. As the carriage bowled along, Paul and Gontran sat smoking in silence ; the Marquis was dozing and Christian stargazing. Charlotte, who had had three glasses of champagne, could hardly restrain her tears.

When they arrived at the hotel, Christian said to her father :

" As it's dark, you had better see the child home."

The Marquis gave Charlotte his arm and they set out at once.

Paul seized Gontran by the shoulders and murmured in his ear :

" Come and have five minutes' talk with your sister and me."

They went up to the little sitting-room, communicating with the Andermatts' bedrooms.

" Listen," said Christian, as soon as they had seated themselves, " Monsieur Paul and I are going to lecture you."

" Lecture me? What about? I have been a model of propriety, for lack of opportunity to be otherwise."

" Do be serious. Without thinking, you are doing a very unwise and very dangerous thing. You are compromising that girl."

Gontran appeared to be greatly surprised.

" Whom do you mean? Charlotte? "

" Yes. Charlotte."

" You say I'm compromising Charlotte? "

" Yes. Everyone here is talking about it, and this afternoon in the park at Royat you were both very . . . very indiscreet. You agree with me, Monsieur Brétigny? "

" Yes, I'm entirely of your opinion."

Gontran turned his chair round, straddled it, took a fresh cigar, lighted it and broke into a laugh.

" Ah! So I'm compromising Charlotte Oriol? "

He waited a moment to see the effect of his answer. Then he continued :

" Well, how do you know I don't intend to marry her? "

Christian gave a start of surprise.

" Marry her? You? You must be mad."

" Why? "

" That . . . that little peasant girl."

" Pooh! Silly prejudices! Whom do you get them from? Your husband? "

As she made no reply to this direct attack, he continued, himself supplying both question and answer :

" Is she pretty? Yes. Well-educated? Yes. And more ingenuous, more charming, more simple, more straightforward than girls in society. She is as well educated as anyone else. She can talk both English and Auvergnat and that makes two foreign languages. She will be quite as rich as any heiress from that played-out suburb, St. Germain, which ought to be rechristened St. Stony-broke. Besides all this, she comes of sound peasant stock, and is all the more likely to present me with healthy children. So there you are."

As he still seemed to be laughing and joking, she said doubtfully :

" Do you mean it seriously? "

" Why not? She's a charming girl. She has a kind heart, a pretty face, a merry, happy disposition, rosy cheeks, bright eyes, white teeth, red lips, long, thick, glossy, wavy hair; and, thanks to your husband, my dear sister, her old wine-grower of a father will be as rich as

Croesus. What more do you want? The daughter of a peasant? Well, isn't the daughter of a peasant worth all the daughters of corrupt finance, who pay fancy prices for doubtful dukes? Isn't she worth all the daughters of the rotten aristocracy bequeathed to us by the Empire; worth all the daughters of dubious paternity whom one meets in society? Why, if I marry this girl, it will be the first wise and sensible act of my life."

After a moment's thought, Christian suddenly embraced the idea with enthusiasm.

"Why, everything he says is true," she exclaimed. "Perfectly true, perfectly right. Are you really going to marry her, Gontran darling?"

It was now his turn for caution.

"Not so fast, not so fast. You must give me time to consider, too. All I say is, that if I marry her, it will be the first wise and sensible act of my life. It doesn't follow that I shall do it. But I'm thinking it over, I'm studying her and paying her a little attention, so as to discover if she really would suit me. At present the answer is neither yes nor no, but it's nearer yes."

Christian turned to Paul.

"What do you think, Monsieur Brétigny?"

Sometimes she called him Monsieur Brétigny, sometimes Monsieur Paul.

Paul was always fascinated by a situation in which he thought he could discern a certain magnanimity; by an unequal marriage which had a redeeming element of generosity: in short, by all the sentimental claptrap which masks the human heart.

"Personally I am disposed to think that he's right. If he cares for her, let him marry her. He couldn't do better."

At this moment the Marquis and Andermatt entered and the subject was dropped. The two young men adjourned to the Casino to see if the gambling room was still open.

From that day onwards Christian and Paul smiled upon Gontran's undisguised courtship of Charlotte. She was invited more frequently than ever, and made to stay to dinner, and was treated, in short, as if she were already one of the family. Conscious of all this, Charlotte realised its significance and was beside herself with joy. Her little head was completely turned, and she built ravishing castles in the air. As yet Gontran had said nothing definite, but his manner, his remarks, his attitude towards her, the increasing seriousness of his courtship, his caressing gaze, all seemed tacitly to repeat to her day after day :

" I have chosen you. You shall be my wife."

The tone of gentle friendliness, of discreet surrender, of maidenly reserve, which now characterised her attitude towards him, implied :

" I know. And when you ask for my hand, the answer will be yes."

Her own family whispered among themselves. Louise never spoke to her, except to wound her with spiteful allusions and cutting, bitter words. Her father and Jacques, however, appeared to be gratified. Nonetheless, she had never yet asked herself if she loved this fascinating suitor of hers, whose wife she was doubtless to become. He attracted her; he was always in her mind; she thought him handsome, clever, distinguished. But chiefly she dreamed of all that the future would hold for her, once they were married. At Enval, the bitter rivalries between the doctors and between the owners of the springs, the conjectures concerning the Duchess's sentiments towards her medical adviser, the gossip which, in every spa, flows as freely as its waters : all was forgotten in the interest aroused by this astonishing business of Count Gontran de Ravenel's prospective marriage to the little Oriol girl.

At last Gontran thought that the moment had come. One day, as they rose from luncheon, he took Andermatt by the arm and said :

" My dear fellow, strike while the iron is hot. This is how things stand. The child is waiting for me to propose, although I haven't committed myself in any way. But you may be sure she won't refuse me. It is up to you now to approach the father, in your own interests and mine."

" Be easy," replied Andermatt. " Leave it to me. I'll sound him this very day, without compromising you or committing you. As soon as the situation is perfectly clear, I'll make a formal proposal."

" Excellent."

After a moment's silence, Gontran resumed :

" This may be my last day of freedom, so I shall go over to Royat, where I saw some friends of mine the other afternoon. I'll be back some time to-night, and will knock at your door to hear your news."

He ordered his horse and rode across the mountain, breathing the pure, exhilarating air, and breaking now and then into a gallop, so as to feel the swift caress of the breeze fanning his cheeks and his moustache. He spent a festive evening with his friends and their young women. They lingered over supper and it was very late when he returned home. Everyone in the Mont-Oriol Hôtel had gone to bed when he knocked at Andermatt's door. At first there was no reply. Then, as his knocking grew more insistent, a hoarse, drowsy voice growled from within :

" Who's there? "

" It's I, Gontran."

" Wait a moment. I'll let you in."

Andermatt appeared in his nightshirt. His face was puffy, his chin bristly and his head was wrapped in a silk handkerchief. He returned to bed, and, sitting up with his hands stretched out on the sheet, he remarked :

" Well, my dear fellow, it won't do. This is how the matter stands. I sounded that old fox Oriol without, however, mentioning you. I merely said that a friend of mine—and I may have given him to understand that I meant Paul Brétigny—might suit one of his daughters and I asked what dowry he would give. In reply he asked me what fortune the young man possessed and I fixed the figure at three hundred thousand francs and expectations."

" But I haven't a penny," murmured Gontran.

" I'll lend it to you, my dear fellow. If we pull it off, your land will bring in enough to repay me."

" Splendid! " sneered Gontran. " The girl for me. The money for you."

Andermatt flared up at once.

" If you are only going to insult me, in return for my trouble, I'll wash my hands of you. We'll drop it."

Gontran hastened to apologise.

" I beg your pardon, Will. Don't be angry. I know you're a man of the most spotless integrity in business matters. If I were your coachman, I would never dream of asking you for a tip. But if I were a millionaire, I'd trust you with my whole fortune."

William calmed down.

" We'll return to that presently. We must first settle the important question. The old man saw through my game and said : ' It depends which of my girls you mean. If it's Louise, her dowry is as follows.' And he detailed all the land round about the Baths, between the Baths and the hotel and between the hotel and the Casino; in fact, all the land which is absolutely indispensable to our scheme and of incalculable value to me. To the younger daughter he allotted the land on the other side of the mountain, which will no doubt be worth a great deal later on, but is no use to me whatever at present. I tried every possible means to induce him to reconsider his distribution and to interchange the plots of land. But I found myself up against the most mulish obstinacy. He has made up his mind and there's an end. Now what do you think about it? "

" What do you think yourself? " asked Gontran, greatly troubled and perplexed. " Do you suppose he had his eye on me, when he divided the property in this way? "

" I have no doubt he had. He said to himself, the old yokel : ' As he has taken a fancy to the child, we will stick to the money bags.' His idea was to give you his daughter and keep the best of the land himself. Or perhaps he did it to benefit his elder daughter. Who knows? She's his favourite. She is more like him, more shrewd, more calculating, more practical than her sister. I think she's a young woman of ability. If I were you I'd transfer my affections."

"The devil!" muttered Gontran in consternation. "The devil! And Charlotte's land ... you wouldn't look at it, you say?"

"No, a thousand times, no. I must have that land between my Baths and my hotel and between my hotel and my Casino. It's perfectly clear. I wouldn't give a farthing for the other land; it will not be saleable till later on and then only in small plots to private individuals."

"The devil! The devil!" muttered Gontran again. "What a maddening business! What do you advise?..."

"I don't advise anything. But I think you would do well to reflect, before deciding between the two sisters."

"Yes, yes, you're right. I'll think it over. I'll go to bed and sleep on it. Night brings counsel."

He rose to leave the room, but Andermatt called him back.

"Excuse me, my dear fellow, just two words on another subject. I pretend not to see, but I really understand perfectly, all the innuendoes you are always aiming at me, and I have had enough of it. You reproach me with being a Jew—that is to say, a money-grubber, a miser, a speculator who sails very near the wind. Well, my friend, the money I make, not without some trouble, I spend my days lending, or, in other words, giving, to you. Never mind that. But there is one accusation to which I do not plead guilty. I am no miser. In proof of this I may mention that I make your sister presents of twenty thousand francs at a time, that I gave your father a Théodore Rousseau he wanted, worth ten thousand francs, and when you came here, I presented you with the horse you rode over to Royat this afternoon. Then in what respect am I a miser? Because I decline to let myself be robbed? All my race are like that, and we are right. Let me explain our point of view to you once and for all. People call us misers simply because we know the exact value of things. To you a piano is a piano, a chair a chair, a pair of trousers a pair of trousers; so they are to us, but at the same time each object represents a certain monetary value, a definite and appreciable market value, which a practical man ought to recognise at a glance, not from motives of economy, but to avoid being cheated. What would you say if a tobacconist charged you twopence for a penny stamp or for a box of wax vestas? You would be so angry, sir, that you would send for the police, all for a copper, a paltry copper. And that merely because you happened to know the value of these particular objects. Well, personally, I know the value of everything saleable, and that same feeling of indignation which you would experience, if you were charged twopence for a penny stamp, comes over me when I am asked to pay twenty francs for an umbrella worth fifteen. Do you see what I mean? I protest against this deep-rooted, never-ending, abominable thieving on the part of shopkeepers, servants, coachmen. I protest against the commercial dishonesty of your whole race, who look down on us. The tips I give are in proportion to the services rendered, not like the ridiculous tips you fling right and left indiscriminately, which vary from five sous to five francs according to your mood. Do you see what I mean?"

Gontran had risen to his feet with that smile of delicate irony which, on his lips, was so attractive.

" Yes, perfectly, my dear fellow; you are quite right. I am all the more convinced of it because my grandfather, the old Marquis de Ravenel, left my poor father hardly a penny, and all because of a bad habit of his of never accepting change from a tradesman when he bought anything. He considered it beneath his dignity as a nobleman, and always gave a round sum or a whole coin."

Whereupon Gontran marched off with an air of perfect complacency.

IIII

THE next day, just as the Andermatts and the Ravenels were going in to dinner in their private dining-room, Gontran opened the door and announced:

"Mademoiselle Oriol and Mademoiselle Charlotte Oriol."

Laughing at their confusion, he pushed the two girls into the room.

"I carried them off, both of them, in the open street. I created quite a scandal. I brought them here by main force, because I have a bone to pick with Mademoiselle Louise and I couldn't do it in the middle of the town."

He took their hats and the sunshades they were carrying, for he had met them going home from a walk, and made them sit down. He kissed his sister, shook hands with his father, Andermatt and Paul, and then returned to Louise Oriol.

"Now, then, Mademoiselle Louise, will you kindly tell me what grudge you've been nursing against us all this time?"

She seemed as frightened as a captive bird in the hand of a fowler.

"Nothing, Monsieur Gontran, nothing. What makes you think that?"

"Everything, Mademoiselle Louise, everything. You never come near us. You never go for drives with us in Noah's Ark "—(as he had dubbed the big landau)—"And you put on such a forbidding air when I meet you and try to talk to you."

"No, no, I really don't."

" Oh, yes, you do. But whatever it is, I don't want it to continue, and I'm going to make peace with you this very day. You know how determined I am. You may look as black as you please, I shall manage to get round you, until you are as charming to us as your sister, who is an angel of kindness."

Dinner was announced and Gontran took Louise's arm as they went into the dining-room. He devoted himself to both girls, dividing his attentions with admirable tact :

" You," he remarked to Charlotte, " are one of us, so I shall neglect you for a few days. One doesn't put one's self out for one's friends, you know, as much as for other people. As for you, Mademoiselle Louise, I give you fair warning, like an honourable foe, that I'm going to make a conquest of you. I'm even going to pay court to you. Ah! you're blushing. That's a good sign. You will find that I can be very charming when I take the trouble. Can't I, Mademoiselle Charlotte? "

By this time both girls were blushing and Louise said in her solemn way :

" Oh, Monsieur Gontran, how absurd you are! "

" Pooh, you'll hear more thrilling things than that later on, when you come out and get married, as you will very soon. Then people will really pay you compliments."

Christian and Paul praised him for recapturing Louise; the Marquis smiled at his boyish nonsense, while Andermatt thought to himself :

" He's no fool, that fellow."

Nonetheless Gontran was exasperated at the part he had to play, his senses urging him towards Charlotte, while his interests impelled him towards Louise. As he smiled at the elder sister, he muttered through his clenched teeth :

" Your old villain of a father thought he would score off me, but I shall carry you off with flying colours. You'll see how cleverly I shall set about it."

Glancing from one to the other, he compared the two girls. Undoubtedly he preferred the younger. She was more amusing, more vivacious, with her tip-tilted nose, her sparkling eyes, her narrow forehead, her splendid teeth, which, like her mouth, were a trifle large. Yet her sister, too, was pretty, though not so sympathetic, not so gay. In private relations, Louise would never reveal either humour or charm. But when the Countess de Ravenel was announced at a ball, she was more likely than Charlotte to do credit to her title, after a little practice and association with well-bred people. Yet he was raging inwardly. He was angry with both of them, as well as with their father and brother, and he vowed to himself that later on, when he was master, he would make them all pay for his disappointment.

When they returned to the drawing-room, he made Louise, who was something of an expert, tell his fortune by cards. The Marquis, Andermatt and Charlotte listened attentively, attracted irresistibly by the mystery of the unknown, the possibility of the improbable, by that invincible faith in the miraculous that haunts mankind and exposes even a confirmed sceptic to the most transparent deceptions of the charlatan.

Paul and Christian were talking in the embrasure of an open window. For some time, her consciousness that he no longer cared for her as before, had made her miserable, and the rift between the lovers was deepened each day by their own fault. The first hint of this calamity had come to her during their walk on the evening of the fête. But although she realised that his eyes no longer held the same tenderness, the same passionate desire, nor his voice the same caress, she did not suspect the cause of this change in him. Yet it had begun long ago, the very moment when, as they met at their daily tryst, she had exclaimed joyfully :

" Do you know, I really think that I'm going to have a baby."

He had at once experienced a faint shudder of distaste. At every subsequent meeting, with a heart thrilling with delight, she had spoken to him of her condition. Her preoccupation with a matter which he privately considered a troublesome, sordid, squalid business, cast a blight upon his ecstatic worship of his idol. Later, when he saw her changed, hollow-cheeked, sallow and wasted, he felt that she ought to have spared him this spectacle. She should have vanished for a few months, to reappear again more blooming and lovely than ever, either drawing a veil over the incident, or cunningly enhancing the seductions of the mistress by the new and piquant charm of the young mother, wise enough to permit only a distant view of her baby, a mere bundle of laces and pink ribbons. Her summer visit to Mont-Oriol afforded her a unique opportunity for exercising the tact he expected of her. She had only to let him remain in Paris, and spare him the sight of her diminished bloom and grace. He sincerely hoped she would understand the situation. But hardly had she arrived in Auvergne when she summoned him with letter after letter, so piteous, so unremitting, so insistent, that he had yielded in weak compassion. And now she overwhelmed him with her grotesque and lachrymose caresses. He felt an irresistible impulse to flee from her, to escape from the sight of her and from her exasperating and unseasonable maunderings of love. If only he could unburden his heart, explain to her the folly and tactlessness of her behaviour! But he could not do it. He dared not leave her, and yet he could not refrain from betraying his irritation with unkind and bitter words. Physically uneasy, more and more oppressed with the tribulations peculiar to her condition, she felt his conduct all the more deeply with her increasing need to be petted, comforted and cherished. She adored him with that utter surrender of herself, body and soul, which sometimes makes of love a sacrifice knowing no bounds, no reserves. She ceased to regard herself as his mistress; she was his wife, his trusty, devoted companion, his humble slave, his chattel. For her there was no longer any question of gallantry and coquetry between them, of

N   193

incessant effort to please and to attract. She was now too completely his own, since they were linked together by that strong and tender bond, the child so soon to be born.

The moment they were alone in the recess in the window, she began her tender reproaches.

" Paul, my dear Paul, tell me, do you still love me as you used to?'

" Of course I do. You know, you ask me that every day. It gets a little monotonous."

" Forgive me. It's because I can't believe it now, and I long to be reassured. I long to hear those precious words again and again. And you don't say them as often as you used to. I have to ask and entreat and beg for them."

" Very well, then, I love you. And now, for heaven's sake, let's talk of something else."

" Oh, how unkind you are ! "

" No, I'm not unkind. Only . . . Only . . . you don't understand . . . you don't understand."

" Oh, yes I do. You don't love me any longer. If you only knew what I suffered ! "

" Christian, you're getting on my nerves. If you only realised what a mistake you're making."

" If you loved me, you wouldn't talk like that."

" But, confound it, if I didn't love you I shouldn't be here."

" Listen," she said. " You belong to me now; you are mine and I am yours. This little new life is a bond between us, which nothing can break. But will you promise that some day, when you no longer love me, you will tell me so?"

" Yes, I promise."

" You swear it? "

" I swear it."

" But even then we should remain friends, shouldn't we? "

" Of course we should."

" The day you are no longer in love with me, you will come to me and say : ' My dear little Christian, I am still very fond of you, but it's not the same thing. Let us be friends, just friends.' "

" Quite so. I promise."

" You swear it? "

" I swear it."

" All the same I should be very unhappy. How you worshipped me only a year ago ! "

" The Duchess de Ramas-Aldavarra," announced a voice behind them.

The Duchess had come to pay a friendly call, for Christian was at home every evening to Enval's distinguished visitors, like a princess holding a court. The handsome Spaniard was attended by Dr Mazelli, obsequiously smiling and bowing. The two women shook hands, sat down and began to talk.

" Come over here, my dear fellow," Andermatt called to Paul, " Mademoiselle Oriol is wonderful with the cards ; she has told me the most surprising things."

He seized Paul by the arm.

" What a queer creature you are, to be sure," he continued. " At Paris we hardly see you once a month, in spite of my wife's entreaties. It took fifteen letters to get you to Enval. And now that you are here, anyone would think you were losing a million a day, you look so depressed. Are you worrying about something? Could I help you in any way? You must let me know."

" No, it's nothing, my dear fellow. If I don't come to see you oftener in Paris . . . well, Paris, you know. . . ."

" Quite so. But here at least you ought to be in good spirits. I am getting up some entertainments for you all, which ought to be very successful."

Professor Cloche and his daughter, Madame Barre, were announced, the latter a dashing young widow with red hair, and immediately afterwards Professor Mas-Roussel and his wife, a pale elderly woman with her hair plastered down over her temples.

Professor Rémusot had left Enval the previous evening, after buying his châlet, it was whispered, on exceptionally favourable terms. His two colleagues were anxious to know what these terms were, but Andermatt merely rejoined :

" Oh, we made a little arrangement, which was satisfactory to all concerned. If you wish to do the same, we'll see what we can manage, we'll see. As soon as you have decided, let me know, and we'll have a talk about it."

Presently Dr Latonne came in, and later Dr Honorat without his wife, whom he always left at home.

The drawing-room was humming with voices, raised in animated conversation. Gontran never left Louise the whole evening, but stood behind her chair talking to her. From time to time he said laughingly to a passing guest :

" This is an enemy of mine, and I've undertaken her conquest."

Mazelli had taken a seat beside Professor Cloche's daughter. For some days he had been in hot pursuit of her, and she had received his advances with a boldness that put him on his mettle. The Duchess, who never took her eyes off him, was quivering with exasperation. Suddenly she sprang up, crossed the room, and broke in upon her medical adviser's tête-à-tête with his red-haired charmer.

" Come along, doctor. I want to go home. I'm not feeling very well."

As soon as they had gone, Christian returned to Paul.

" Poor woman," she exclaimed, " how she must be suffering ! "

" Whom do you mean ? " he asked absently.

" The Duchess. Don't you see how jealous she is ? "

" If you're going to weep over every tiresome limpet of a woman, you'll be kept busy."

Reduced almost literally to tears by his unkindness, she turned away and took a chair beside Charlotte Oriol, who was sitting by herself, surprised and perplexed at Gontran's behaviour.

" There are days when one wishes one were dead," she said to the girl, who, however, failed to penetrate her meaning.

Surrounded by the doctors, Andermatt was describing the extraordinary case of old Clovis, who was beginning to recover the use of his legs. He himself seemed so thoroughly convinced, that no one could doubt his good faith. As soon as he had seen through the trick played by the two peasants and the paralytic, and had realised that, thanks to his own burning desire to believe in the efficacy of the waters, he had allowed himself to be bluffed, and particularly when he found that the old humbug's damaging complaints could not be silenced without payment, he had turned him into a most effective advertisement, which he exploited with the utmost skill.

After escorting his patient home, Mazelli returned to the drawing-room, a free man. Gontran seized him by the arm :

" Give me your advice, my bonny lad. Which of the two Oriol girls do you prefer? "

" The younger one to flirt with," the handsome doctor whispered back, " the elder one to marry."

" That's exactly my own opinion. Splendid ! " laughed Gontran.

He went up to his sister, who was still talking to Charlotte.

" You haven't heard yet. I have just arranged a picnic to the Puy de la Nugère on Thursday. It's the finest crater in the range. We are all going. Everything is settled."

" Just as you please," returned Christian indifferently.

Professor Cloche and his daughter came to say good-bye, and Mazelli, who had offered to escort them to their door, left the room in the wake of the young widow. In a few minutes the whole party broke up, for Christian always went to bed at eleven. Paul and Gontran saw Louise and Charlotte home. Gontran walked on ahead with Louise, and Brétigny, following a few paces behind with Charlotte, could feel her arm trembling a little within his own. As they said good-night, they all agreed to lunch together at the hotel at eleven o'clock on Thursday.

On their return the men come upon Andermatt, who

had been buttonholed by Professor Mas-Roussel in a corner of the garden.

"Very well," the Professor was remarking, " if you're not engaged to-morrow morning, I'll come to discuss that little affair of the châlet with you."

William turned towards the hotel with Paul and Gontran. Raising himself on tiptoe, he whispered into Gontran's ear :

"Congratulations, my dear fellow. You were magnificent."

For the last two years, his dire need of money had poisoned Gontran's whole existence. While he was running through his mother's fortune, he had let himself drift, with the careless nonchalance inherited from his father, in the company of that set of wealthy, blasé, dissipated young men, whose names figure in the daily papers, and, who, although they belong to the fashionable world, seldom frequent it, but acquire in the society of light women the manners and morals of cocottes. About a dozen of them formed a clique, which could be seen night after night, from twelve o'clock to three in the morning, in the same café on the boulevard. Always immaculately dressed in tail coats and white waistcoats, with shirt studs which cost them twenty louis at the principal jewellers and which they changed every month, they lived entirely for enjoyment, hunting women, courting notoriety and raising money by every possible expedient. Ignorant of everything beyond the latest scandal, the gossip of stables and backstairs, stories of duelling and gambling, their ideas were confined within these narrow bounds. They had possessed all the professional courtesans on the market, passing them on, lending them among themselves, and they discussed their peculiar qualities as they would discuss the points of a race horse. They associated, too, with the flashy, titled set, who are always in the limelight, whose women are nearly all involved in open liaisons under the very eyes, indifferent, averted, closed or shortsighted, of their husbands. These ladies they judged by the same standard as the professionals and had no higher respect for them, though they recognised some slight difference due to birth and social standing. By dint of their subterfuges for raising the necessary funds for this mode of life, tricking moneylenders, borrowing left and right, putting off tradespeople, laughing in their tailor's face, when he presented his half-yearly bill with another three thousand francs tacked on; by dint of listening to their women's stories of female rapacity, seeing men cheat at the clubs, feeling themselves robbed by everyone, servants, shopkeepers, the proprietors of the big restaurants, witnessing and taking a hand in doubtful transactions on the Stock Exchange and other shady proceedings for the sake of a few louis, their moral sense had become blunted and atrophied till their one remaining point of honour was to fight a duel, as soon as they found themselves suspected of acts of which they were potentially, if not actually, guilty. After some years of this existence, their careers generally ended in a wealthy marriage, or failing that, in scandal, suicide, or in mysterious disappearances as absolute as death. But it was to a wealthy marriage that they all looked for salvation. Some trusted to their families to arrange it; others, without seeming to do so, fended for themselves and had lists of heiresses, just as people have lists of houses for sale. They kept a special watch on the exotic beauties of North and South America, whom they could dazzle with their dash, their romantic reputations, the rumours of their conquests and their personal elegance. Their tradespeople, too, pinned their hopes to the same happy consummation.

This pursuit of a wealthy bride might, however, prove a long one. In any case it entailed careful investigation as well as all the trouble and boredom of courtship and visits : an expenditure of energy of which Gontran's congenital indolence rendered him utterly incapable. For a long time now, as his plight grew daily more critical, he had been telling himself that he must really take steps.

But he never did, and he came no nearer his object. At last he was reduced to the painful pursuit of trifling sums of money, to all the doubtful expedients of persons at the end of their resources, and finally to quartering himself for long periods on his family. It was at this very moment that Andermatt suddenly suggested to him the idea of marrying one of the Oriol sisters. At first he had preserved a discreet silence. The girls had seemed too far beneath him for him to consent to such an unequal match. But a few minutes' reflection had speedily modified his views, and he at once made up his mind to embark upon a playful courtship, a summer season flirtation, which would not compromise him, but would leave the way of retreat open. Knowing his brother-in-law intimately, he was convinced that he had given his proposal long and careful thought and preparation, and that, coming from him, it had a solid value, rare enough in other quarters.

And then, it would cost him no trouble. He had only to bend down and pick up a charming girl. The younger one attracted him greatly; he had often said to himself that it would be very pleasant to meet her again some day.

Thus his choice had fallen on Charlotte Oriol, and in a very short time he had brought her to the point when a formal proposal could be made. But when her father settled upon his elder daughter the dowry coveted by Andermatt, Gontran had either to abandon all idea of such a marriage, or to transfer his attentions from Charlotte to her sister. His disgust had been acute and his first impulse had been to tell his brother-in-law to go to the devil, while he himself remained a bachelor till something else turned up. But, as it happened, his exchequer just then was so completely exhausted that even to go to the Casino, he had to borrow another twenty-five louis from Paul, who had already frequently subsidised him with sums that were never returned. And then he would have to hunt for the problematic heiress, find her, fascinate her, and perhaps conciliate a disapproving family, while he had only to stay where he was, and with a few days of attention and flattery win the elder girl as easily as he had captivated her younger sister. By the same operation he would gain a hold over his banker brother-in-law, whom he could hold responsible for the marriage, and load with eternal reproaches, while helping himself out of his purse. As for his wife, he would take her to Paris and introduce her as the daughter of Andermatt's partner. After all, she had the same name as the spa, whither, on the principle that a river never flows back to its source, he would never, never, never let her return. Her face and figure were pleasing; she had already a certain air of distinction, capable of development, and she was sufficiently intelligent to grasp the ins and outs of polite society, hold her own, and even cut a figure which would do him positive credit.

People would say :

"That young spark has married a pretty girl for whom he does not care a straw," which was exactly his idea. Once married to her and with her money in his pockets, he proposed to resume his former bachelor ways. Thus planning, he had transferred his attentions to Louise. Unconsciously taking advantage of the jealousy aroused in that sullen heart, he had stirred her latent instinct of coquetry together with a vague desire to deprive her sister of this handsome suitor, whom people called "Count." She had never acknowledged this even to herself; she had neither schemed nor plotted, but was completely taken by surprise when he met her and Charlotte that evening and carried them off to the hotel. But when she saw him so assiduous in his attentions to herself, she felt, from his manner, his gaze, his whole attitude, that he was not in the least in love with Charlotte, and without looking ahead, she went to bed happy and content, almost exultant.

Thursday's expedition to the Puy de la Nugère hung for some time in the balance. The air was sultry and there was a threat of rain in the overcast sky. Gontran, however, was so determined that he over-ruled all objections. Luncheon had not been cheerful. Christian and

Paul had quarrelled the evening before, for no particular reason. Andermatt was anxious about the prospects of Gontran's marriage, for old Oriol had alluded to him only that morning in ambiguous terms, while Gontran, who had been informed of this, was furious and firmly resolved to succeed. Although she could not explain Gontran's change of front, Charlotte had a premonition of her sister's triumph. She had made up her mind to stay behind, and was with difficulty prevailed upon to go.

Noah's Ark, with a full complement of its usual occupants, lumbered along towards the lofty plateau overlooking Volvic. Suddenly eloquent, Louise Oriol did the honours of the expedition. She explained how Volvic stone, which is simply lava from the surrounding hills, had been used for building all the churches and houses in the neighbourhood, whence the sinister and volcanic aspect of the towns of Auvergne. She pointed out the yards where the stone was hewn and the lava tracks whence the rough rock was quarried, and she called their attention to a great, black image of the Virgin on the summit of the hill above Volvic, brooding protectingly over the city. The road leading to the upper plateau, which was studded with extinct volcanoes, lay through beautiful, shady woods. The horses toiled slowly up the long, steep slope. No one spoke. Christian was thinking of Tazenat. The same carriage! The same people! But how changed the hearts! Everything seemed as before. And yet, and yet! What was the difference? A mere nothing! A little more love on her part. A little less love on his. That was all. Just the difference between the birth of passion and its end. A mere nothing. The invisible stab that satiety deals to the loving heart. Oh, a mere nothing, a mere nothing! A changed look in eyes to whom the same face is no longer the same. What's in a look? A mere nothing.

The coachman drew up.

" It's over there to the right, through the wood. You have only to follow the path."

With the exception of the Marquis, who thought it too hot for walking, everyone alighted. Louise and Gontran hurried on ahead, while Charlotte and Paul followed with Christian, who could scarcely walk.

It seemed to them a long way till they emerged from the woods on to the grassy brow of the hill, which sloped steadily upwards to the edge of the extinct crater. Louise and Gontran had arrived at the crest and stood there, two slim figures, who seemed to be floating among the clouds. Presently the others reached them.

Paul Brétigny's enthusiastic soul felt a thrill of lyrical rapture. They were surrounded by conical hills, curiously truncated; some of them rose high in the air; others were crushed flat, but all presented the peculiar aspect of extinct volcanoes. These great stumps of mountains with their flattened tops, ran from southeast to northwest, springing up from a vast desolate plateau, itself more than three thousand feet above Limagne, which stretched away to east and north, beyond range of sight, to the invisible horizon, beneath its eternal veil of bluish mist. To the right, the Puy de Dôme towered above the other seventy or eighty extinct craters. In the distance rose Gravenoire, Crouel, La Pedge, Sault, Noschamps, La Vache, and in the foreground, Le Pariou, Côme, Jumes, Tressoux, Louchadière : one vast cemetery of dead volcanoes.

The five visitors gazed around them in amazement. At their feet yawned the first crater, La Nugère, a deep turfy hollow; at the bottom lay three great blocks of brown lava, vomited forth with the monster's last breath, only to fall back into its dying jaws, there to remain throughout the ages till the end of time.

" I'm going down," cried Gontran. " I want to see how these fellows gave up the ghost. Come, ladies, a little run down the slope."

Seizing Louise by the arm, he carried her off. Charlotte ran after them. But suddenly she stopped and watched them skipping along arm in arm. Then, turning abruptly away, she went back to Christian and Paul, who were seated on the grass at the top of the incline. When she reached them she fell on her knees, and, hiding her face in Christian's gown, burst into sobs. Christian understood. Of late she had felt the sorrows of others as keenly as if they were her own. Throwing her arms round the girl's neck and herself moved to tears, she murmured :

"Poor child, poor child! "

Prostrate on the ground, her face hidden, Charlotte went on crying, her hands mechanically plucking at the grass.

Brétigny had sprung up and was pretending not to notice. But the sight of this girlish sorrow, this innocent grief, filled him with sudden indignation against Gontran. This man, whom Christian's deep anguish merely exasperated, was moved to the soul at the spectacle of a girl's first disillusion. He returned and knelt down beside her.

"Come, come," he said. "Do try to calm yourself. The others will be back in a minute. You don't want them to see you crying."

Horrified at the idea of her sister finding her in tears, she started up. She choked down her sobs, but, repressed within her heart, they served merely to increase its anguish.

"No, no," she faltered. "I'm all right now. It's nothing. It's over. You don't think they'll notice anything? It doesn't show now, does it? "

Christian dried the girl's cheeks and then passed the handkerchief over her own eyes.

"Go and see what they're doing," she said to Paul. "They're hidden behind those blocks of lava. I'll look after the child and cheer her up."

Brétigny had risen to his feet.

"Yes, I'll go and bring them back," he replied in quivering tones. "But I'll have it out with your brother this very day. I'll make him explain his abominable behaviour, after what he said to us the other evening."

He ran down the slope towards the heart of the crater.

Gontran had dragged Louise away with him and had then pushed her as hard as he could down the steep side of the hollow, so that breathless, frightened and bewildered she had to cling to him for support. Carried away by his impetuosity, Louise tried to stop him:

"Oh, not so fast!" she gasped. "I shall fall . . . you're quite mad. . . . I shall fall."

They were brought up sharp by the blocks of lava and stood leaning against them, panting. Then they walked round them examining certain wide fissures which formed at the base a kind of cave with a double entrance. The expiring volcano had emitted its final vomit of foam, which no longer spouted sky high but was ejected, already chilled and thickened, only to congeal upon its dying lips.

"Let's go in," said Gontran, pushing the girl before him.

"Now then, Mademoiselle Louise," he exclaimed as soon as they had entered the grotto, "this is the moment for a declaration."

"A declaration!" she cried in amazement. "To me?"

"Why, yes. In four words: I think you charming."

"You ought to say that to my sister."

"Oh, you know perfectly well that I have no declaration to make to your sister."

"Oh, come now."

"You're not a woman for nothing. You must have realised that I only paid her attention to see how you took it. What looks you gave me! Looks of fury! How pleased I was! I then tried to show you, with all possible respect, what I thought of you."

No one had ever spoken to her like this before. She felt at once embarrassed and charmed, and her heart swelled with joy and pride.

"I know I have behaved abominably to your little sister," he continued. "But it can't be helped. After all, she was under no delusion. You noticed how she stayed at the top and wouldn't come with us. Oh, she understood, she understood."

He had seized Louise's hand and was airily kissing her finger-tips.

"How charming you are," he murmured. "How charming you are."

She leaned against the lava wall, without uttering a word, listening to the excited beating of her heart. The only thought which was clear in her bewildered mind was one of triumph : she had defeated her sister.

A shadow darkened the entrance to the cave. Paul Brétigny was standing there looking at them. With an air of unconcern, Gontran released the little hand he was pressing to his lips.

"Oh, it's you!" he said. "Are you alone?"

"Yes, we were surprised to see you disappear down here."

"Well, we're just coming up, my dear fellow. We were only having a look at the cave. A curious place, isn't it?"

Blushing to the roots of her hair, Louise emerged from the cave and began to climb the slope. Talking in undertones, the two men followed her.

Christian and Charlotte were standing hand in hand waiting for them. They all returned to the carriage, where they had left the Marquis, and Noak's Ark set out for home. In the middle of a small pine wood the landau came to a sudden halt, and the coachman began to swear. An old dead donkey was blocking the way. Everyone got out of the carriage to gaze at it, as it lay there, a sombre patch on the dark dust. It was so thin that the bones looked as though they must have pierced through the worn hide, had the wretched animal lived another day. All its ribs stood out, and the head looked gigantic, the pitiful head with its closed eyes, lying on its pillow of stone so still, so still and dead, as if it were rejoicing in this new and surprising peace. The huge ears hung limp like scraps of cloth. Two open cuts on its knees showed that it had fallen more than once that day, before it collapsed, never to rise again. A sore on its side marked the spot where for years its master had goaded it with an iron spike at the end of a stick, to hasten its lagging paces.

The coachman seized it by the hindlegs and dragged it closer to the ditch. Its neck was stretched out, as if to utter one last bray as a final protest.

" What brutes to leave it in the middle of the road like that ! " exclaimed the man, when he had deposited it on the grass.

Without another word, they all returned to the landau.

Cut to the heart by this harrowing spectacle, Christian visualised all the poor brute's wretched existence, terminated thus by the roadside. She saw the frolicsome little foal, so quaint and playful, with its big head and great bright eyes, its rough coat and long ears, as it frisked in freedom round its mother; then the first cart, the first hill, the first blows. And then, and then, the terrible, endless, plodding along interminable roads. Blows and more blows ! Overwhelming burdens ! Burning suns ! And for food, only a little straw, a handful of hay, a few leaves, while green meadows beckoned on either side of the rough road. And later on, in old age, the iron spike substituted for the supple switch, the terrible martyrdom endured by the wornout animal, exhausted, tortured, still dragging cruel loads, and aching in every limb, in every inch of its poor old body, worn threadbare like a beggar's coat. And then death, merciful death, three paces away from the green grass by the roadside, whither some passer-by drags it with an oath. For the first time in her life Christian realised the misery of creatures in bondage, and she, too, felt that death might sometimes wear the aspect of a blessing.

Presently they passed a small cart drawn by a half-naked man, a woman in rags and an emaciated dog, all of them panting, sweating and dropping with fatigue. The lean, mangy cur, its tongue hanging out, was harnessed between the wheels. The cart was loaded with wood, probably stolen, picked up here and there, roots, stumps, broken branches, beneath which other articles seemed to be concealed. On the top lay a bundle of rags, and on the bundle a child, with only its head emerging from a heap of grey tatters, a round, bullet head, two eyes, a nose, a mouth.

And this was a family, a human family. After the donkey had died of exhaustion, the man, without a pang of pity for his dead slave, without even dragging him into the ditch, had left him in the middle of the road, in the way of passing vehicles. Then he and his wife had harnessed themselves between the empty shafts and had set to work to draw the cart, as the donkey had done before them. Onwards they fared. Whither were they bound? What were they going to do? Had they as much as a few coppers? And the cart, would they always have to draw it themselves, unable to afford another donkey? How would they live? Where would they find an end to their labours? Probably they would die the same death as their donkey. Were they married, this wretched pair, or merely mated, with that child, that little undeveloped animal, huddled in squalid rags, to follow in their footsteps?

All these thoughts passed through Christian's mind, and new ideas rose from the depths of her horrified soul. She had caught a glimpse of the sufferings of the poor.

" I don't know why," exclaimed Gontran suddenly, " but I think it would be jolly to dine all together at the Café Anglais. I should like to see a boulevard again."

" Nonsense ! " replied the Marquis. " We're very comfortable at our own hotel; it's much better than the old one."

As they passed Tournoël, Christian recognised a certain chestnut tree and her heart beat with a thrill of remembrance. She glanced at Paul, but his eyes were closed and he did not see her pathetic appeal. Presently on the road in front of the carriage, they saw two vine-dressers with their hoes over their shoulders, coming back from work and walking with the lagging stride of the weary labourer. Louise and Charlotte blushed to the roots of their hair, as they recognised their father and brother, who had resumed their work in the vineyards, and spent their days with the sun beating down on their bent backs, tending in the sweat of their brow, the land that had enriched them, turning up the soil from morning till night, while their fine frock coats lay, carefully folded, in the chest of drawers and their tall hats reposed in the wardrobe.

The two peasants greeted the party with a friendly smile, and everyone in the landau waved to them.

When they reached home, Gontran alighted from the Ark, and set out for the Casino. Brétigny accompanied him but stopped him after they had gone a few steps.

" Listen, my dear fellow, you're not behaving well, and I promised your sister to speak to you about it."

" About what? "

" Your conduct during the last few days."

" My conduct? " returned Gontran, with the insolent air he sometimes wore. " What do you mean? "

" The scandalous way in which you've been playing fast and loose with that poor girl."

" That's your opinion, is it? "

" Yes, . . . and I'm right."

" Dear me, you've become very particular all of a sudden."

" My dear Gontran, it's not a question of a cocotte, but of an unmarried girl."

" I'm aware of that, and I haven't seduced her. There's a very distinct difference."

They walked on side by side. Paul was exasperated by Gontran's manner.

" If you weren't my friend, I should tell you some very unpleasant home truths."

" I shouldn't let you."

" Listen, my dear fellow, I'm sorry for that child. She was in tears this afternoon."

" What, in tears? I do feel flattered."

" Do be serious. What do you propose to do? "

" To do? Nothing."

" You know you went far enough to compromise her.

The other day you told your sister and me that you were thinking of marrying her."

Gontran halted suddenly. In a sarcastic voice, which contained a veiled threat, he exclaimed :

" You and my sister had better not interfere with other people's little flirtations. All I said was that I had taken a fancy to the girl and that if I married her, it would be a wise and sensible act. That was all. It so happens that I now prefer the elder. I've changed my mind, just as others do."

He looked his friend full in the face.

" What do you do, may I ask, when you're tired of a woman? Do you show her much consideration? "

Paul Brétigny was startled; as he tried to grasp the concealed, inner meaning of Gontran's remarks, he, too, became a little heated.

" Again, I say, it's not a question of a cocotte or a married woman," he exclaimed vehemently, " but a girl deceived by your behaviour, if not by your promises. And that, let me tell you, is conduct unbecoming a man of honour and a gentleman."

Gontran turned pale.

" Not another word," he broke in, in cutting tones. " You have said more than enough and I ought never to have stood it. In your own words, if you weren't my friend, I would show you that there are limits to my patience. Another word, and I'll have nothing more to do with you."

Then deliberately weighing his phrases, he flung them at Paul.

" I am not accountable to you for my actions. It is rather the other way. What is far more unbecoming a man of honour and a gentleman is a certain lack of delicacy, which may take various forms. There are cases when friendship ought to be a safeguard, and even love is no excuse."

With a sudden change of manner, he continued almost playfully :

" As for little Charlotte, if you're sorry for her and like her, marry her yourself. Marriage is often a way out of certain difficulties. It's a solution. It's a stronghold, a barricade against the pertinacity of the desperate. She's rich, she's pretty. Sooner or later you will have to come to it. It would be fun if both of us were to be married here on the same day. I propose to marry the elder girl myself. I tell you this in confidence. Don't let it go any farther for the present. . . . And just remember that you're the last person in the world with any right to talk about sentimental scruples and delicacy in love affairs. Now go and mind your own business, and leave me to mine. Good-night."

Suddenly changing direction, he went down the hill towards the village, while Paul, uneasy in mind and heart, returned slowly to the hotel. As he tried to recall every word that Gontran had said and to fathom his meaning, he felt aghast at the secret shifts, the shameful artifices, that lurk unavowed within the souls of men.

When Christian asked him what Gontran had said, he stammered :

" Why, good heavens . . . he . . . he prefers the elder girl now. . . . I think he actually means to marry her. At my rather strongly worded remonstrances, he shut me up with awkward insinuations about you and me."

Christian collapsed into a chair.

" Good God," she gasped. " Good God ! "

Dinner had just been announced, and at that moment Gontran came in. He kissed Christian lightly on the forehead.

" Well, little sister," he said gaily, " how are you? Not too tired? "

He shook hands with Paul and then turned to Andermatt, who had entered the room after him.

" Can you tell me, pearl among brothers-in-law, husbands and friends, can you tell me the exact value of an old dead donkey lying by the wayside? "

IV

Andermatt and Dr Latonne were strolling up and down the terrace, ornamented with imitation marble vases, in front of the Casino.

" He never recognises me now," said the doctor, alluding to his colleague Bonnefille. " He's sulking down there in his lair like a wild boar. I think he would poison our springs if he had the chance."

Andermatt, his hands behind his back, his hat, a small grey felt bowler, pushed off his bald forehead, was thinking deeply.

" In three months' time they will all have knuckled under. They've cost us nearly ten thousand francs already. It's that wretched Bonnefille who eggs them on and makes them think that I shall give in. But he's mistaken."

" You know they closed their Casino yesterday," remarked the Inspector. " They hadn't a single visitor."

" Yes, I know. But we don't get enough people here ourselves. They keep too much to their hotels, and then of course they feel bored. We've got to amuse our visitors, find occupation for them, and make the season seem too short. People from our Mont-Oriol Hôtel come every evening, because they are so near, but the others think twice about it and stay at home. It's a question of roads, that's all. Success always depends on minute causes, which one has to be clever enough to discover. The walk to a place of entertainment ought to be in itself a pleasure, a fitting preliminary to the evening's enjoyment. Now the roads leading to the Casino are bad : they're steep, stony and tiring. If a place that vaguely attracts you, is reached by a smooth, wide road, shady in the daytime, and not too trying for an after-dinner stroll, you instinctively choose it in preference to other roads. If you only knew how the body stores up thousands of impressions, which the mind never troubles to retain. I believe that is what constitutes the memory of animals. If on your way to some place or other, you felt too hot, found the rough surface tiring to your feet, or the gradient unpleasantly steep, although you may have been thinking of something quite different, you will nevertheless experience an invincible physical reluctance to visit that spot again. You were perhaps talking to a friend and paid no attention to the little inconveniences of the walk. You did not look about you or notice things, but your legs, your muscles, your lungs, your whole body, haven't forgotten, and when the mind attempts to direct them along the same road again, they say : ' No thank you. Once was enough.' And the mind docilely accepts this refusal, submits to the silent protest on the part of the comrades who have to carry it round.

" Well, then, we must have good roads, and that means that I must get hold of the land belonging to that old mule Oriol. But patience ! . . . And that reminds me, Mas-Roussel has acquired his châlet on the same terms as Rémusot. It's a small concession, for which he will com-pensate us over and over again. Try to discover precisely what Cloche's intentions are."

" He will do as the others," replied the doctor. " But there's another thing I have been thinking about the last few days. We have quite overlooked the necessity for a meteorological report."

" A meteorological report ? "

" Yes, in all the great Paris newspapers. It's absolutely essential. A health resort must be known to possess a better climate, less variable, more pleasantly equable, than any of its neighbours and rivals. What you have to do is

to subscribe to the meteorological section of all the principal journals, and I will telegraph the atmospheric conditions every evening. I shall see to it that at the end of
the year the mean temperature works out higher than the
best records of other spas in the district. The first thing
that strikes one as one opens the newspapers, is the temperature of Vichy, Royat, Mont-Dore, Châtel-Guyon in
the summer, and that of Cannes, Mentone, Nice, St.
Raphaël in the winter. The weather in those regions
must always be fine, must always be warm, so that the
Parisian may say to himself :

" ' Good Lord, what luck those people have who are
able to go there.' "

" Upon my word," cried Andermatt, " you're perfectly
right. Fancy my not thinking of it ! I'll see about it this
very day. And while we are on the subject of profitable
suggestions, have you written to Professors de Larenard
and Pascalis? I should like specially to attract these two."

" Unapproachable, my dear sir, . . . unless they are
personally convinced . . . after frequent experiments, of
the efficacy of our waters. In their case, you will gain
nothing by attempting to influence them prematurely."

They passed Paul and Gontran, who were having coffee
on the terrace. Other visitors made their appearance,
most of whom were men, as the ladies generally retired
to their rooms for an hour or two after luncheon. Petrus
Martel was superintending the waiters and calling for
kümmel, cognac, aniseed, in the same deep sonorous voice
in which he would presently conduct a rehearsal and
direct the youthful prima donna along the right lines.

Andermatt stopped for a moment to talk to the two
young men, then resumed his walk with Dr Latonne.
With crossed legs and folded arms, Gontran lay back in
his chair, smoking, in a state of perfect bliss, with his
eyes on the sky and his cigar cocked heavenwards.

" Would you care to come for a stroll in the Sans-
Souci valley presently? " he suddenly asked. " The girls
will be there."

" Yes, certainly," replied Paul after a moment's hesitation.

" Are things going well? " he added.

" By Jove, yes. She's mine. She can't escape me now."

Gontran had adopted his friend as confidant and favoured him with a daily account of his successful progress. He even made him accessory to his assignations with Louise Oriol, which he had shown great ingenuity in arranging. After the drive to the Puy de la Nugère, Christian had put a stop to their expeditions. She hardly ever went out and this made it difficult for the pair to meet. Disconcerted at first by her attitude, Gontran had presently sought a solution of the problem. Accustomed to the ways of Paris, where, by men of his calibre, women are accounted fair game, sometimes involving an arduous chase, he was well acquainted with various stratagems for approaching his quarry. He had a special aptitude for making use of intermediaries and a keen eye for interested and obliging parties of either sex, who were ready to further his designs. When Christian's involuntary assistance was suddenly withdrawn, he had looked about for the necessary link, for some accommodating soul, as he put it, who would replace his sister. His choice had fallen on the wife of Dr Honorat. There were many points indicating her suitability. In the first place, her husband was an intimate friend of the Oriols and had been their doctor for the last twenty years. He had brought the children into the world, and he dined with the family every Sunday, returning their hospitality at his own table every Tuesday. His wife was a stout, elderly woman, not quite a lady, full of affectations and susceptible to flattery. She could be counted upon to show herself only too ready to further any project of the Count de Ravenel, brother-in-law of the owner of Mont-Oriol. One glance at her walking down the street had revealed to Gontran's experienced eyes her natural talents as a go-between. She looked the part, and Gontran held that physical aptitude for a profession generally implied corresponding mental qualities.

One day when he had walked home with her husband, he called on her and stayed talking to her and flattering her till dinner time.

"What a delicious smell!" he remarked as he rose to go. "You keep a better cook than ours at the hotel."

"If I might venture," faltered Madame Honorat, swelling with pride, "If I might venture, Count . . . ?"

"Venture what, dear Madame Honorat?"

"Venture to ask you to share our frugal meal?"

"Why, I should be only too delighted."

"But there's nothing for dinner," protested the doctor. "Just *pot-au-feu*, a joint, and a chicken, nothing else."

"And quite enough, too," laughed Gontran. "Then I may stay?"

So he had dined with the Honorats. His stout hostess kept jumping up to snatch the dishes out of the maid's hands, for fear she should spill the gravy on the cloth. To her husband's exasperation, she did all the waiting herself.

The Count congratulated her on her cook, her house, her charm of manner, and left her bubbling over with enthusiasm. He had paid his after-dinner call, had accepted a second invitation and was soon always in and out of the house. Louise and Charlotte, too, were continually dropping in, in a friendly way, just as they had done for years.

Thus he spent hours in the three ladies' company, but though he made himself pleasant to both sisters, his decided preference for Louise became daily more marked. The mutual jealousy, which his earlier attentions to Charlotte had aroused, had in Louise taken the form of bitter hostility, to which her sister replied with disdain. For all her air of reserve, Louise contrived to invest her prim, reticent manner towards Gontran with more coquetry and provocation than her sister with all her frank and merry ways. Wounded to the heart, Charlotte was too proud to betray her feelings; she pretended neither to see nor understand, and with a brave show of indifference came to all these meetings at Madame Honorat's house. She would not stay at home for fear the others should think that she was unhappy and in tears, and that she had allowed her sister to supplant her. Too proud of his own cleverness to make a secret of it, Gontran confided in Paul. Paul thought the situation amusing and laughed. Ever since his friend's ambiguous remarks, he had vowed never to meddle with his affairs again, and he often wondered uneasily if Gontran had any inkling of his relations with Christian. He knew Gontran too well not to believe him capable of shutting his eyes to his sister's indiscretions. But why had he not hinted long ago that he knew or suspected? Gontran was the kind of man who credits every woman of the world with at least one lover; a man to whom the family is merely a society for mutual assistance, morality a pose to conceal the various appetites implanted in us by nature, and worldly honour a façade to screen our pleasant vices. If he had urged his little sister to marry Andermatt, it was surely with the vague, perhaps even definite, idea that the Jew could be exploited in every possible way by the whole family. Had Christian remained faithful to a husband selected on utilitarian grounds, Gontran would probably have despised her, much as he would have despised himself, had he refrained from dipping into his brother-in-law's purse. All this occurred to Paul and troubled his soul, the soul of a Don Quixote, but a modern Don Quixote, ready to accept compromises. He had thus begun to treat his enigmatic friend with extreme reserve. When Gontran confided to him the convenience he was making of Madame Honorat, Brétigny merely laughed, and of late he had allowed Gontran to take him to her house, where he greatly enjoyed talking to Charlotte.

Madame Honorat accepted the part assigned to her with the best grace in the world. At five o'clock, like the Paris ladies, she dispensed tea and little cakes, which she had made with her own hands. The first time Paul accompanied Gontran to her house, she welcomed him like an old friend, made him sit down, and insisted on relieving him of his hat, which she deposited on the mantelpiece beside the clock. She went fussily from one visitor to the other, her vast corporation well to the fore.

" Can I offer you some light refreshments " she asked.

Completely at his ease, Gontran laughed and joked, and presently, under Charlotte's anxious gaze, drew Louise into the recess of the window. Madame Honorat, who was chatting to Paul, remarked in motherly tones :

" These dear children come here to see each other for a few moments now and then. It's very innocent, Monsieur Brétigny, isn't it ? "

" Very innocent indeed, Madame Honorat."

The next time he came, she called him familiarly " Monsieur Paul," and treated him almost like an old crony. After this, Gontran related to him with his usual racy cynicism every instance of the lady's readiness to oblige.

He said to her one evening :

" Why don't you ever take the girls for a walk along the Sans-Souci road? "

" Oh, I will, Count, I will."

" What about to-morrow about three o'clock? "

" Certainly, Count, to-morrow about three o'clock."

" You are kindness itself, Madame Honorat."

" I am at your disposal, Count."

" You see," Gontran explained to Paul, "in the drawing-room I can't say anything rather special to Louise with her sister there. But in the wood I can go on ahead with Louise or fall behind. You'll come? "

" Yes, certainly."

" Then let's start."

They rose and strolled slowly along the highroad. After passing through Roche-Pradière, they turned to the left and made their way through the tangled undergrowth of the wooded valley. They crossed the little stream and then sat down by the wayside to wait. Soon the three ladies made their appearance, walking in single file, Louise in front, Charlotte behind her, and Madame Honorat bringing up the rear. One and all seemed surprised at this encounter.

"What an inspiration of yours to come this way!" exclaimed Gontran.

"It was quite my own idea," replied Madame Honorat.

They continued their walk together. Gradually Gontran and Louise increased their pace till they were far ahead of the others and disappeared round one of the bends of the narrow path.

"Oh, they've got young legs," panted the stout chaperone, with an indulgent glance in their direction. "I can't possibly keep up with them."

"Never mind, I'll call them back," cried Charlotte. She was just darting off, when Madame Honorat checked her.

"Don't worry them, my dear, if they want to talk. It wouldn't be kind to disturb them. They'll come back of their own accord."

She sank down on the grass in the shade of a pine tree and fanned herself with her handkerchief. Charlotte cast at Paul an appealing glance, a piteous, despairing glance, which he was quick to interpret.

"Well, Mademoiselle Charlotte, suppose we leave Madame Honorat here to rest, while we catch up your sister?"

"Oh, yes," exclaimed Charlotte impetuously.

Madame Honorat raised no objection.

"Run away, children, run away. I'll wait here for you. Don't be too long."

At first, seeing no sign of the others, they walked quickly in the hope of overtaking them. But after some minutes they came to the conclusion that Louise and Gontran must have turned off through the wood. Charlotte called to them in a subdued and trembling voice. But there was no reply.

"Good heavens," she murmured, "where can they be?"

Again Paul felt a wave of that intense pity, that poignant sympathy, which had swept over him that day by the crater of la Nugère. He did not know what to say to this heart-broken child. He felt an impulse, an overwhelming and fatherly impulse, to take her in his arms, to kiss her and soothe her with kind and comforting words, if only they would occur to him. She kept turning this way and that, peering through the branches with distraught eyes, and listening to every sound.

" I think they're over here . . . no, over there. Don't you hear anything? "

" No, nothing. We had better stop and wait for them."

" Oh, heavens, no! We must find them."

After a moment's hesitation, he said, in a very low voice :

" Do you mind so very much? "

She raised to him despairing eyes, swimming in rising tears, crystal drops that trembled upon the long, brown lashes. She tried in vain to speak, but she could not trust herself, though her heart, brimming over with its pent-up sorrows, yearned to break its bounds.

" You must have been very fond of him," he continued, " but really, he is not worthy of your love."

No longer able to control herself, she buried her face to hide her tears.

" No, no," she sobbed. " I don't love him at all . . . he has behaved too badly. He was only playing with me . . . it was too base, too mean . . . but it hurt all the same . . . it was so unkind, so very unkind. But what I mind most is my sister. She doesn't love me any more, and she has been worse than he. She hates me, I know she does. And she was all I had. Now I have nobody. And it's not as if I had done anything."

All he could see of her was her ear and her girlish neck, rising from the collar of her dainty gown, which veiled her rounded bosom. He felt overwhelmed with compassion and sympathy; inspired with that mysterious impulse to devotion, which seized upon him, whenever a woman touched his heart. His inflammable soul kindled at the sight of that innocent distress, so touching, so childlike, so poignantly charming. With an instinctive gesture, as one pets or soothes a child, he put his hand on her back just behind the shoulder. He could feel her heart fluttering like the little heart of a captured bird. The quick, continuous throbs travelled along his arm till they reached his own heart and made it beat. He was conscious of the rapid pulsations, which, proceeding from her, took possession of himself, body, nerves and muscles, until his own heart seemed one with hers, rent with the same sorrow, thrilled with the same vibrations, instinct with the same life, like two clocks, connected by a wire and made to keep time with each other, moment by moment. She drew her hands away from her flushed face and hastily dried her eyes.

" Oh, I oughtn't to have spoken to you," she exclaimed. " I must be crazy. Let us go back at once to Madame Honorat, and you must forget. You promise to forget? "

" I promise."

She gave him her hand.

" I can trust you. I do believe that you are sincere."

They turned back. He lifted her over the stream, as he used to lift Christian the previous summer. Christian! How often he had wandered with her along this very path in the days when he adored her! Astounded at the change in his feelings, he thought to himself how short-lived that passion of his had been.

Charlotte touched him on the arm.

" Madame Honorat is asleep," she whispered. " Let us sit down very quietly."

With her back to the fir tree Madame Honorat was indeed fast asleep, her handkerchief over her face and her hands crossed on her waist. They sat down a few paces away and did not talk for fear of disturbing her. The woods enfolded them in a silence so deep that it was almost oppressive. All they could hear was the water trickling over the stones just below them; the almost inaudible flutter of tiny insects, the floundering of big black beetles among the dead leaves; the infinitesimal murmur of flies.

Where could they be, Louise and Gontran? What were they doing? Suddenly they could be heard, far away in the distance. They were coming back.

Madame Honorat woke up with a start.

" Oh, you're there, are you? I never heard you. Did you find the others? "

" Here they are," replied Paul, " they're just coming."

Gontran's laugh rang out, and at this a great load seemed to slip from Charlotte's heart, she knew not why. They were soon in sight, Gontran almost running and pulling Louise, who was scarlet in the face, along by the arm. He could hardly wait till he reached the others to tell his story.

" You'd never guess whom we caught, not if you had a thousand shots; it was that handsome fellow Mazelli, with the daughter of the illustrious Professor Cloche, as Will would say; in other words, the pretty, red-haired widow. It was a complete surprise . . . complete. The rascal was actually kissing her. Upon my word! "

At this unseemly merriment, Madame Honorat bridled a little.

" Count, you forget that young ladies are present."

Gontran bowed deeply.

" You are perfectly right, dear Madame Honorat, to call me to order. You have the highest principles."

To avoid returning together, the two men took leave of the ladies and walked home through the wood.

" Well? " said Paul.

" Well, I told her I adored her and would be charmed to marry her."

" What did she say to that? "

" She replied with very pretty discretion that the matter concerned her father, and that she would give her answer through him."

" Then you intend . . . ? "

222

" I intend to instruct my ambassador Andermatt to make an official proposal. And if the old yokel raises objections I shall compromise the girl irretrievably."

Andermatt was still talking to Dr Latonne on the terrace. Gontran drew his brother-in-law aside and informed him of the latest developments.

Meanwhile Paul wandered by himself along the Riom road. He wanted to be alone. He felt utterly overcome by that tumult of body and soul, which is produced in a man by the proximity of the woman with whom he is falling in love. For some time he had been unconsciously influenced by the fresh and winning charm of this deserted child. He thought her so sweet and good, so simple, frank and ingenuous, that at first he had been moved with compassion, that tender compassion, which a woman's sorrow invariably inspires. Seeing her often, he had allowed a little seed to germinate in his heart, that tiny seed of affection, which a woman is so swift to sow, and which grows so quickly. And now, especially during the last hour, he was beginning, in her absence, to have that feeling of her presence, which is the first sign of love. As he wandered along, he was haunted by the memory of her gaze, the sound of her voice, by her face, wreathed in smiles or wet with tears, by her walk, her carriage, and even the colour and rustle of her gown.

" I believe I'm fairly caught," he reflected. " I recognise the symptoms. What a bore ! Perhaps I had better go back to Paris. Confound it, she's an unmarried girl. I can't possibly make her my mistress."

Then he began to think about her, as he used to think about Christian only a year ago. This girl, too, was different from all the city-born and city-bred women when he had known. She was different even from other girls, who from infancy had had before them the example of coquetry, whether of the domestic or the public variety. She possessed nothing of the artificial manner of women trained to fascinate. There was nothing studied in her words, nothing conventional in her gestures, nothing insincere in her gaze. Not only was she pure and unspoilt, but she came of primitive stock; she was a true daughter of the soil, just on the point of developing into a woman of the world. Roused to enthusiasm, he pleaded for her against his own vague prejudice, of which he was still conscious. Before his eyes flitted romantic forms, the creations of Walter Scott, Dickens, George Sand, which stimulated an imagination straightway spurred to passion by the idea of woman.

"Paul," Gontran sometimes reflected, "is like a runaway horse with a Cupid on his back. No sooner does he throw off one than a second springs up."

Night was falling, and as he had walked far, he turned homewards. As he passed the new Baths, he caught sight of Andermatt and the two Oriols, who were busy surveying and measuring the vineyards. It was evident from their gesticulations that this task was provocative of excited controversy.

An hour later Will entered the drawing-room in which the family were assembled.

"My dear Marquis," he exclaimed, "I beg to announce that your son Gontran, within the next six weeks or two months, is going to marry Mademoiselle Louise Oriol."

"What? Gontran?" the Marquis cried in amazement.

"What I said was that he would, within the next few weeks, and subject to your consent, marry Mademoiselle Louise Oriol. She will be very well off."

"Well, well!" said the Marquis simply, "if that's his fancy, I'm sure I don't object."

Andermatt proceeded to recount his negotiations with old Oriol. The moment he was informed by Gontran that the girl was willing, he had determined to leave the old man no time to play any tricks, but to hustle him into immediate consent. He accordingly hastened with all speed to his house, where he found him laboriously casting up his accounts on a greasy scrap of paper. Colosse, who did the additions on his fingers, was helping him.

" I could do with a glass of your excellent wine," Andermatt began, taking a seat.

As soon as Colosse had fetched the glasses and a brimming pitcher of wine, Andermatt, hearing that Louise was in, asked that she might be sent for. When she entered the room he rose and bowed deeply.

" Mademoiselle Louise, are you willing on this occasion to regard me as a friend worthy of your entire confidence? You are? Very well. I have taken on myself a very delicate mission concerning you. My brother-in-law, Count Raoul-Olivier-Gontran de Ravenel, has fallen in love with you, and in my opinion very wisely, and has charged me with the office of asking for your hand, in the presence of your family."

Taken thus by surprise, Louise turned anxious eyes on her father, who in turn gaped in amazement at his customary adviser Colosse. Colosse for his part kept his eyes on Andermatt. Andermatt resumed with a certain arrogance :

" You understand, Mademoiselle Louise, that I have undertaken this mission only on a promise to secure an immediate reply for my brother-in-law. He is quite aware that his proposal may be unwelcome to you, and if that be the case, he will leave this place to-morrow, never to return. I am also satisfied that you know him well enough to be able to give me, in my simple capacity of intermediary, a plain answer, Yes, or No."

Blushing and with drooping head, but resolutely, she replied :

" It is yes, Monsieur Andermatt."

Thereupon she turned and fled with such precipitancy that she bumped against the doorway.

Resuming his seat, Andermatt helped himself peasant-fashion to a glass of wine.

" Now," said he, " we are going to talk business."

Without admitting the bare possibility of any hesitation, he attacked the question of dowry, taking as his base the statements made to him three weeks previously by old Oriol himself. He assessed Gontran's fortune, exclusive of expectations, at three hundred thousand francs. It was, of course, an understood thing that if a man of Count de Ravenel's rank sought the hand of Oriol's daughter, charming young lady as she was, the girl's family would naturally recognise the honour by making a corresponding pecuniary sacrifice. Greatly taken aback by this suggestion, but at the same time flattered almost into helplessness, Oriol roused himself to defend his property, and a lengthy discussion ensued. Andermatt, however, made the path easy by a preliminary declaration :

"We don't want ready money or securities, only land, the land you have already pointed out to me as constituting your daughter's dowry, with the addition of one or two other plots which I shall indicate."

At the idea that the loss of Louise would not entail any simultaneous loss of actual cash, a deep peace stole into the souls of father and son, a desire to come to terms, and a secret joy which they could hardly contain. They would not have to disburse any of the money which they had so slowly amassed; the money which had come into the house, franc by franc, sou by sou; those fair gold and silver coins polished by time, flung down on café tables, passed from hand to hand, into purses, pockets, deep drawers in old cupboards, those coins which tinkled their tale of sorrow, of care, of weariness and of toil, those coins so dear to the peasant's heart and eyes and fingers, more precious to him than cow or vine, than field or house, those coins with which it is sometimes more difficult to part than with life itself.

The Oriols, however, prolonged the discussion, with the idea of saving an odd corner of land here and there. A large-scale plan of the estate was laid out on the table, and on it, one by one, the portions allotted to Louise were marked by crosses. It took Andermatt a good hour to establish a claim to the last two plots. Finally, to avoid any danger of a misunderstanding on either side, the three of them went over the actual ground, and with the aid of the plan, identified with meticulous care all the areas which had already been inscribed with crosses, and verified them anew.

But Andermatt's mind was not at ease. He suspected that the two Oriols were capable of challenging, at the first opportunity, some of the concessions to which they now agreed. They would try to recover patches here and there which were essential to his plans. He endeavoured to hit upon some practical and trustworthy scheme for clinching the agreement. An idea occurred to him, which at first made him smile, then seemed to him the very thing, in spite of its eccentricity.

" If you like," he suggested, " we will put this all down in writing so that we shan't forget anything later on."

When they returned to the village he stopped at the tobacconist's and bought two registration sheets. He knew that the list of lots, would, in the eyes of the Oriols, acquire a character almost inviolable, once it was inscribed on this legal stationery, which symbolised the Law, ever invisible yet ever threatening, upheld by the police, by fines and imprisonment. He accordingly drew up a document, in duplicate, in the following terms :

" It is hereby agreed pursuant to the promise of marriage mutually exchanged between Count Gontran de Ravenel and Mademoiselle Louise Oriol that the father of the aforesaid Louise Oriol do surrender as dowry to his daughter the property hereinafter designated. . . ."

Here followed a carefully drawn-up list, with correct references to the Cadastral Register of the Commune. Having added the date and affixed his own signature, he insisted on the signature of old Oriol, who, had, for his part, stipulated that mention be made of the amount of the Count's estate.

Then Andermatt set out for the hotel with the document in his pocket.

Everyone was greatly amused at his story, especially

Gontran. When it was finished, the Marquis, with great dignity, said to his son:

"We must both of us go this evening and pay a call on the Oriols. I shall repeat in person the request already made by my son-in-law. That will put matters on a more regular footing."

V

GONTRAN proved a delightful fiancé, and as attentive as
he was charming. Drawing upon Andermatt for money,
he gave presents at large, and he was continually going to
see his betrothed either at her own house or at Madame
Honorat's. Paul rarely failed to accompany him. He
wanted to meet Charlotte, although after every visit he
would firmly resolve never to go near her again.

Charlotte had resigned herself bravely to the idea of
her sister's marriage and could even speak of it without
constraint and without betraying a sense of injury. There
was perhaps some slight change in her character; she
seemed more composed and less frank than hitherto.
While Gontran was murmuring his pretty speeches to
Louise in a corner of the room, Paul would converse
gravely with Charlotte, yielding gradually to her fascination, and suffering this new love to surge over his heart
like a rising tide. Fully conscious of the situation, he
accepted it none the less, reflecting that he could always
run away when danger threatened. From Charlotte he
would go straight to Christian, who now spent the whole
day on a sofa. The moment he set foot in her room, he
felt nervous and irritable, and hardened himself to con-
front the querulousness which is begotten of physical
prostration. Her every thought and utterance exasperated him in advance. Her airs of suffering, her attitude
of resignation, her glances of reproach and supplication
brought angry words to his tongue. These, however, he
was sufficiently man of the world to suppress. While in
her presence, he was forever haunted by the constant remembrance, the persistent image, of the girl whom he
had just left.

Christian's anguish at seeing so little of him prompted her to overwhelm him with questions as to how he spent his days, and he invented stories to which she listened eagerly, seeking to detect in them some indication of interest in another woman. Aware that she had lost her power of inspiring in Paul even a little of the love that tortured her, conscious of her physical inability to please him, to give herself to him, to reconquer by caresses all that she could not gain through the finer emotions, she became obsessed by vague suspicions, although she could find no definite focus for her fears. She was vaguely aware that danger was looming, some great unknown danger; her jealousy hovered in mid-air, ready to pounce. She mistrusted even the women whom she saw from her window and whose charms she acknowledged, although she did not even know whether Paul had ever spoken to them.

" Have you noticed a very pretty tall dark woman? " she asked him. " I've only just seen her. She must have arrived within the last few days."

" No, I don't know her," he replied.

At once suspecting him of falsehood, she turned pale.

" It isn't possible," she persisted. " You must have seen her. She is quite beautiful, I think."

Surprised at her insistence, he assured her that he had not see the newcomer, but would do his utmost to meet her.

" That's the woman ! " she said to herself. " I'm convinced of it."

There were days when she was persuaded that he was concealing a liaison with some one in the neighbourhood. He must have sent for his mistress, that actress of his, perhaps. Then she would question her father, her brother, her husband, everybody, about all the young and desirable women they knew at Enval. If only she had been well enough to walk about and see for herself and watch his movements, her mind would have been more at rest, but her present inability to move amounted to unendurable martyrdom. When she spoke to Paul, the mere tone of her words revealed her anguish, and provoked in him the fretful impatience which is the aftermath of outworn passion. There was only one topic, Gontran's approaching marriage, which they could discuss peacefully together. This theme enabled him to mention Charlotte and to give vocal expression to his thoughts of her. He derived, moreover, a mysterious, confused, inexplicable pleasure from hearing Christian pronounce the girl's name, commend her charm and attractiveness, pity her, regret that her brother had sacrificed her, and express a wish that she should be loved and wedded by some honest fellow.

"Really," he would comment, "Gontran was a fool. She is a charming young creature, quite charming."

"Quite charming," echoed the unsuspecting Christian. "She is a pearl among girls. Simply perfect."

It never occurred to her that a man of Paul's stamp could fall in love with a girl of that class and marry her. It was only of Paul's mistresses that she was afraid. And yet, so curious is the psychology of love, the praises of Charlotte on Christian's lips had an extraordinary potency; they excited his love, whipped up his passion, invested the girl with irresistible attractions. One day when he accompanied Gontran to Madame Honorat's house to meet Louise and her sister, they found Dr Mazelli in the drawing-room, obviously quite at home. He held out a hand to each of them, smiling that Italian smile of his, and seeming to bestow his whole heart with every word and gesture. Gontran and he had struck up a superficial friendship, based on certain secret affinities and resemblances, on a sort of complicity of instincts, rather than on genuine trust and affection.

"Well, how about your red-haired charmer of Sans-Souci wood?" asked Gontran.

"Pooh!" The Italian smiled. "We have both cooled off. She is one of those women who promise everything and give nothing."

In the conversation that ensued, the handsome doctor laid himself out to please the sisters, especially Charlotte. When he addressed a woman, his voice, his gestures, his glances, expressed a never-failing adoration. From head to foot, his whole physical frame declared his devotion with an eloquence of attitude which made its way irresistibly to the feminine heart. Combining the airs and graces of an actress, the light pirouettes of a dancer, the supple movements of a juggler, he deployed a whole science of seduction, at once natural and studied, of which he continually availed himself.

On his way back to the hotel with Gontran, Paul exclaimed peevishly :

" What on earth is that mountebank after in that house ? "

" Who can tell with these adventurers ? " Gontran rejoined placidly. " They are the sort of people who slip in everywhere. This one is probably tired of his vagabond life, and of obeying the caprices of his Spanish woman, to whom he is not so much a doctor as a valet, or worse. He is on the look-out for something better. Professor Cloche's daughter was a pleasing morsel ; but he says he has missed fire there. Charlotte Oriol would please his fancy equally. So he keeps trying, feeling his way, following the scent, taking soundings. If he became co-proprietor of the springs, he could devote his attention to ousting that imbecile Latonne, and in any case during the summer he could work up an excellent practice for the following winter. I'll swear that's his plan. There's no doubt about it."

Dull anger, jealous hostility, arose in Paul's heart.

They heard a voice calling to them to stop. Mazelli was pursuing them.

Paul addressed him in a sarcastic and aggressive manner :

" Where are you running so fast, Doctor? One would think you were pursuing the goddess Fortune."

Without checking himself in his stride, the smiling

Italian skipped backwards, thrust his hands with a graceful, pantomimic gesture into his pockets, and turned them
gaily inside out, seizing the seams between finger and
thumb and stretching them out to display their emptiness.

" I haven't caught her yet," he replied.

Then, pivoting elegantly on his toes, he made off like
a man with a pressing engagement.

On several occasions during the following days they
found him at Dr Honorat's, where he ingratiated himself
with the ladies by a thousand trifling and pleasing services,
doubtless the same delicate attentions as had availed him
with the Duchess. There was nothing, from compliments
to macaroni, that he could not turn out in perfection.
He was really an excellent cook. He would don a blue
apron and a chef's hat made out of paper. Singing his
Neapolitan songs, and handling the pots and pans in a
way which was comical without being absurd, he amused
and charmed everyone, down to the half-witted maid-of-
all-work who vowed that he was an angel.

His projects were not long in disclosing themselves.
In Paul's mind there was no longer any doubt that he was
endeavouring to gain the affections of Charlotte. And he
seemed to be succeeding. He was so flattering, so assiduous, so skilled in every trick of giving pleasure that the
mere sight of him brought to her face that gratified expression which reveals an inward joy. Paul for his part,
without quite realising all that his manner implied,
adopted the attitude of a rival lover. The moment
Mazelli approached Charlotte, Paul was on the spot,
exerting himself in his more direct fashion to win the
girl's affections. His tender speeches had a touch of
bluntness; he was ardent and at the same time brotherly.
He would remark to her, "You know I'm very fond of
you," but his manner was so sincere, so unconstrained,
and his tone so frank, that one could hardly interpret it
as a serious declaration.

Surprised at this unexpected rivalry, Mazelli deployed
all his forces. A prey to that instinctive jealousy, which

grips a man in relation to any woman who attracts him, even if he is not actually in love with her, Paul, who was of a naturally violent temperament, became aggressive and arrogant, while Mazelli, self-controlled and insinuating, countered with subtle witticisms and adroit compliments that had a hint of mockery in them. Every day the struggle between them became more acrimonious, though probably neither had a very clear idea of his real intentions. Like two dogs holding by their teeth to the same prey, neither was willing to yield to the other.

Charlotte was her merry self again, but there was a change in her; there was now a certain asperity in her humour; her smile and her glance held a hint of reserve, a certain lack of frankness. It seemed as if Gontran's desertion had been a lesson to her, had inculcated suppleness and wariness, and opened her eyes to possible deceptions. She played off one lover against the other with skill and self-possession. She had the right word for each; never bringing them into conflict, never allowing either to imagine that she preferred him to his rival, making fun of each in turn in the other's presence, leaving it a drawn match between them, and not even appearing to take either of them seriously. All this was carried out with a simplicity that suggested the schoolgirl rather than the coquette and with the roguishness that often lends irresistible charm to girls of that age.

Then suddenly Mazelli appeared to be gaining the upper hand. He seemed to have become more intimate with her, as though some secret understanding had been established between them. When he spoke to her, he would trifle with her umbrella or with a ribbon on her gown in a way that Paul interpreted as a sort of moral ownership, and which exasperated him till he longed to box Mazelli's ears.

One day at the Oriols' house, it chanced that Paul was talking to Louise and Gontran, and at the same time keeping a watchful eye on Mazelli, who was speaking in undertones to Charlotte and making her smile. Paul saw the girl blush suddenly with so obvious an air of perturbation that he could not for a moment doubt that Mazelli had been talking love to her. With downcast eyes and unsmiling countenance she was listening intently. Conscious that he was on the point of losing his temper, Paul asked Gontran to come outside with him for a few minutes. Gontran made his excuses to Louise, and followed his friend into the street.

" Look here, Gontran," Paul exclaimed, " at all costs we must prevent that scoundrelly Italian from seducing that girl. She is quite defenceless against him."

" What do you expect me to do about it? Me of all people? "

" You must warn her what sort of man this adventurer is."

" My dear fellow, it's none of my business."

" Isn't it? She is going to be your sister-in-law."

" Quite so. But I have no positive proof that Mazelli has any reprehensible designs on her. He flirts with every woman. He has never said or done anything improper."

" Very well, then, if you won't do it, I will, though it is far less my business than yours."

" Oh! Then you are in love with her, are you? "

" I? . . . No . . . but I can see through that rascal's games."

" You are treading on dangerous ground, my friend, . . . unless . . . unless . . . you're in love with her yourself."

" I tell you I'm not in love with her. But I'll put a spoke in the wheel of that foreign blackguard, see if I don't."

" What do you propose doing, may I ask? "

" Slap the scoundrel's face for him."

" Just the very thing to make her really fall in love with him. He will fight you and then, whether he wounds you or gets wounded himself, he forthwith becomes a hero in her eyes."

" What would you do? "

" In your place? "

" Yes. In my place."

" I would have a friendly talk with her. She has great faith in you. So I would just tell her simply, in so many words, what these parasites of society are. You have the knack of saying that sort of thing. You know how to put a little warmth into it. I should make her understand in the first place, why he became a hanger-on of that Spanish woman; secondly, why he has been trying to get round Professor Cloche's daughter; and thirdly, why, after failing in that attempt, he is now, as a last resort, setting himself to make a conquest of Mademoiselle Charlotte Oriol."

" Why won't you do it yourself, as her future brother-in-law? "

" Because . . . because . . . well, because of what has passed between us. Come now, it is hardly for me to do it."

" You are right. I'll speak to her myself."

" Would you like me to arrange for you to see her alone at once? "

" Yes, do."

" Very well. Go for a ten minutes' walk. I'll take Louise and Mazelli away. You will find Charlotte all by herself when you come back."

As he walked away towards the Enval gorges, Paul was puzzling how best to approach this delicate subject. On his return to the cold, white-washed drawing-room of the paternal dwelling, he found Charlotte alone, as Gontran had promised. Taking a chair near her, he began :

" It was at my special request, Mademoiselle Charlotte, that Gontran procured me this interview with you."

With her clear eyes fixed on him, she asked :

" Indeed? Why? "

" Oh, it wasn't to talk insipid nonsense to you in the Italian fashion. I wanted to speak to you as a friend, a very devoted friend, who feels bound to give you some advice."

" Go on, please."

At first he skirted the subject carefully. Laying stress on his experience and her own ingenuousness, he very gently conveyed, in discreet but lucid phrases, his opinion of fortune-hunting adventurers who exploit with professional ability the innocent and unsuspecting creatures of both sexes, into whose purses and affections they worm their way. At this she turned a little pale and gave him her serious and entire attention.

" I understand, and yet I don't," she remarked. " You are thinking of some particular person."

" I mean Dr Mazelli."

Lowering her eyes she was silent for a few instants. Then in hesitating tones she said :

" You have been so frank that I must follow your example. Since . . . since . . . since my sister's engagement I have become a little less—a little less foolish. I confess I already had my suspicions, and I got a good deal of quiet amusement out of his visits."

She lifted her eyes to his, and there was so much gracious sincerity, lively humour, charming archness in her smile, in the subtlety of her glance, in her small tip-tilted nose, in the white teeth that flashed between her lips, that Paul felt himself swept towards her by one of those tumultuous impulses that hurled him, distracted with passion, at the feet of whatever woman had captivated him for the time being. So Mazelli was not the favoured rival ! His heart leaped with joy. He, Paul, was the victor !

" Then you really don't care for him? " he asked.

" For whom? Mazelli? "

" Yes."

She cast at him a glance of such reproach that he felt overwhelmed. In beseeching tones he faltered :

" Then . . . there is no one . . . you care for? "

With downcast eyes she replied :

" I don't know . . . I love those who love me."

He seized her hands and kissed them in a sudden frenzy, in one of those moments of rapture, when a man loses his head and utters words, begotten of physical excitement rather than of a spirit in tumult.

"But I love you, Charlotte; I love you, darling."

Quickly freeing one of her hands, she placed it on his lips.

"Don't say another word," she implored him. "It would hurt me too terribly if I were again deceived."

She had risen to her feet. He jumped up, and, throwing his arms around her, caught her to his heart in a transport of love.

A sudden noise made them spring apart. Old Oriol had entered the room and was gazing at them, dumbfounded.

"*Bouggre! bouggre! bouggre!* You blackguard!" he shouted.

Charlotte fled and the two men were left facing each other. After a few moments of embarrassment, Paul attempted to explain.

"My dear sir. I have . . . it is quite true . . . my behaviour. . . ."

But old Oriol was possessed by raging fury, and would not listen to a word. He advanced on Paul with his fists clenched.

"*Bouggre!* You blackguard!" he kept repeating.

He thrust his face into Paul's, and seized him by the collar with his gnarled peasant's hands. But Paul was as tall as old Oriol and possessed the added strength of the athlete. With a single effort he shook himself free from his assailant's clutches. Then pinning him to the wall, he cried:

"Now listen to me, Oriol. It's not a question of fighting, but of understanding each other. It is true that I have kissed your daughter, but I swear I have never done it before, and I also swear to you that I mean to marry her."

The old man's physical fury had succumbed to the impetus of his antagonist, but his wrath had in no way abated.

" Ah, that's it," he spluttered. " Stealing my daughter because you want her money. *Bouggre!* You black-guard ! "

Then came a torrent of despairing words which re-vealed the pent-up grievances in his heart. He was still inconsolable, as he thought of the dowry promised to his elder daughter, of his vineyards passing into the hands of those *Parigiens.* He now suspected Gontran of being a pauper and Andermatt a sharper. He entirely forgot the unexpected wealth which the latter had brought him, and belched forth all his secret bile and rancour against those scoundrels who would no longer let him sleep in peace. He spoke as if Andermatt and all his relations and friends were in the habit of coming night after night to rob him, now of his land, now of his mineral springs, now of his daughters. Hurling these charges into Paul's face, he accused him of having similar designs on his property, of being a swindler, who was stealing his daughter for the sake of her acres.

Paul soon lost patience, and shouted back into Oriol's face :

" You old dunderhead ! I'm a richer man than you are. I could buy you up."

Incredulous, but eager to hear more, the old man was silent for a moment; then he renewed his recriminations, but with less vehemence. Paul was able to make his ex-planations heard. Believing himself compromised, and by his own act, he proposed to marry Charlotte and forego a dowry altogether. But old Oriol merely shook his ears, and made him repeat his offer. He could not grasp it. To him, Paul was still only a beggar, a penniless adven-turer. Paul continued to shout in his face :

" I have an income of more than a hundred and twenty thousand francs, you old dodderer. Do you understand? A capital of three million francs."

Oriol replied like a flash :

" Will you put that in writing, give it to me on paper? "

" Yes, certainly."

" Will you sign it? "

" Yes."

" On stamped paper? "

" Yes, on stamped paper."

The old man rose and went to his cupboard. Thence he took a couple of registration sheets, and with the help of the agreement which Andermatt had a few days before extracted from him, he composed a grotesque promise of marriage which covenanted for a guarantee of three million francs on the part of the male betrothed. To this Paul had to affix his signature.

Once he was outside the house, it seemed to Paul that the whole world was revolving in the wrong direction. It appeared that he was betrothed, and betrothed in spite of himself, in spite of the girl, by one of those accidents, those tricks of destiny, which preclude all escape.

" What madness ! " he said to himself.

But presently he reflected that after all he might not perhaps have fared better, had he searched the whole world through. At the bottom of his heart he rejoiced to find himself caught in this snare, which fate had laid for him.

VI

The following day opened inauspiciously for Andermatt. On arriving at the Baths, he was informed that Monsieur Aubry-Pasteur had died of apoplexy during the night, at the Hôtel Splendid. With his wide knowledge, his disinterested zeal, and the love he had conceived for Mont-Oriol, which he had regarded more or less as his own offspring, Aubry-Pasteur had been very useful to Andermatt. But apart from all this, it was most unfortunate that a patient who had come for the purpose of combating a tendency to congestion, should die of that very complaint, under full medical treatment, at the height of the season and in the first flush of the town's dawning success .

Greatly perturbed, Andermatt paced to and fro in Dr Latonne's empty consulting-room, busily devising some means of attributing the misfortune to a different cause, to some kind of accident, to a fall, an act of carelessness, the rupture of an aneurism; and he awaited Dr Latonne's arrival with impatience; anxious to have the death certified in terms which would arouse no suspicion as to its true cause.

Dr Latonne entered hurriedly; his face was pale and showed traces of intense emotion. Before he had crossed the threshold he enquired :

" You have heard the deplorable news? "

" Yes. The death of Monsieur Aubry-Pasteur."

" No, no. Dr Mazelli has run away with Professor Cloche's daughter."

Andermatt felt a cold shudder coursing down his spine.

"What! You mean to say that. . . ."

" My dear Andermatt! It is a frightful calamity, a crushing blow."

Dr Latonne dropped into a chair and wiped his forehead. Then he recounted the facts as he had them from Petrus Martel, who had just learned them directly through the Professor's valet. Mazelli had paid marked attentions to the pretty, red-haired widow, a shameless and wanton flirt, whose first husband had died of consumption, the result, it was said, of excessive conjugal indulgence. Professor Cloche had, however, got wind of Mazelli's projects and having no desire to have this adventurer, whom he had surprised kneeling at his daughter's feet, imposed upon him as a second son-in-law, he forcibly turned him out of the house. But Mazelli, having gone out by the door, came in by the window, with the aid of the silken ladder sacred to lovers. There were two versions current. According to the first, he had reduced the widow to an insane state of love and jealousy; according to the second, he had continued visiting her secretly, while making a pretence of paying his attentions to another woman. Convinced at last by his mistress that her father remained obdurate, he had eloped with her that very night, thus creating a scandal which made a marriage inevitable. Dr Latonne rose to his feet and leaned his back against the mantelpiece, while Andermatt paced to and fro in consternation.

" A doctor! " exclaimed Latonne. " A doctor to do such a thing! A doctor of medicine! How utterly unprincipled! "

In his distress, Andermatt was weighing the consequences, which he figured out as if he were doing a sum in arithmetic.

In the first place, vexatious reports would be circulated in the neighbouring health resorts and would spread as far as Paris. But if one went the right way about it, this elopement could be made to serve as an advertisement. A dozen or so attractively worded paragraphs inserted in the papers with the largest circulations, would focus much attention on Mont-Oriol.

Secondly, Professor Cloche would leave Enval: an irreparable loss.

Thirdly, the Duke and Duchess of Ramas-Aldavarra would go away, and their departure would constitute another disaster, for which nothing could compensate.

In short, Dr Latonne was right. It was a frightful catastrophe. Andermatt turned to Latonne.

"You had better go at once to the 'Splendid' and draw up a death-certificate in terms that will arouse no suspicion as to the true cause."

As Latonne picked up his hat to go, he remarked:

"Ah, there's still another item of news. Is it true that your friend Paul Brétigny is going to marry Charlotte Oriol?"

Andermatt started.

"Brétigny? What an idea! Who told you that?"

"Petrus Martel again. He had it from old Oriol's own lips."

"Old Oriol?"

"Yes, old Oriol, who affirmed that his future son-in-law had a fortune of three million francs."

Andermatt was almost past thinking.

"Well, well," he muttered, "after all, it is possible. He has been pretty hot on her track for some time past. But in that case . . . the whole hillside is ours, the whole hillside. I must verify that at once."

He left directly after the doctor, so as to catch Paul before luncheon. On entering the hotel he was informed that his wife had asked for him several times. He found her still in bed, talking to her father and brother. The latter was rapidly scanning the morning papers with a casual glance.

Christian was feeling unwell, very unwell, and ill at ease. She was afraid, without knowing why. Moreover she was possessed by one of those fancies which haunt a woman in her condition, a fancy which had been growing upon her for several days. She wanted to consult Dr Black. She had heard people making jokes at the expense of Dr Latonne, with the result that she had lost all confidence in him. She was anxious to have another opinion, that of Dr Black, whose reputation was steadily growing. All day long she was tortured by the fears and obsessions by which women are afflicted when their delivery draws near. Ever since the night before, in consequence of a dream, she had the idea that her child was so placed that a natural delivery would be impossible and the Cæsarian operation prove necessary. In imagination she stood by, watching all the horrible details of this operation performed upon herself. Every few minutes she closed her eyes in order to recall again and again this vision of her own frightful and agonizing travail. It was then that she took it into her head that Dr Black was the only person who could tell her the truth. She insisted on seeing him; nothing would content her. He must come and examine her at once, at once, at once.

Andermatt was greatly perplexed and hardly knew what to say.

" My dear child, it is a very delicate matter, in view of my relations with Dr Latonne. In fact it is . . . frankly impossible. But, listen, I have an idea. I will send for Professor Mas-Roussel; he is worth a hundred Blacks. He is sure to come if I ask him."

But no. She stuck to her point. She would have Black, nobody but Black; she must have Black and his bulldog face at her bedside. It was a craving, a wild, superstitious obsession; she would not be denied.

At this, Andermatt endeavoured to divert her ideas into another channel.

" Did you know that sly fellow Mazelli had eloped with Professor Cloche's daughter last night? They are off. They have decamped, no one knows where. There's a pretty kettle of fish ! "

In wide-eyed distress, she raised herself on her pillow.

" Oh, the poor Duchess! Poor woman, how sorry I am for her."

Her heart had long since come to understand that other wounded and passionate soul. They wept the same bitter tears, for they were racked by the same sufferings.

Nevertheless she repeated her demand.

" Will, do send for Dr Black. I know I shall die if he doesn't come."

Andermatt seized her hand and kissed it affectionately.

" Christian, my pet, do be reasonable. You must consider . . ."

He saw her eyes fill with tears, and he turned to her father :

" This is your affair, Marquis. Personally I can do nothing. But Black comes here every day about one o'clock to see the Princess von Maldeburg. Stop him in the passage and bring him in to see your daughter. You won't mind waiting another hour, Christian, will you? "

She agreed to this, but she refused to get up and join the men at luncheon. Leaving her, they went into the dining-room, where Paul was already waiting. As soon as he saw him, Andermatt exclaimed :

" I say, what is this story I have just heard? Are you really going to marry Charlotte Oriol? Surely it can't be true? "

Paul looked uneasily at the closed door and said in subdued tones :

" As a matter of fact, it is."

They all listened to his news in consternation.

" What can have come over you? " William asked. " Why should you marry at all, with a fortune like yours? Why burden yourself with one woman, when all women are at your disposal? And really you must admit that the girl's family is hardly up to the mark. It's all very well for Gontran, who hasn't a sou."

" My father," Paul rejoined, laughing, " made his pile out of flour. He was just a miller, if you come to think of it; a wholesale miller. If you had known him, you might have said he was not quite up to the mark either. As for Charlotte herself . . ."

" Oh, she is perfect," Andermatt broke in. " Delicious. . . . Perfect. And . . . you know—she will be as well off as you, if not more so. I guarantee that personally."

" Quite so," Gontran concurred. " Marriage is no obstacle and it comes in useful for getting you out of a scrape. But you ought to have let us know, Paul. How the deuce did it happen? "

Paul thereupon gave an account of the affair, with some slight modifications. He laid undue stress on his vacillations and emphasized the sudden nature of his decision at a word from Charlotte, which revealed her love for him. He described the unexpected entrance of old Oriol, their high words, which lost nothing in the telling, Oriol's incredulity on the subject of his fortune, and the production of the stamped paper from the cupboard. Andermatt laughed till he cried. He thumped the table with his fist.

" Ah, he played that trick on you, did he? The stamped paper! Why, that was my invention."

Colouring and stammering, Paul asked Andermatt not to mention the engagement to his wife.

" We are such friends," he said, " that I would rather tell her myself. . . ."

Gontran looked at his friend with a queer smile of amusement on his face.

" That's the style," it seemed to say. " That's right. This is how these little affairs ought to end. No noise, no scandal, no scenes."

" If you like," he suggested, " we'll go and see her after luncheon. She will be up by then, and you can tell her your news."

His eyes met Paul's; the two young men gazed at each other fixedly, full of unutterable thoughts. Then they looked away.

" Why, certainly," Paul replied carelessly; "we can talk that over presently."

One of the hotel servants entered and announced that
Dr Black had come to see the Princess. The Marquis
went out into the passage to waylay him. Having explained the situation fully, his son-in-law's predicament,
his daughter's craving, he had no difficulty in persuading
him to see Christian. As soon as the little man with the
big head entered her room, the patient said :

" Papa, you can leave us."

The Marquis having retired, Christian described her
fears, her nervous dread, her nightmares. She spoke in
a low soft voice, as if confessing to a priest, and the
doctor listened like a father-confessor. Every now and
then he fixed his great round eyes on her, and nodded his
head to show that he was attending, murmuring, " Precisely, precisely," in a way which suggested that he had
her case at his finger-ends and could cure her as soon as
he pleased.

Having heard her out, he set himself to question her
with extreme minuteness as to her habits, her diet, the
medical treatment prescribed to her. Sometimes a gesture
would indicate his approval, sometimes a pregnant " Oh "
would convey the contrary. When at last she confided
her haunting dread that the child might be wrongly
placed, he rose to his feet and passed his hands gently
over her body, but with ecclesiastical modesty and without uncovering her.

" No," he announced finally. " All is as it should be."

She could have thrown her arms round his neck. What
a splendid doctor he was !

He took a sheet of notepaper from the table and wrote
a prescription, a very long prescription. Then returning
to the bedside, he began to converse in a different tone,
which implied that for the present he had finished with his
sacred professional duties. He had a deep, unctuous
voice, one of those powerful voices peculiar to men of
thick-set, dwarfish stature. His most commonplace remark concealed an interrogation, and he gossiped about
everything and everyone. Gontran's marriage seemed to

interest him greatly, and, at last, with the ugly smile of deformity, he remarked :

"I suppose I oughtn't to talk to you yet about Monsieur Brétigny's engagement, though it is hardly a secret. Old Oriol is telling everybody."

She felt overcome by sudden faintness. It began at her finger-tips and then swept over her whole body, arms, bosom, abdomen, legs. She had not quite grasped the truth, but a horrid dread of being kept in the dark inspired her with swift cunning.

"Ah!" she faltered. "So old Oriol has been telling everybody, has he?"

"Yes, yes. He told me about it himself not ten minutes ago. Apparently Monsieur Brétigny is very well off and has been in love with little Charlotte for a long time. And you know it was Madame Honorat who made both those matches. She put her services and her house at the disposal of the young people. . . ."

Christian's eyes were closed. She had lost consciousness. At the doctor's summons a chambermaid came hurrying in, and on her heels the Marquis, Andermatt and Gontran, who went in search of smelling-salts, ether, ice, and a score of useless things.

Suddenly Christian moved. She opened her eyes and threw up her arms, and, writhing about in bed, she uttered a piercing scream. Then with a violent effort she gasped :

"Oh . . . the pains . . . my God, . . . the pains . . . in my back. . . . I'm being torn in pieces—oh, my God. . . ."

Then her shrieks rang out anew. The symptoms of childbirth were obvious. Andermatt made off at full speed for Dr Latonne, whom he found finishing his luncheon.

"Come at once," he exclaimed. "There's something wrong with my wife. Be quick."

Then an idea flashed upon him and he mentioned that Dr Black happened to be in the hotel when his wife was taken ill. Dr Black corroborated this falsehood.

"I was just on my way to the Princess," he assured his

colleague, " when they told me that Madame Andermatt wasn't feeling well, so I came straight here. It was high time, I assure you."

Andermatt, who was in a great state of emotion, excitement and distress, was suddenly seized with doubts as to the skill of these two practitioners. Out he went again, bare-headed, and ran to Professor Mas-Roussel's house, to implore him to come. The Professor consented immediately, buttoned his frock coat with the mechanical movements of a doctor setting out on his rounds, and walked to the hotel with the long, quick, purposeful stride of the eminent specialist whose presence is a matter of life and death.

The two other physicians received him with the utmost deference, and consulted him with extreme humility, saying repeatedly, almost in the same breath :

" This is exactly what happened, *cher maître*. . . . Isn't that your opinion, *cher maître?* . . . Isn't that the case, *cher maître?* "

Andermatt for his part was beside himself with agony at his wife's groans. He harassed the Professor with questions, and, like the two doctors, kept fulsomely addressing him as *cher maître.*

Christian, lying almost unclothed in the presence of all these men, was past hearing, seeing, understanding. Her sufferings were so appalling that thought was impossible. It seemed to her as if someone were driving a saw through her sides and back, about the level of her hips; a long saw with blunt teeth that hacked slowly, jerkily, at bones and muscles, with momentary respites, succeeded by yet more excruciating torments. Sometimes the paroxysms abated for some instants, but with the relief from physical anguish, her soul was racked by a thought which was more cruel, more piercing, more dreadful, than the throes that rent her body : Paul loved another woman and was going to marry her. In order to exorcise this mental torment which gnawed at her heart and spirit, she purposely provoked new paroxysms of physical pain by violently moving her limbs, and when the pain seized her once more, she had at least a respite from her agony of mind.

For fifteen hours she endured this martyrdom. She was so utterly worn out by suffering and despair that she longed to die, strove to die, in the agonies which convulsed her. But at last, after a pang more prolonged and more violent than any that had preceded it, the child was born. The ordeal was over. Her agonies abated, as when the waves of the sea subside, and so intense was the relief that even the bitterness of her heart was for a time assuaged. When spoken to, she replied in a voice that was low and inexpressibly weary.

Suddenly she became aware of Andermatt leaning over her and saying :

"The child will live. It was almost the full time. It is a girl."

Christian could only murmur :

" Oh, my God, my God."

So she had a child, a living child, a child that would grow up. And it was Paul's. Again she could have cried aloud, so grievously was her heart stricken by this new calamity. A daughter! She would have none of her. She would never see her, never touch her.

Gentle hands had laid her back in bed and tended her. Someone had kissed her. Who was it? Doubtless her husband and her father. She did not know. But Paul, where was Paul? What was he doing? How happy she would have felt at this hour if only he loved her.

Time passed; hour followed hour; she could not distinguish between day and night; she was conscious only of the one burning thought that he loved another woman. Suddenly it occurred to her that after all it might not be true. Surely the news of the engagement would have reached her ears sooner than Doctor Black's? On further reflection, however, she realised that she had been kept in the dark. Paul had taken care that she should learn nothing. She looked about her room to see who was there. A strange woman, a woman of the people, was watching by her bedside. She dared not question her. From whom then could she find out the truth?

The door flew open, and her husband entered on tip-toe. Seeing that she was awake, he came to her bedside.

" Are you feeling better? "

" Yes, thank you."

" You gave us a terrible fright yesterday. However, the danger is over. And that reminds me that I am in rather a difficulty about you. I telegraphed to our friend Madame Icardon, who was to have looked after you. I told her of your sudden seizure and begged her to come at once, but she is nursing her nephew, who has scarlatina. All the same you can't be left without someone to attend you, someone more or less suitable. There is a lady here who has volunteered to be with you and keep you company during the daytime, so I just accepted her offer. It's Madame Honorat."

Christian suddenly remembered Dr Black's words. With a thrill of horror she moaned:

" Oh, no . . . no . . . anyone but her."

Andermatt was puzzled.

" Look here. I am quite aware that she is a common person, but your brother has a great regard for her. She has been most useful to him. And people do say that she used to be a midwife, and that Honorat made her acquaintance over a case. If you dislike her very much, I can get rid of her to-morrow. But we can try her at any rate. Let her come once or twice."

She reflected in silence. Then an imperious need to know the truth, the whole truth, seized her, and with the idea of inducing the woman to gossip, of extracting from her, one by one, the words that would rend her heart, she now could hardly refrain from exclaiming:

" Yes, yes, go and fetch her at once, at once. Be quick. Why are you waiting? "

This irresistible desire to know the worst was followed by a strange craving, a yearning to suffer yet more intensely, to toss upon her bed of sorrow as upon a bed of thorns : the mysterious, morbid ecstasy of the martyr welcoming his agonies.

"Very well," she faltered. "I agree. Send for Madame Honorat."

Suddenly she realised that she could no longer endure to wait without confirmation, unimpeachable confirmation, of Paul's treachery. In a voice that hardly rose above a whisper, she asked :

"Is it true that Monsieur Brétigny is going to be married?"

"Yes," he replied calmly. "You would have been told sooner if you had been well enough."

"To Charlotte?" she pursued.

"Yes."

Andermatt himself had a fixed idea already firmly implanted in his mind : his new-born daughter, at whom he was always peeping. He was a little hurt because Christian's first demand had not been for the child. He reproached her gently :

"Come now, my dear, you haven't asked about the baby yet. I suppose you know that she's doing splendidly?"

She started as if he had touched an open wound. But this was her Calvary; she must not shirk one station of her Cross.

"Bring her to me," she said.

Diving behind a curtain at the foot of the bed, he reappeared with a bundle of white linen in his arms, which he held clumsily enough, but his face was aglow with pride and happiness. He placed the child on the embroidered pillow by Christian's head. Christian was almost choking with emotion.

"There !" he said. "Isn't she a beauty?"

He drew back the filmy laces that veiled the child's features. Christian saw a small red face, so absurdly small, so grotesquely red; the eyes were closed and the little mouth was working.

"This is my daughter," she reflected, as she bent over this atom on the threshold of life; "my daughter, and

Paul's. This is the little creature that caused me all those agonies. This . . . this . . . is my daughter."

The repulsion she had felt for the child, whose coming had worked such havoc in her heart and in her tender body, vanished in a moment; she gazed at her now with a curiosity, ardent yet melancholy, and with deep astonishment, the amazement of an animal witnessing the emergence of its first-born.

Andermatt, who was waiting to see her caress the child passionately, remained surprised and shocked.

" Won't you kiss her? " he asked.

She leaned very gently towards the tiny crimson countenance. As her lips came closer to it, she felt a growing attraction, an irresistible appeal. And when at last they touched it and felt its moist warmth, a warmth derived from her own life, it seemed as if she could never again take them away from that baby face, but must go on kissing it for ever. She felt something brushing her cheek. It was her husband's beard. He was leaning down to kiss her. With tender gratitude he pressed her to him in a lingering embrace. Then he must needs have his turn of caressing his daughter, and with eager lips he showered light, soft kisses on her tiny nose.

Christian's heart contracted at his caresses, and she looked at the two, her husband and her daughter, there beside her.

Presently Andermatt offered to put the child back in her cradle, but Christian protested.

" No. Leave her here a few more minutes. I want to feel her close to my face. Don't speak or move. Just wait here and let us alone."

She laid one arm across the minute body in its swaddling clothes; put her face close to the small, puckered countenance, closed her eyes and lay still, her mind a blank. After a few minutes, however, William touched her gently on the shoulder.

" Come, my dear. You must be sensible. Don't let your emotions get the better of you."

He took the child away; but the mother's eyes followed her until she disappeared behind the curtains of the bed.

"Very well, then," said Andermatt, when he came back to her, " I'll send you Madame Honorat to-morrow morning to keep you company."

"Yes, dear," she replied in a firmer voice, " do send her. To-morrow morning."

Then she lay back in bed, utterly exhausted, but perhaps a shade less unhappy.

Her father and her brother came to see her the same evening, and told her all the gossip of the neighbourhood. Professor Cloche had departed hastily in search of his daughter, and the Duchess of Ramas, too, was nowhere to be seen. It was supposed that she had gone to give chase to Mazelli. Gontran, who laughed heartily over these escapades, pointed the moral in his humorous way.

"These watering-places are incredible. They are the only true fairylands left on earth. In two months, more things happen there than during the remaining ten in the rest of the world. You would really think that the springs were not so much mineralised as bewitched. It is the same in all the other spas, Aix, Royat, Vichy, Luchon, as well as at seaside places like Dieppe, Etretat, Trouville, Biarritz, Cannes, Nice. You meet specimens there of every race and class, magnificent adventurers, and such a medley of nationalities as you find nowhere else, and the most astonishing incidents occur every day. The women reveal an exquisite aptitude and readiness in playing the fool. In Paris they resist. In watering-places, they fall, flop! Some men find fortunes there, like Andermatt, some find death, like Aubry-Pasteur. Others fare even worse and get married . . . like myself . . . and like Paul. Isn't that a silly, farcical affair? You have heard about Paul's engagement, I suppose?"

"Yes," said Christian. " William has just been telling me."

"Paul is right, quite right," Gontran resumed. " True, she is only a peasant's daughter. But what of that? It's better than being connected with adventurers, or having no connections at all. I know Paul. He would have ended up by marrying any riff-raff who could stand out against him for six weeks. And no one could resist Paul except a thoroughly bad lot or an absolute innocent. He has picked up the innocent. So much the better for him."

Christian listened. Every word that entered her ear caused a pang to her heart, an agonising pang.

"I am dead tired," she said at last, closing her eyes. "I must have a little rest."

They kissed her and went away. But Christian was unable to sleep. Her reawakened imagination was busy at its work of torture. The idea that Paul no longer preserved even the slightest vestige of love for her became so intolerable that had it not been for the sight of her nurse asleep in her armchair, she would have opened the window and thrown herself down on to the steps outside. A slender ray of moonlight, shining in through a slit in the curtains, threw a small round patch of light upon the floor. As soon as she caught sight of it she was assailed by a host of memories : the lake, the wood, the first whisper of love, that had so thrilled her, Tournoël, all the kisses they had exchanged on dark paths of an evening and on the Roche-Pradière road. Of a sudden she saw that road white in the starlight, and Paul was wandering there, with his arm round a woman's waist, and at every step he kissed her on the mouth. She recognised the woman. It was Charlotte. He pressed her to him, smiling that smile of his and murmuring in her ears the tender words that rose so swiftly to his lips. Then throwing himself on his knees he kissed the ground at her feet, just as he had kissed it at Christian's. It was hard to bear, so hard that she turned round, hid her face in the pillow and sobbed. She could hardly restrain herself from crying aloud, as torments of despair racked her soul. Each throb of her heart, repeated by the pulses in her throat and humming temples, hammered out, over and over again, the word, "Paul, Paul, Paul." To shut out the sound, she covered her ears with her hands and put her head under the bedclothes, but in vain. " Paul, Paul, Paul," the name echoed in her bosom, with every beat of her inconsolable heart.

The nurse woke up.

" Are you feeling worse, Madam? "

Christian turned to her, her face wet with tears.

" No. I was asleep. Dreaming. I felt frightened."

She asked for a couple of candles to be lit, so that she might no longer see the ray of moonlight. Towards morning, however, she became drowsy, and she had been asleep for several hours, when Andermatt came in with Madame Honorat.

That stout dame lost no time in making herself at home. Seating herself by the bedside, she took Christian's hands in hers and questioned her like a doctor. Satisfied with the patient's replies, she announced :

" There, there ! We are getting on famously."

Taking off her bonnet, gloves and shawl, she turned to the nurse :

" You may go now, my good girl. You can come when we ring for you."

Christian at once felt a qualm of disgust at the sight of Madame Honorat.

" Let me have my baby for a while," she said to Andermatt.

As on the previous evening, William brought the child tenderly in his arms and put her down on the pillow. Once more a healing calm stole over Christian, as soon as she felt through the clothes the warmth of the tiny stranger swathed in its linen wrappings. Suddenly the infant began to cry in a shrill, piping voice.

" She wants the breast," said Andermatt.

He rang the bell for the nurse, a huge red-faced woman, with an ogreish mouth, full of great glistening teeth that almost frightened Christian. Opening her bodice she produced a ponderous breast, smooth, distended with milk, like the udder of a cow. When Christian saw her baby drinking from this turgid vessel, she felt a pang of jealousy and disgust and longed to snatch the child out of her arms. Meanwhile Madame Honorat was giving instructions to the nurse, who presently left the room, taking the baby with her. Then Andermatt, too, went away, and the two women remained alone.

Christian hardly knew how to introduce the subject that was torturing her mind. She trembled, lest in her excessive agitation she should lose her head and burst into tears, or in some way betray herself. But Madame Honorat needed no prompting, and began at once to pour out all the gossip of the neighbourhood, till she at last arrived at the Oriols.

"They are worthy people," she said. "Very worthy people. If only you had known the mother. Such a good, capable woman! She was worth ten ordinary women. And what is more, her daughters take after her."

As she threatened to diverge to another subject. Christian asked her:

"Which do you prefer, Louise or Charlotte?"

"Personally, I prefer Louise, your brother's fiancée. She is more sensible, more settled than her sister; a very capable girl, and such a good organiser. But my husband prefers Charlotte. Men's tastes are different from ours, you know."

She stopped talking for a moment. Christian's courage was failing her.

"My brother used often to meet Louise at your house," she faltered.

"Why, yes, Madame Andermatt. To be sure. Every day. The whole thing happened at my house. I gave the young people a chance to talk to each other. I understood how things lay. But what really pleased me was when I saw Monsieur Paul taking a fancy to little Charlotte."

In almost inaudible tones Christian asked:

"Is he very much in love with her?"

"In love with her? Oh, Madame Andermatt! He was quite wild about her. And when that Italian, the one who

ran away with Dr Cloche's daughter, started paying attention to her, just to see how far he could go with the girl,
I thought they would come to blows. Ah, if you had seen
Monsieur Paul's eyes! He looked at her as if he were
gazing on a holy Virgin. It's a perfect delight to see
anyone so much in love."

Christian questioned her on all that had passed in her
presence, everything they had said and done during their
walks in the valley of Sans-Souci, where Paul had so
often told her of his love. Madame Honorat was surprised by the odd questions she asked about trifling
matters, which would never have occurred to most people.
As Christian recalled a thousand details of the previous
year, Paul's exquisite lovemaking, his thoughtfulness, his
ingenuity in pleasing her, his mustering of all the tender
solicitude, all the charming little attentions, which reveal
a man's imperious desire to win his lady's love, she never
ceased from making comparisons. She wanted to discover whether he had devoted all these arts to her rival,
whether he had addressed himself to this new siege of a
soul with the same ardour, the same rapture, the same
irresistible passion. Every time she recognised some
small characteristic action, some exquisite trifle, one of
those acts of thrilling and palpitating unexpectedness of
which Paul was prodigal when he loved, Christian, lying
in bed, could not restrain an exclamation of suffering.
Surprised at these strange ejaculations, Madame Honorat
would affirm even more positively:

"Yes, indeed, I assure you it all happened exactly as
I am telling you. I have never seen a man so deeply in
love."

"Did he repeat poetry to her?"

"Indeed he did, Madame Andermatt. Beautiful
poetry."

When a silence fell between them, the only sound to be
heard was the gentle monotonous voice of the nurse, as
she sang the infant to sleep in the adjoining room.

Steps were heard approaching along the corridor. Pro-

fessor Mas-Roussel and Dr Latonne were coming to visit
their patient. They found her excited and hardly so well
as on the previous evening. After their departure, Andermatt opened the door and put his head into the room.

" Dr Black wants to see you. You have no objection? "

Starting up in bed, she exclaimed :

" No, no. I won't see him. I won't."

Utterly dumbfounded, William came towards her.

" But look here, you really must; it's his due; you
ought to . . ."

With her dilated eyes and quivering lips, she seemed
almost out of her mind. In a voice so piercing and loud
that it must have been heard through the walls, she
repeated :

" No, no. Never. Never let him come near me again.
Do you understand? Never."

And then, hardly knowing what she was saying, she
stretched out her arm and pointed at Madame Honorat,
who was standing in the middle of the room.

"That woman, too, send her away. I can't bear the
sight of her. Turn her out."

Andermatt sprang to his wife's side, and, putting his
arms round her, kissed her on the forehead.

" Christian, darling, don't excite yourself. What is the
matter with you? You must keep calm."

She could scarcely speak. The tears were streaming
from her eyes.

" Send everyone away," she sobbed, " and stay with me
yourself."

Distracted, he ran to Madame Honorat and pushed her
gently towards the door.

" Leave us for a moment," he begged her; " it is fever,
milk-fever. I'll calm her down. I'll come and see you
again presently."

When he returned to the bedside, Christian had sunk
back exhausted and was quietly weeping; and for the first
time in his life he, too, shed tears.

Fever did, in fact, set in during the night, and was

accompanied by delirium. After several hours of extreme restlessness, Christian began suddenly to speak. The Marquis and her husband, who were sitting up with her over a game of cards and counting their scores in undertones, fancied they heard her call them and went to the bedside. But she did not see them, or did not recognise them. Her colourless face showed pale against the white pillow. Her fair hair fell about her shoulders. With her clear blue eyes she gazed out into an unknown world, the mysterious, fantastic world of the insane. Her hands, which lay stretched out on the sheets, quivered and twitched spasmodically. At first she did not seem to be conversing, but inconsequently and ramblingly describing some particular scene. She had come to a rock. It was too high for her to jump down. She was afraid of spraining her ankle, and did not quite trust the man who was holding out his arms to catch her. Then she began to talk about perfumes, and seemed to be searching her mind for forgotten phrases.

" Could anything be sweeter? . . . It intoxicates like wine. . . . Wine intoxicates one's thoughts, perfumes intoxicate one's dreams. . . . In perfumes you inhale the very essence, the pure essence of things, of the world itself ; of flowers, trees, grass. You can discern the very soul of ancient dwellings as it slumbers amongst old furniture, old carpets, old curtains. . . ."

In the next phase of delirium, her face took on a strained expression, as if she had undergone protracted exertion. With slow, heavy steps she was toiling up a hill, and pleading with someone :

" Oh, do carry me again, I implore you. I shall die here. I can't go another step. Carry me as you used to carry me, up above the gorges. Do you remember? How you loved me ! "

Then she uttered a cry of anguish, and a look of horror came into her eyes. She was gazing at some dead animal which was lying at her feet. She begged that someone would remove it, but without hurting it.

The Marquis explained in a low voice to his son-in-law :

"She is thinking of a donkey we saw on the way back from la Nugère."

Now she was talking to the dead animal, comforting it, telling it that she, too, was very unhappy, even more unhappy, because she had been forsaken. Then suddenly she protested against some task imposed on her :

"Oh, no, not that," she exclaimed. "Oh, it is you, you of all people, . . . who want me to drag that cart."

She panted as if she were actually drawing a cart. For more than half-an-hour, with tears and moans and cries, she continued to climb the hill, dragging behind her, with fearful effort, a cart, which was obviously the cart that the dead donkey had once drawn. And someone was beating her cruelly, for she cried out :

"Oh, how you are hurting me! For heaven's sake don't beat me any more. I'll go on. But don't beat me any more, I implore you. I'll do what you please, but stop beating me."

Then her distress abated gradually, and until daybreak her mind wandered, but without violence, till at last she grew drowsy and fell asleep. At about two in the afternoon she awoke. Her temperature was still very high, but the delirium had left her, though until the following day her thoughts remained dull, confused, fleeting. She had difficulty in finding the words she wanted, and wore herself out racking her head for them. After a night's rest, however, her mind was perfectly clear again. None the less she was conscious of a change in herself. The ordeal through which she had passed had left its mark upon her soul. While she suffered less, she reflected the more. All her terrible experiences, recent as they were, had receded into a past that already seemed remote. She was able to contemplate them with a clearness of vision such as her mind had never known before. This new light, which had suddenly dawned upon her, visits certain individuals in their hours of trial; it revealed to her, as never before, life, men, material objects; in short, the whole earth and everything on its surface. Once more it was borne in upon her that she was utterly alone and deserted in the universe. This feeling of desolation came home to her even more keenly than on that night in her room, after the expedition to Lake Tazenat. She realized that although all mankind marches shoulder to shoulder along the highroad of fate, no two human beings are ever merged in a true union. Through her betrayal by the man in whom she had placed her whole trust, she felt that others, all the others in the world, would never to her be more than casual travelling companions, moving with her, on a journey that might prove long or short, grave or gay, towards a mysterious to-morrow. She realised that even while she was in her lover's arms, when she believed her being to be mingled and interfused with his, when she imagined that their bodies, their souls were merged into one body, one soul, they had drawn only a very little nearer, just close enough to bring into contact the walls of those impenetrable prisons in which nature has mysteriously isolated each human being. She saw only too clearly that no one has ever succeeded, or will ever succeed, in breaking down that invisible barrier which cuts off each individual from every other in life as completely as star from star in the firmament. There came to her a sense of that effort, never relinquished since the beginning of the world, that impotent yet unwearied effort, by which men seek to break through the sheaths, in which their souls struggle forever in dungeon-like solitude; the effort of arms, lips, eyes, of quivering flesh, the strivings of a love that exhausts itself in kisses, and, as its sole consummation, bequeaths life to some creature destined to be equally forlorn.

Then she was seized by an irresistible yearning to see her baby. When the child was brought in, Christian asked the nurse to undress her, as she had hitherto seen only the tiny face. The swaddling clothes were unwound, revealing the pathetic little, undeveloped body of the new-born infant, which stirred with the vague, instinctive movements of dawning life. Christian touched her with timid, trembling fingers. Then, with a sudden impulse, she kissed her all over, body, back, legs and feet.

Full of bewildering thoughts, she gazed at her child. A man and a woman had met and had loved in a delicious ecstasy, and behold the result! The baby in her arms was Paul and herself, blended together in this little being until the day of her death. He and she were united in this new life, which combined something of Paul and something of herself with an element of the unknown, through which would be evolved a personality different from theirs. Both of them would be reproduced in the child's physical frame, in her mind, in her ways, gestures, movements, tastes, passions, in her eyes, in the actual tones of her voice, in her gait and bearing. And yet, none the less, she would be a new individual.

Paul and she were now parted for ever. Never again would their glances mingle in one of those transports of love which secure the indestructibility of the human race. Straining the infant to her bosom, she murmured:

" Farewell, farewell."

She whispered it in the ear of her child, but it was Paul to whom she was bidding adieu, the brave but heart-broken leavetaking of a proud soul, the farewell of a woman who had before her long, perhaps life-long, suffering, but who at least would know how to conceal her tears from the world.

Her husband's voice was heard through the half-opened door.

" Ah! I've caught you at it. Just give me back my daughter, will you? "

He came running to the bedside, and caught up the child in arms already skilled in holding her. Lifting her above his head, he said:

" Good-morning, Mademoiselle Andermatt. Good-morning, Mademoiselle Andermatt."

" That," reflected Christian, " is my husband."

She looked at him in astonishment as if she beheld him

for the first time. That was the man to whom the law had united her and given her. That was the man who, by all human standards, religious and social, was half herself; nay, more, master of her days and her nights, of her heart and of her body. She could hardly restrain herself from smiling, so grotesque, just then, did it seem to her. Nothing could ever unite them. Never could they be linked together in those bonds, which, though, alas, so quickly broken, seem at the time eternal, ineffably sweet, almost divine. She felt not the slightest pang of remorse for having betrayed and deceived him. Why was that, she wondered. Why? Doubtless it was because they were too different, too remote from each other, too alien in race. If he understood her not at all, no more did she understand him. None the less he was kind, loyal, indulgent. Perhaps it is only persons of the same mould, of the same nature, the same moral essence, who can feel bound to each other by the sacred chain of voluntary duty.

While the nurse was dressing the baby, William took a seat.

" Christian, my dear," he said, " I hardly like to suggest any more visitors to you since your famous reception of Dr Black. All the same I should be much pleased if you would receive a friend of mine—I mean Dr Bonnefille."

Then, for the first time, she laughed, but it was the mere ghost of a laugh, proceeding from the lips, not from the soul.

" Dr Bonnefille! What a miracle! You and he are friends again? "

" Certainly. But now listen. I am going to tell you a great piece of news, which is still a deep secret. I have just bought the old establishment. I own the whole countryside now. Eh? What a triumph! Dr Bonnefille, poor fellow, was of course the first to know about it, and he at once started his little manœuvres, coming to enquire about you every day and leaving his card inscribed with a few sympathetic words. I responded by calling on him, and now we are on the best of terms."

" He can come when he pleases," said Christian. " I shall be glad to receive him."

" That's right. Thank you. I'll bring him to-morrow morning. I needn't tell you that Paul is always sending you messages through me and enquiring for the baby; he is most eager to see her."

Despite her resolutions, Christian felt perturbed. But she controlled herself sufficiently to say :

" Please thank him for me."

" Paul was very anxious," Andermatt resumed, " to know whether you had heard about his engagement. I told him you knew, and since then he has asked me several times what you thought about it."

Summoning up all her fortitude she murmured :

" Tell him it has my entire approval."

With unconscious cruelty, William continued :

" He was particularly eager to know what name you were going to give the child. I told him we hadn't decided whether it was to be Marguerite or Geneviève."

" I have changed my mind," she said. " I want to call her Arlette."

In the early days of her approaching motherhood, she and Paul had discussed what name they should choose for a boy or a girl, as the case might be. For a girl they had hesitated between Geneviève and Marguerite. But now she would have neither of these names.

" Arlette, Arlette," William repeated. " That's very pretty. You have chosen well. Personally I should have liked to call her Christian after you. An adorable name, Christian ! "

" Oh, no," she sighed deeply, " the name of the Crucified Saviour is too ominous of suffering."

Such an association of the names had never occurred to him. He blushed and rose to go.

" In any case," he said, " Arlette is charming. Goodbye, my dear, for the present."

When he had left the room, she called the nurse and directed that the cradle should henceforward be placed beside her. The light, swaying coracle-shaped cot, bearing its white curtains, like a sail, upon a mast of twisted copper, was rolled up to Christian's big bed. Christian stretched out her hand to touch the sleeping infant and said softly :

" Sleep, my child. You will never find anyone who will love you as I do."

The following days Christian passed in tranquil sadness and in deep thought. She was forging for herself a new heart and spirit, proof against the trials of everyday life. Her chief interest now lay in gazing into her baby's eyes and endeavouring to surprise in them the first look of intelligence, but all that she could see were two bluish circles, which were invariably turned towards the bright light of the window. A profound melancholy swept over her when she reflected that those eyes, as yet unawakened, would look on the world, just as she herself had done, through that illusive inner vision which fills a girl's soul with happiness, confidence and gaiety. Those eyes would love all that she had loved; bright days of sunshine, flowers, and, alas ! human beings too. They would love a man. A man ! Their depths would harbour his familiar and cherished image; they would behold him even when he was far away and they would light up on his return. And after that . . . after that . . . they would know what it was to weep. Tears, tears of bitterness, would course down those tender cheeks. The frightful agonies of love betrayed would eclipse their brightness; those pitiful, vague eyes, which would some day be as blue as her own, would have their beauty marred by anguish and despair. Covering her infant with distracted kisses, she cried :

" Never love anyone but me, my child."

At last the day arrived when Professor Mas-Roussel, who came every morning to see her, declared that she might get up. When the doctor had gone, Andermatt said :

" It's a great pity you are not quite well yet. We are having a very interesting demonstration to-day at the Baths. Dr Latonne has accomplished an absolute miracle with old Clovis. He has given him a course of automatic gymnastics. You would hardly believe it, but the old vagabond can walk now almost as well as anybody. More than that, there is a noticeable improvement in him after every treatment."

To please her husband she asked :

" Are you going to have a public demonstration? "

" More or less. The doctors and some friends will be there."

" At what o'clock? "

" Three."

" Will Monsieur Brétigny be present? "

" Yes, certainly. He promised me to come. All the members of the Board will be there. From the medical point of view it will be very interesting."

" Very well," she said. " I shall be up just about that time, so you can ask Monsieur Brétigny to come and see me. He shall keep me company while you are watching the experiment."

" Certainly, my dear."

" You won't forget? "

" No, no. Don't worry."

He went out to beat up an audience. After having been tricked by the Oriols on the occasion of the paralytic's first course of baths, he had in his turn played on the credulity of the invalids, who are readily persuaded when there is any prospect of a cure. He had now reached the stage of playing the comedy for his own delectation. He spoke of it so frequently, and with such ardour and conviction, that he would have had great difficulty in avowing whether he did or did not believe in it.

About three o'clock, all the people he had whipped up, were collected together in a group outside the door of the Baths, awaiting old Clovis, who arrived, supported on two walking-sticks and dragging his legs as usual. He bowed politely to all the spectators. He was followed by the two Oriols with Louise and Charlotte, who were accompanied by Paul and Gontran.

In the great hall in which the jointed apparatus had been set up, Dr Latonne was passing the time in conversation with Dr Honorat. When he caught sight of old Clovis a happy smile passed over his clean-shaven lips.

" Well," he asked. " How are you getting on to-day? "

" Oh, not so bad. Not so bad."

Presently Petrus Martel and Saint-Landri arrived, anxious to see for themselves. The former was inclined to believe, the latter to doubt. Behind them the spectators noted with amazement the advent of Dr Bonnefille, who greeted his rival and then shook hands with Andermatt. Dr Black was the last to appear.

Dr Latonne bowed to Louise and Charlotte.

" Well, ladies and gentlemen," he began, " you are about to witness a most interesting event. Bear in mind that this honest fellow could only walk a little, a very little, before the treatment. Can you walk at all without your sticks, Clovis? "

" Oh, no, sir.'

" Very good. Now let us begin."

The old man was hoisted into the armchair, and his limbs were strapped into the moveable legs that were attached to the seat. Dr Latonne gave the word : " Now, gently ! " and a bare-armed attendant turned the hand-winch. Clovis's right knee was then seen to rise, and straighten out, bend, straighten out again; then the left was put through similar movements. A sudden gaiety seized the old man and he began to laugh. He seemed to be wagging his head and his long beard and keeping time to the compulsory movements made by his legs. Andermatt and the four doctors leaned over him, examining him with the gravity of augurs, while Colosse Oriol exchanged knowing winks with the old vagabond.

The doors having been left open, there was a constant influx of visitors, some convinced, others still sceptical, but all anxious to look on.

" Quicker," said Dr Latonne, and the stalwart attendant

increased the speed. Old Clovis's legs began to move at a running pace, and he was overcome by irresistible mirth like a child that is being tickled. He laughed uproariously, threw his head about madly, and through his paroxysms of laughter he kept shouting out, "*Rigolo, Rigolo*," an expression he had doubtless picked up from some stranger. Colosse, too, burst into laughter. He stamped his foot on the floor, slapped his thighs, and exclaimed:

"Oh, that old devil, Clovis . . . that old devil, Clovis," until Dr Latonne had to call him to order.

The patient having been relieved from his fastenings, the doctors went to one side to record the result. Old Clovis was seen to rise unaided out of the armchair and to begin to walk. His steps were short, to be sure; he was all doubled up and every effort was signalised by a grimace. Still the fact remained: he was walking!

Dr Bonnefille was the first to give his opinion:

"It is a most extraordinary case."

Dr Black promptly went one better than his colleague. Dr Honorat alone preserved silence.

Gontran muttered in Paul's ear:

"I'm frankly puzzled. Look at their faces. Are they fools, or are they backing each other up?"

Andermatt at all events had plenty to say. He narrated the history of the case from the first day: the improvement, relapse and final cure, which purported to be definite and absolute. He added gaily:

"And even if our patient has a slight relapse every winter, we will cure him again every summer."

Then followed a pompous eulogy of the waters of Mont-Oriol and all their properties.

"I have personally had the opportunity," he said, "of testing their potency in the person of one very dear to me, and if the line of Andermatt is not doomed to extinction, it is to the waters of Mont-Oriol that it owes its survival."

Then he suddenly remembered that he had promised his wife to ask Paul Brétigny to call on her. His remorse was keen, for he was always loath to disappoint her. He looked round for Paul.

"My dear Brétigny, I entirely forgot to tell you that Christian is waiting to see you."

"Me?" stammered Paul. "Now?"

"Yes. She is up to-day. She wants to see you before anyone else. So run along as quick as you can. And forgive my remissness."

His heart palpitating with emotion, Paul set off towards the hotel. On the way he met the Marquis de Ravenel, who said:

"My daughter is up. She is surprised at not seeing you."

None the less, when he set foot on the staircase, he paused to reflect on what he should say to her. How would she receive him? Would she be alone? If she referred to his marriage, what was he to reply? Ever since he had learnt of her confinement he could not think of her without a tremor of uneasiness. Whenever it crossed his mind, the thought of their first meeting brought to his cheek a sudden flush or a sudden pallor. His troubled thoughts turned upon the new-born child, of whom he was the father. He was torn by conflicting emotions, a yearning mingled with fear, at the prospect of seeing her. Morally he felt himself plunged in the mire with which a man's conscience is besmirched till the day of his death. But above all he dreaded the eyes of the woman for whom his love had been so ardent, yet so brief. Would she greet him with reproaches, with tears, or with scorn? Had she sent for him merely to dismiss him? And what ought his own attitude to be? Should he be humble, distressed, supplicating, or cold? Should he seek to justify himself, or should he listen to her in silence? Should he sit or stand? And when he was shown the child, what should he do, or say? What emotion ought he to display?

He halted again outside the door, and as he touched the electric bell he noticed that his hand was trembling.

Pressing the little ivory button he heard it ringing within the apartment. A maid opened the door to him. Standing on the threshold of the drawing-room, he caught sight of Christian at the far end of the room beyond, where she was lying in a long chair. She was looking at him. It seemed an interminable journey across the two rooms. His footsteps were so unsteady that he was afraid he would knock against the furniture. But he had to keep his eyes on Christian's, and dared not look down to watch his steps. Motionless and silent, Christian waited until he was near her. Her right hand lay stretched out on her gown, while the left rested upon the rim of the curtained cradle.

Three steps from her, he halted, at a loss what to do. The maid had closed the door upon them. They were alone.

His first impulse was to fall upon his knees and beg Christian's forgiveness. But she slowly raised her right hand and held it out to him.

"How do you do?" she said gravely.

He dared not clasp her hand, but bent over it and lightly touched it with his lips.

"Won't you sit down?" she said.

He took a low chair at her feet. He felt that he ought to speak, but he could not summon up a word or an idea. And he hardly ventured even to look at her. At last he stammered out:

"Your husband forgot to tell me that you were expecting me. Otherwise I should have been here sooner."

"No matter," she replied. "A little sooner, . . . a little later . . . as long as we were to meet."

She fell silent.

"I hope you are feeling better now?" he asked eagerly.

"Yes, thank you. As well as one can expect after such a series of shocks."

She was very pale, and had grown thin, but she was prettier than ever. Her eyes especially had gained a depth of expression which was strange to him. They

271

seemed darker; their blue was less bright, less transparent, but more intense than formerly. Her hands were as white as the hands of one dead.

"I have come through a fearful ordeal," she said. "But such sufferings give one strength that lasts till death."

Deeply affected by her words, he replied:

"It must have been terrible indeed."

"Terrible," she echoed.

For some moments the light stirring, the hardly audible sounds of a baby on the point of waking, had proceeded from the cradle. Paul could no longer keep his eyes away from it. He was tortured with an increasing longing to see the tiny living creature hidden behind those draperies. Then he noticed that the curtains were fastened from top to bottom with the gold, crescent-shaped brooches which Christian usually wore in her bodice. In the old days Paul had often amused himself by taking them out and pinning them in her gown again. He caught the significance of her action. Overcome by poignant emotion, he shrank before the barrier of tiny golden spikes which separated him for ever from his child. From the interior of that white prison rose the weak piping wail of an infant. Christian at once began to rock the cradle.

"I must apologise," she said rather curtly, "for giving you so short a time. You see I have to attend to my little girl."

Rising, he kissed once more the hand which she held out to him, and as he turned to go, she murmured:

"I shall pray for your happiness."

LaVergne, TN USA
17 December 2009
167454LV00001B/25/A